INTERNATIONAL ACCLAIM FOR *Pirate Latitudes*

"As with many of his classic thrillers, Crichton makes place and time come alive with a wealth of engaging detail."—*Boston Globe*

"Crichton writes superbly. . . . The excitement rises with each page."—*Chicago Tribune*

"*Pirate Latitudes* is a lusty, rollicking 17th-century adventure. . . . History as entertainment. . . . Crichton has done his homework."
—*USA Today*

"*Pirate Latitudes* forms a fascinating snapshot-in-time from within the craftsman's studio. . . . The plot itself seems carefully outlined and skilfully written. . . . A compelling read."
—*The Washington Times*

"Hilariously exciting. . . . If you're on the lookout for some light adventure . . . thar she blows!"—*Washington Post*

"An entertaining tale filled with crafty privateers, despicable villains, treasure hoards, double crosses, and a sea monster."—*San Francisco Chronicle*

"Crichton's great talent was writing books that were virtually impossible to put down. . . . *Pirate Latitudes* is no exception. The plot sucks you in like the giant kraken monster that nearly sinks our hero's galleon as he's being chased by a Spanish warship."
—*Entertainment Weekly*

"The story of the raid on a Spanish outpost by a captain and his colourful crew will satisfy his fans. Verdict: Up there with the best of his work."—*The Daily Telegraph* (Australia)

"Offers unexpected turns and plenty of yo ho ho's."—*People* (Starred Review)

"Crichton has combined highly descriptive battles, vivid locations, a memorable cast of characters, and a gripping plot to great effect. An addictive, enjoyable read."—*Canberra Times* (Australia)

"It's visual, it's compelling. . . . Crichton jumps from one spectacular adventure to another without pause."—*Associated Press*

"Characteristically riveting and marvelously improbable. . . . What distinguishes this book and gives it a particular savor is its feel for the sea and sailing, something you sense the author held in particular reverence."—*The Plain Dealer* (Cleveland)

"And so we come to the close of a spectacularly successful writing career. . . . What [Crichton] wrote—escapist fiction, with a cunning and critical eye to the world around us, and to the worlds beyond—he wrote very well, indeed."—*The Charlotte Observer*

"Crichton knows how to craft a tale, one that keeps the reader turning the pages."—*Houston Chronicle*

"A superb period piece. Crichton's typically exhaustive research provides a brilliant glimpse into 17th-century colonial society, both culture and politics."—*The Providence Journal-Bulletin*

"*Pirate Latitudes* is Crichton at his polished best and a fitting requiem for one of the most successful popular novelists of our times."—*The Courier-Journal* (Louisville)

"One of the masters of modern fiction, Crichton effortlessly enmeshes solid naturalism and scientific research with all the thrills and spills of a blockbuster read."—*The West Australian*

PIRATE
LATITUDES

MICHAEL CRICHTON

PIRATE LATITUDES

A NOVEL

Harper Weekend

Harper **Weekend**

Pirate Latitudes
Copyright © 2009 by Michael Crichton

Published by Harper Weekend, an imprint of HarperCollins Publishers Ltd

First published in Canada by HarperCollins Publishers Ltd
in a hardcover edition: 2009
This Harper Weekend trade paperback edition: 2010

HarperCollins books may be purchased for educational, business, or sales promotional use through our Special Markets Department.

HarperCollins Publishers Ltd
2 Bloor Street East, 20th Floor
Toronto, Ontario, Canada
M4W 1A8

www.harpercollins.ca

Library and Archives Canada Cataloguing in Publication

Crichton, Michael, 1942–2008
        Pirate latitudes / Michael Crichton.

ISBN 978-1-55468-811-1

        I. Title.
PS3553.R48P57 2010   813'.54   C2010-900418-3

Designed by Lucy Albanese

Printed and bound in the United States
RRD 10 9 8 7 6 5 4 3 2

Part I

PORT ROYAL

CHAPTER 1

SIR JAMES ALMONT, appointed by His Majesty Charles II Governor of Jamaica, was habitually an early riser. This was in part the tendency of an aging widower, in part a consequence of restless sleep from pains of the gout, and in part an accommodation to the climate of the Jamaica Colony, which turned hot and humid soon after sunrise.

On the morning of September 7, 1665, he followed his usual routine, arising in his chambers on the third floor of the Governor's Mansion and going directly to the window to survey the weather and the coming day. The Governor's Mansion was an impressive brick structure with a red-tile roof. It was also the only three-story building in Port Royal, and his view of the town was excellent. In the streets below he could see the lamplighters making their rounds, extinguishing streetlights from the night before. On Ridge Street, the morning patrol of garrison soldiers was collecting drunks and dead bodies, which had fallen in the mud.

Directly beneath his window, the first of the flat, horse-drawn carts of water carriers rumbled by, bringing casks of fresh water from Rio Cobra some miles away. Otherwise, Port Royal was quiet, enjoying the brief moment between the time the last of the evening's drunken revelers collapsed in a stupor, and the start of the morning's commercial bustle around the docks.

Looking away from the cramped, narrow streets of the town to the harbor, he saw the rocking thicket of masts, the hundreds of ships of all sizes moored in the harbor and drawn up to the docks. In the sea beyond, he saw an English merchant brig anchored past the cay, near Rackham's reef offshore. Undoubtedly, the ship had arrived during the night, and the captain had prudently chosen to await daylight to make the harbor of Port Royal. Even as he watched, the topsails of the merchant ship were unreefed in the growing light of dawn, and two longboats put out from the shore near Fort Charles to help tow the merchantman in.

Governor Almont, known locally as "James the Tenth," because of his insistence on diverting a tenth share of privateering expeditions to his own personal coffers, turned away from the window and hobbled on his painful left leg across the room to make his toilet. Immediately, the merchant vessel was forgotten, for on this particular morning Sir James had the disagreeable duty of attending a hanging.

The previous week, soldiers had captured a French rascal named LeClerc, convicted of making a piratical raid on the settlement of Ocho Rios, on the north coast of the island.

On the testimony of a few townspeople who had survived the attack, LeClerc had been sentenced to be hanged in the public gallows on High Street. Governor Almont had no particular interest in either the Frenchman or his disposition, but he was required to attend the execution in his official capacity. That implied a tedious, formal morning.

Richards, the governor's manservant, entered the room. "Good morning, Your Excellency. Here is your claret." He handed the glass to the governor, who immediately drank it down in a gulp. Richards set out the articles of toilet: a fresh basin of rosewater, another of crushed myrtle berries, and a third small bowl of tooth powder with the toothcloth alongside. Governor Almont began his ministrations to the accompanying hiss of the perfumed bellows Richards used to air the room each morning.

"Warm day for a hanging," Richards commented, and Sir James grunted his agreement. He doused his thinning hair with the myrtle berry paste. Governor Almont was fifty-one years old, and he had been growing bald for a decade. He was not an especially vain man—and, in any case, he normally wore hats—so that baldness was not so fearsome as it might be. Nonetheless, he used preparations to cure his loss of hair. For several years now he had favored myrtle berries, a traditional remedy prescribed by Pliny. He also employed a paste of olive oil, ashes, and ground earthworms to prevent his hair from turning white. But this mixture stank so badly that he used it less frequently than he knew he should.

Governor Almont rinsed his hair in the rosewater, dried it with a towel, and examined his countenance in the mirror.

One of the privileges of his position as the highest official of the Jamaica Colony was that he possessed the best mirror on the island. It was nearly a foot square and of excellent quality, without ripples or flaws. It had arrived from London the year before, consigned to a merchant in the town, and Almont had confiscated it on some pretext or other. He was not above such things, and indeed felt that this high-handed behavior actually increased his respect in the community. As the former governor, Sir William Lytton, had warned him in London, Jamaica was "not a region burdened by moral excesses." Sir James had often recalled the phrase in later years—the understatement was so felicitously put. Sir James himself lacked graceful speech; he was blunt to a fault and distinctly choleric in temperament, a fact he ascribed to his gout.

Staring at himself in the mirror now, he noted that he must see Enders, the barber, to trim his beard. Sir James was not a handsome man, and he wore a full beard to compensate for his "weasel-beaked" face.

He grunted at his reflection, and turned his attention to his teeth, dipping a wetted finger into the paste of powdered rabbit's head, pomegranate peel, and peach blossom. He rubbed his teeth briskly with his finger, humming a little to himself.

At the window, Richards looked out at the arriving ship. "They say the merchantman's the *Godspeed*, sir."

"Oh yes?" Sir James rinsed his mouth with a bit of rosewater, spat it out, and dried his teeth with a toothcloth. It was an elegant tooth-cloth from Holland, red silk with an edging of lace. He had four such cloths, another minor delicacy of his position within the Colony. But one had already been ruined by a mindless servant girl who cleaned it in the native manner by pounding with rocks, destroying the delicate fabric. Servants were difficult here. Sir William had mentioned that as well.

Richards was an exception. Richards was a manservant to treasure, a Scotsman but a clean one, faithful and reasonably reliable. He could also be counted on to report the gossip and doings of the town, which might otherwise never reach the governor's ears.

"The *Godspeed*, you say?"

"Aye, sir," Richards said, laying out Sir James's wardrobe for the day on the bed.

"Is my new secretary on board?" According to the previous month's dispatches, the *Godspeed* was to carry his new secretary, one Robert Hacklett. Sir James had never heard of the man, and looked forward to meeting him. He had been without a secretary for eight months, since Lewis died of dysentery.

"I believe he is, sir," Richards said.

Sir James applied his makeup. First he daubed on cerise—white lead and vinegar—to produce a fashionable pallor on the face and neck. Then, on his cheeks and lips, he applied fucus, a red dye of seaweed and ochre.

"Will you be wishing to postpone the hanging?" Richards asked, bringing the governor his medicinal oil.

"No, I think not," Almont said, wincing as he downed a spoonful. This was oil of a red-haired dog, concocted by a Milaner in London and known to be efficacious for the gout. Sir James took it faithfully each morning.

He then dressed for the day. Richards had correctly set out the governor's best formal garments. First, Sir James put on a fine white silk tunic, then pale blue hose. Next, his green velvet doublet, stiffly quilted and miserably hot, but necessary for a day of official duties. His best feathered hat completed the attire.

All this had taken the better part of an hour. Through the open windows, Sir James could hear the early-morning bustle and shouts from the awakening town below.

He stepped back a pace to allow Richards to survey him. Richards adjusted the ruffle at the neck, and nodded his satisfaction. "Commander Scott is waiting with your carriage, Your Excellency," Richards said.

"Very good," Sir James said, and then, moving slowly, feeling the twinge of pain in his left toe with each step, and already beginning to perspire in his heavy ornate doublet, the cosmetics running down the side of his face and ears, the Governor of Jamaica descended the stairs of the mansion to his coach.

CHAPTER 2

FOR A MAN with the gout, even a brief journey by coach over cobbled streets is agonizing. For this reason, if no other, Sir James loathed the ritual of attending each hanging. Another reason he disliked these forays was that they required him to enter the heart of his dominion, and he much preferred the lofty view from his window.

Port Royal, in 1665, was a boomtown. In the decade since Cromwell's expedition had captured the island of Jamaica from the Spanish, Port Royal had grown from a miserable, deserted, disease-ridden spit of sand into a miserable, overcrowded, cutthroat-infested town of eight thousand.

Undeniably, Port Royal was a wealthy town—some said it was the richest in the world—but that did not make it pleasant. Only a few roads had been paved in cobblestones, brought from England as ships' ballast. Most streets were narrow mud ruts, reeking of garbage and horse dung, buzzing with flies and mosquitoes. The closely packed buildings were wood or brick, rude in construction and crude in purpose: an endless succession of taverns, grog shops, gaming places, and bawdy houses. These establishments served the thousand seamen and other visitors who might be ashore at any time. There were also a handful of legitimate merchants' shops, and a church at the north end of town, which was, as Sir William Lytton had so nicely phrased it, "seldom frequented."

Of course, Sir James and his household attended services each Sunday, along with the few pious members of the community. But as often as not, the sermon was interrupted by the arrival of a drunken seaman, who disrupted proceedings with blasphemous shouts and oaths and on one occasion with gunshots. Sir James had caused the man to be clapped in jail for a fortnight after that incident, but he had to be cautious about dispensing punishment. The authority of the Governor of Jamaica was—again in the words of Sir William—"as thin as a parchment fragment, and as fragile."

Sir James had spent an evening with Sir William, after the king had given him his appointment. Sir William had explained the workings of the Colony to the new governor. Sir James had listened and had thought he understood, but one never really understood life in the New World until confronted with the actual rude experience.

Now, riding in his coach through the stinking streets

of Port Royal, nodding from his window as the commoners bowed, Sir James marveled at how much he had come
to accept as wholly natural and ordinary. He accepted the
heat and the flies and the malevolent odors; he accepted
the thieving and the corrupt commerce; he accepted the
drunken gross manners of the privateers. He had made a
thousand minor adjustments, including the ability to sleep
through the raucous shouting and gunshots, which continued uninterrupted through every night in the port.

But there were still irritants to plague him, and one of
the most grating was seated across from him in the coach.
Commander Scott, head of the garrison of Fort Charles and
self-appointed guardian of courtly good manners, brushed
an invisible speck of dust from his uniform and said, "I
trust Your Excellency enjoyed an excellent evening, and is
even now in good spirits for the morning's exercises."

"I slept well enough," Sir James said abruptly. For the
hundredth time, he thought to himself how much more haz-
ardous life was in Jamaica when the commander of the garrison was a dandy and a fool, instead of a serious military man.

"I am given to understand," Commander Scott said,
touching a perfumed lace handkerchief to his nose and
inhaling lightly, "that the prisoner LeClerc is in complete
readiness and that all has been prepared for the execution."

"Very good," Sir James said, frowning at Commander Scott.

"It has also come to my attention that the merchant-man *Godspeed* is arriving at anchor even as we speak, and that among her passengers is Mr. Hacklett, here to serve as your new secretary."

"Let us pray he is not a fool like the last one," Sir James said.

"Indeed. Quite so," Commander Scott said, and then mercifully lapsed into silence. The coach pulled into the High Street Square where a large crowd had gathered to witness the hanging. As Sir James and Commander Scott alighted from the coach, there were scattered cheers.

Sir James nodded briefly; the commander gave a low bow.

"I perceive an excellent gathering," the commander said. "I am always heartened by the presence of so many children and young boys. This will make a proper lesson for them, do you not agree?"

"Umm," Sir James said. He made his way to the front of the crowd, and stood in the shadow of the gallows. The High Street gallows were permanent, they were so frequently needed: a low braced crossbeam with a stout noose that hung seven feet above the ground.

"Where is the prisoner?" Sir James said irritably.

The prisoner was nowhere to be seen. The governor waited with visible impatience, clasping and unclasping his hands behind his back. Then they heard the low roll of drums that presaged the arrival of the cart. Moments later, there were shouts and laughter from the crowd, which parted as the cart came into view.

The prisoner LeClerc was standing erect, his hands bound behind his back. He wore a gray cloth tunic, spattered with garbage thrown by the jeering crowd. Yet he continued to hold his chin high.

Commander Scott leaned over. "He does make a good impression, Your Excellency."

Sir James grunted.

"I do so think well of a man who dies with *finesse*."

Sir James said nothing. The cart rolled up to the gallows, and turned so that the prisoner faced the crowd. The executioner, Henry Edmonds, walked over to the governor and bowed deeply. "A good morning to Your Excellency, and to you, Commander Scott. I have the honor to present the prisoner, the Frenchman LeClerc, lately condemned by the Audencia—"

"Get on with it, Henry," Sir James said.

"By all means, Your Excellency." Looking wounded, the executioner bowed again, and then returned to the cart. He stepped up alongside the prisoner, and slipped the noose around LeClerc's neck. Then he walked to the front of the cart and stood next to the mule. There was a moment of silence, which stretched rather too long.

Finally, the executioner spun on his heel and barked, "Teddy, damn you, look sharp!"

Immediately, a young boy—the executioner's son—
began to beat out a rapid drum roll. The executioner turned
back to face the crowd. He raised his switch high in the air,
then struck the mule a single blow; the cart rattled away,
and the prisoner was left kicking and swinging in the air.

Sir James watched the man struggle. He listened to
the hissing rasp of LeClerc's choking, and saw his face
turn purple. The Frenchman began to kick rather violently, swinging back and forth just a foot or two from the
muddy ground. His eyes seemed to bulge from his head.
His tongue protruded. His body began to shiver, twisting
in convulsions on the end of the rope.

"All right," Sir James said finally, and nodded to the
crowd. Immediately, one or two stout fellows rushed forward, friends of the condemned man. They grabbed at
his kicking feet and hauled on them, trying to break his
neck with merciful quickness. But they were clumsy at
their work, and the pirate was strong, dragging the other
men through the mud with his vigorous kicking. The
death throes continued for some seconds and then finally,
abruptly, the body went limp.

The men stepped away. Urine trickled down LeClerc's
pants' legs onto the mud. The body twisted slackly back
and forth on the end of the rope.

"Well executed, indeed," Commander Scott said, with
a broad grin. He tossed a gold coin to the executioner.

Sir James turned and climbed back into the coach, thinking to himself that he was exceedingly hungry. To sharpen his appetite further, as well as to drive out the foul smells of the town, he permitted himself a pinch of snuff.

IT WAS COMMANDER SCOTT'S suggestion that they stop by the port, to see if the new secretary had yet disembarked. The coach pulled up to the docks, as near to the wharf as possible; the driver knew that the governor preferred to walk no more than necessary. The coachman opened the door and Sir James stepped out, wincing, into the fetid morning air.

He found himself facing a young man in his early thirties, who, like the governor, was sweating in a heavy doublet. The young man bowed and said, "Your Excellency."

"Whom do I have the pleasure of addressing?" Almont asked, with a slight bow. He could no longer bow deeply because of the pain in his leg, and in any case he disliked this pomp and formality.

"Charles Morton, sir, captain of the merchantman *Godspeed*, late of Bristol." He presented his papers.

Almont did not even glance at them. "What cargoes do you carry?"

"West Country broadcloths, Your Excellency, and glass from Stourbridge, and iron goods. Your Excellency holds the manifest in his hands."

"Have you passengers?" He opened the manifest and realized he had forgotten his spectacles; the listing was a black blur. He examined the manifest with brief impatience, and closed it again.

"I carry Mr. Robert Hacklett, the new secretary to Your Excellency, and his wife," Morton said. "I carry eight freeborn commoners as merchants to the Colony. And I carry thirty-seven felon women sent by Lord Ambritton of London to be wives for the colonists."

"So good of Lord Ambritton," Almont said dryly. From time to time, an official in one of the larger cities of England would arrange for convict women to be sent to Jamaica, a simple ruse to avoid the expense of jailing them at home. Sir James had no illusions about what this latest group of women would be like. "And where is Mr. Hacklett?"

"On board, gathering his belongings with Mrs. Hacklett, Your Excellency." Captain Morton shifted his feet. "Mrs. Hacklett had a most uncomfortable passage, Your Excellency."

"I have no doubt," Almont said. He was irritated that his new secretary was not on the dock to meet him. "Does Mr. Hacklett carry messages for me?"

"I believe he may, sir," Morton said.

"Be so good as to ask him to join me at Government House at his earliest convenience."

"I will, Your Excellency."

"You may await the arrival of the purser and Mr. Gower, the customs inspector, who will verify your manifest and supervise the unloading of your cargoes. Have you many deaths to report?"

"Only two, Your Excellency, both ordinary seamen. One lost overboard and one dead of dropsy. Had it been otherwise, I would not have come to port."

Almont hesitated. "How do you mean, not have come to port?"

"I mean, had anyone died of the plague, Your Excellency."

Almont frowned in the morning heat. "The plague?"

"Your Excellency knows of the plague which has lately infected London and certain of the outlying towns of the land?"

"I know nothing at all," Almont said. "There is plague in London?"

"Indeed, sir, for some months now it has been spreading with great confusion and loss of life. They say it was brought from Amsterdam."

Almont sighed. That explained why there had been no ships from England in recent weeks, and no messages from the Court. He remembered the London plague of ten years earlier, and hoped that his sister and niece had had the presence of mind to go to the country house. But he was not unduly disturbed. Governor Almont accepted calamity with equanimity. He himself lived daily in the shadow of dysentery and shaking fever, which carried off several citizens of Port Royal each week.

"I will hear more of this news," he said. "Please join me at dinner this evening."

"With great pleasure," Morton said, bowing once more. "Your Excellency honors me."

"Save that opinion until you see the table this poor colony provides," Almont said. "One last thing, Captain," he said. "I am in need of female servants for the mansion. The last group of blacks, being sickly, have died. I would be most grateful if you would contrive for the convict women to be sent to the mansion as soon as possible. I shall handle their dispersal."

"Your Excellency."

Almont gave a final, brief nod, and climbed painfully back into his coach. With a sigh of relief, he sank back in the seat and rode to the mansion. "A dismal malodorous day," Commander Scott commented, and indeed, for a long time afterward, the ghastly smells of the town lingered in the governor's nostrils and did not dissipate until he took another pinch of snuff.

CHAPTER 3

DRESSED IN LIGHTER clothing, Governor Almont breakfasted alone in the dining hall of the mansion. As was his custom, he ate a light meal of poached fish and a little wine, followed by another of the minor pleasures of his posting, a cup of rich, dark coffee. During his tenure as governor, he had become increasingly fond of coffee, and he delighted in the fact that he had virtually unlimited quantities of this delicacy, so scarce at home.

While he was finishing his coffee, his aide, John Cruikshank, entered. John was a Puritan, forced to leave Cambridge in some haste when Charles II was restored to the throne. He was a sallow-faced, serious, tedious man, but dutiful enough.

"The convict women are here, Your Excellency."

Almont grimaced at the thought. He wiped his lips. "Send them along. Are they clean, John?"

"Reasonably clean, sir."

"Then send them along."

The women entered the dining room noisily. They chattered and stared and pointed to this article and that. An unruly lot, dressed in identical gray fustian, and barefooted. His aide lined them along one wall and Almont pushed away from the table.

The women fell silent as he walked past them. In fact, the only sound in the room was the scraping of the governor's painful left foot over the floor, as he walked down the line, looking at each.

They were as ugly, tangled, and scurrilous a collection as he'd ever seen. He paused before one woman, who was taller than he, a nasty creature with a pocked face and missing teeth. "What's your name?"

"Charlotte Bixby, my lord." She attempted a clumsy sort of curtsey.

"And your crime?"

"Faith, my lord, I did no crime, it was all a falsehood that they put to me and—"

"Murder of her husband, John Bixby," his aide intoned, reading from a list.

The woman fell silent. Almont moved on. Each new face was uglier than the last. He stopped at a woman with tangled black hair and a yellow scar running down the side of her neck. Her expression was sullen.

"Your name?"

"Laura Peale."

"What is your crime?"

"They said I stole a gentleman's purse."

"Suffocation of her children ages four and seven," John intoned in a monotonous voice, never raising his eyes from the list.

Almont scowled at the woman. These females would be quite at home in Port Royal; they were as tough and hard as the hardest privateer. But wives? They would not be wives. He continued down the line of faces, and then stopped before one unusually young.

The girl could hardly have been more than fourteen or fifteen, with fair hair and a naturally pale complexion. Her eyes were blue and clear, with a certain odd, innocent amiability. She seemed entirely out of place in this churlish group. His voice was soft as he spoke to her. "And your name, child?"

"Anne Sharpe, my lord." Her voice was quiet, almost a whisper. Her eyes fell demurely.

"What is your crime?"

"Theft, my lord."

Almont glanced at John; the aide nodded. "Theft of a gentleman's lodging, Gardiner's Lane, London."

"I see," Almont said, turning back to the girl. But he could not bring himself to be severe with her. She remained with eyes downcast. "I have need of a womanservant in my household, Mistress Sharpe. I shall employ you here."

"Your Excellency," John interrupted, leaning toward Almont. "A word, if you please."

They stepped a short distance back from the women. The aide appeared agitated. He pointed to the list. "Your Excellency," he whispered, "it says here that she was accused of witchcraft at her trial."

Almont chuckled good-naturedly. "No doubt, no doubt." Pretty young women were often accused of witchcraft.

"Your Excellency," John said, full of tremulous Puritan spirit, "it says here that she bears the *stigmata of the devil*."

Almont looked at the demure, blond young woman. He was not inclined to believe she was a witch. Sir James knew a thing or two about witchcraft. Witches had eyes of strange color. Witches were surrounded by cold draughts. Their flesh was cold as that of a reptile, and they had an extra tit.

This woman, he was certain, was no witch. "See that she is dressed and bathed," he said.

"Your Excellency, may I remind you, the stigmata—"

"I shall search for the stigmata myself later."

John bowed. "As you wish, Your Excellency."

For the first time, Anne Sharpe looked up from the floor to face Governor Almont, and she smiled the slightest of smiles.

CHAPTER 4

"SPEAKING WITH ALL due respect, Sir James, I must confess that nothing could have prepared me for the shock of my arrival in this port." Mr. Robert Hacklett, thin, young, and nervous, paced up and down the room as he spoke. His wife, a slender, dark, foreign-looking young woman, sat rigidly in a chair and stared at Almont.

Sir James sat behind his desk, his bad foot propped on a pillow and throbbing badly. Sir James was trying to be patient.

"In the capital of His Majesty's Colony of Jamaica in the New World," Hacklett continued, "I naturally anticipated *some semblance* of Christian order and lawful conduct. At the very least, some evidence of constraint upon the vagabonds and ill-mannered louts who act as they please everywhere and openly. Why, as we traveled in open coach through the streets of Port Royal—if they may be called streets—one vulgar fellow hurled drunken imprecations at my wife, upsetting her greatly."

"Indeed," Almont said, with a sigh.

Emily Hacklett nodded silently. In her own way she was a pretty woman, with the sort of looks that appealed to King Charles. Sir James could guess how Mr. Hacklett had become such a favorite of the Court that he would be given the potentially lucrative posting of Secretary to the Governor of Jamaica. No doubt Emily Hacklett had felt the press of the royal abdomen upon her more than once.

Sir James sighed.

"And further," Hacklett continued, "we were everywhere treated to the spectacle of bawdy women half-naked in the streets and shouting from windows, men drunk and vomiting in the streets, robbers and pirates brawling and disorderly at every turn, and—"

"Pirates?" Almont said sharply.

"Indeed, pirates is what I should naturally call those cutthroat seamen."

"There are no pirates in Port Royal," Almont said. His voice was hard. He glared at his new secretary, and cursed the passions of the Merry Monarch that had provided him with this priggish fool for an assistant. Hacklett would obviously be no help to him at all. "There are no pirates in this Colony," Almont said again. "And should you find evidence that any man here is a pirate, he will be duly tried and hanged. That is the law of the Crown and it is stringently enforced."

Hacklett looked incredulous. "Sir James," he said, "you quibble over a minor question of speech when the truth of the matter is to be seen in every street and dwelling of the town."

"The truth of the matter is to be seen at the gallows of High Street," Almont said, "where even now a pirate may be found hanging in the breeze. Had you disembarked earlier, you might have seen it for yourself." He sighed again. "Sit down," he said, "and keep silent before you confirm yourself in my judgment as an even greater idiot than you already appear to be."

Mr. Hacklett paled. He was obviously unaccustomed to such plain address. He sat quickly in a chair next to his wife. She touched his hand reassuringly: a heartfelt gesture from one of the king's many mistresses.

Sir James Almont stood, grimacing as pain shot up from his foot. He leaned across his desk. "Mr. Hacklett," he said, "I am charged by the Crown with expanding the Colony of Jamaica and maintaining its welfare. Let me explain to you certain pertinent facts relating to the discharge of that duty. First, we are a small and weak outpost of England in the midst of Spanish territories. I am aware," he said heavily, "that it is the fashion of the Court to pretend that His Majesty has a strong footing in the New World. But the truth is rather different. Three tiny colonies—St. Kitts, Barbados, and Jamaica—comprise the entire dominion of

the Crown. All the rest is Philip's. This is still the Spanish Main. There are no English warships in these waters.
There are no English garrisons on any lands. There are a
dozen Spanish first-rate ships of the line and several thousand Spanish troops garrisoned in more than fifteen major
settlements. King Charles in his wisdom wishes to retain his
colonies but he does not wish to pay the expense of defend-
ing them against invasion."

Hacklett stared, still pale.

"I am charged with protecting this Colony. How am
I to do that? Clearly, I must acquire fighting men. The
adventurers and privateers are the only source available
to me, and I am careful to provide them a welcome home
here. You may find these elements distasteful but Jamaica
would be naked and vulnerable without them."

"Sir James—"

"Be quiet," Almont said. "Now, I have a second duty,
which is to expand the Jamaica Colony. It is fashionable in
the Court to propose that we instigate farming and agricul-
tural pursuits here. Yet no farmers have been sent in two
years. The land is brackish and infertile. The natives are hostile. How then do I expand the Colony, increasing its numbers and wealth? With commerce. The gold and the goods
for a thriving commerce are afforded us by privateering raids
upon Spanish shipping and settlements. Ultimately this

enriches the coffers of the king, a fact which does not entirely displease His Majesty, according to my best information."

"Sir James—"

"And finally," Almont said, "finally, I have an unspoken duty, which is to deprive the Court of Philip IV of as much wealth as I am able to manage. This, too, is viewed by His Majesty—privately, privately—as a worthy objective. Particularly since so much of the gold which fails to reach Cádiz turns up in London. Therefore privateering is openly encouraged. But not piracy, Mr. Hacklett. And that is no mere quibble."

"But Sir James—"

"The hard facts of the Colony admit no debate," Almont said, resuming his seat behind the desk, and propping his foot on the pillow once more. "You may reflect at your leisure on what I have told you, understanding—as I am certain you will understand—that I speak with the wisdom of experience on these matters. Be so kind as to join me at dinner this evening with Captain Morton. In the meanwhile I am sure you have much to do in settling into your quarters here."

The interview was clearly at an end. Hacklett and his wife stood. Hacklett bowed slightly, stiffly. "Sir James."

"Mr. Hacklett. Mrs. Hacklett."

∞

THE TWO DEPARTED. The aide closed the door behind them. Almont rubbed his eyes. "God in Heaven," he said, shaking his head.

"Do you wish to rest now, Your Excellency?" John asked.

"Yes," Almont said. "I wish to rest." He got up from behind his desk and walked down the corridor to his chambers. As he passed one room, he heard the sound of water splashing in a metal tub, and a feminine giggle. He glanced at John.

"They are bathing the womanservant," John said.

Almont grunted.

"You wish to examine her later?"

"Yes, later," Almont said. He looked at John and felt a moment of amusement. John was evidently still frightened by the witchcraft accusation. The fears of the common people, he thought, were so strong and so foolish.

CHAPTER 5

ANNE SHARPE RELAXED in the warm water of the bathtub, and listened to the prattle of the enormous black woman who bustled around the room. Anne could hardly understand a word the woman was saying, although she seemed to be speaking English; her lilting rhythms and odd pronunciations were utterly strange. The black woman was saying something about what a kind man Governor Almont was. Anne Sharpe had no concern about Governor Almont's kindness. She had learned at an early age how to deal with men.

She closed her eyes, and the singsong speech of the black woman was replaced in her mind by the tolling of church bells. She had come to hate that monotonous, ceaseless sound, in London.

Anne was the youngest of three children, the daughter of a retired seaman turned sailmaker in Wapping. When the plague broke out near Christmastime, her two older brothers had taken work as watchmen. Their jobs were to stand at the doors of infected houses and see that the inhabitants inside did not leave the residence for any reason. Anne herself worked as a sick-nurse for several wealthy families.

With the passing weeks, the horrors she had seen became merged in her memory. The church bells rang day and night. The cemeteries everywhere became overfilled; soon there were no more individual graves, but the bodies were dumped by the score into deep trenches, and hastily covered over with white lime powder and earth. The dead-carts, piled high with bodies, were hauled through the streets; the sextons paused before each dwelling to call out, "Bring out your dead." The smell of corrupted air was everywhere.

So was the fear. She remembered seeing a man fall dead in the street, his fat purse by his side, clinking with money. Crowds passed by the corpse, but none would dare to pick up the purse. Later the body was carted away, but still the purse remained, untouched.

At all the markets, the grocers and butchers kept bowls of vinegar by their wares. Shoppers dropped coins into the vinegar; no coin was ever passed hand to hand. Everyone made an effort to pay with exact change.

Amulets, trinkets, potions, and spells were in brisk demand. Anne herself bought a locket that contained some foul-smelling herb, but which was said to ward off the plague. She wore it always.

And still the deaths continued. Her eldest brother came down with the plague. One day she saw him in the street; his neck was swollen with large lumps and his gums were bleeding. She never saw him again.

Her other brother suffered a common fate for watchmen. While guarding a house one night, the inhabitants locked inside became crazed by the dementia of the disease. They broke out and killed her brother with a pistol-ball in the course of their escape. She only heard of this; she never saw him.

Finally, Anne, too, was locked in a house belonging to the family of a Mr. Sewell. She was serving as nurse to the elderly Mrs. Sewell—mother of the owner of the house—when Mr. Sewell came down with the swellings. The house was quarantined. Anne tended to the sick as best she could. One after another, the family died. The bodies were given over to the dead-carts. At last, she was alone in the house, and, by some miracle, still in good health.

It was then that she stole some articles of gold and the few coins she could find, and made her escape from the second-story window, slipping out over the rooftops of London at night. A constable caught her the next morning, demanding to know where a young girl had found so much gold. He took the gold, and clapped her in Bridewell prison.

There she languished for some weeks, until Lord

Ambritton, a public-spirited gentleman, made a tour of the prison and caught sight of her. Anne had long since learned that gentlemen found her aspect agreeable. Lord Ambritton was no exception. He caused her to be put in his coach, and after some dalliance of the sort he liked, promised her she would be sent to the New World.

Soon enough she was in Plymouth, and then aboard the *Godspeed*. During the journey, Captain Morton, being a young and vigorous man, had taken a fancy to her, and because in the privacy of his cabin he gave her fresh meats and other delicacies, she was well pleased to make his acquaintance, which she did almost every night.

Now she was here, in this new place, where everything was strange and unfamiliar. But she had no fear, for she was certain that the governor liked her, as the other gentlemen had liked her and taken care of her.

Her bath finished, she was dressed in a dyed woolen dress and a cotton blouse. It was the finest clothing she had worn in more than three months, and it gave her a moment of pleasure to feel the fabric against her skin. The black woman opened the door and motioned for her to follow.

"Where are we going?"

"To the governor."

She was led down a large, wide hallway. The floors were wooden but uneven. She found it strange that a man so important as the governor should live in such a rough house. Many ordinary gentlemen in London had houses more finely built than this.

The black woman knocked on a door, and a leering Scotsman opened it. Anne saw a bedchamber inside; the governor in a nightshirt was standing by the bed, yawning. The Scotsman nodded for her to enter the room.

"Ah," the governor said. "Mistress Sharpe. I must say, your appearance is considerably improved by your ablutions."

She did not understand exactly what he was talking about, but if he was pleased then so was she. She curtseyed as she had been taught by her mother.

"Richards, you may leave us."

The Scotsman nodded, and closed the door. She was alone with the governor. She watched his eyes.

"Don't be frightened, my dear," he said in a kindly voice. "There is nothing to fear. Come over here by the window, Anne, where the light is good."

She did as she was told.

He stared at her in silence for some moments. Finally, he said, "You know at your trial you were accused of witchcraft."

"Yes, sir. But it is not true, sir."

"I'm quite sure it is not, Anne. But it was said that you bear the stigmata of a pact with the devil."

"I swear, sir," she said, feeling agitation for the first time. "I have nothing to do with the devil, sir."

"I believe you, Anne," he said, smiling at her. "But it is my duty to verify the absence of stigmata."

"I swear to you, sir."

"I believe you," he said. "But you must take off your clothes."

"Now, sir?"

"Yes, now."

She looked around the room a little doubtfully.

"You can put your clothes on the bed, Anne."

"Yes, sir."

He watched her as she undressed. She noticed what happened to his eyes. She was no longer afraid. The air was warm; she was comfortable without her clothing.

"You are a beautiful child, Anne."

"Thank you, sir."

She stood, naked, and he moved closer to her. He paused to put his spectacles on, and then he looked at her shoulders.

"Turn around slowly."

She turned for him. He peered at her flesh. "Raise your arms over your head."

She raised her arms. He peered at each armpit.

"The stigmata is normally under the arms or on the breast," he said. "Or on the pudenda." He smiled at her. "You don't know what I am talking about, do you?"

She shook her head.

"Lie on the bed, Anne."

She lay on the bed.

"We will now complete the examination," he said seriously, and then his fingers were in her hair, and he was peering at her skin with his nose just a few inches from her quim, and even though she feared insulting him she found it funny—it tickled—and she began to laugh.

He stared angrily at her for a moment, and then he laughed, too, and then he began throwing off his nightshirt. He took her with his spectacles still on his face; she felt the wire frames pressing against her ear. She allowed him to have his way with her. It did not last long, and afterward, he seemed pleased, and so she was also pleased.

AS THEY LAY together in the bed, he asked her about her life, and her experiences in London, and the voyage to Jamaica. She described for him how most of the women amused themselves with each other, or with members of the crew, but she said that she did not—which wasn't exactly true, but she had only been with Captain Morton, so it was very nearly true. And then she told about the storm that had happened, just as they sighted land in the Indies. And how the storm had buffeted them for two days.

She could tell that Governor Almont was not paying much attention to her story. His eyes had that funny look in them again. She continued to talk, anyway. She told about how the day after the storm had been clear, and they had sighted land with a harbor and a fortress, and a large Spanish ship in the harbor. And how Captain Morton was very worried about being attacked by the Spanish warship, which had certainly seen the merchantman. But the Spanish ship never came out of the harbor.

"What?" Governor Almont said, almost shrieking. He leapt out of bed.

"What's wrong?"

"A Spanish warship saw you and didn't attack?"

"No, sir," she said. "We were much relieved, sir."

"Relieved?" Almont cried. He could not believe his ears. "You were relieved? God in Heaven: how long ago did this happen?"

She shrugged. "Three or four days past."

"And it was a harbor with a fortress, you say?"

"Yes."

"On which side was the fortress?"

She was confused. She shook her head. "I don't know."

"Well," Almont said, throwing on his clothes in haste, "as you looked at the island and the harbor, was this fortress to the right of the harbor, or the left?"

"To this side," she said, pointing with her right arm.

"And the island had a tall peak? A very green island, very small?"

"Yes, that's the very one, sir."

"God's blood," Almont said. "Richards! Richards! Get Hunter!"

And the governor dashed from the room, leaving her lying there, naked on the bed. Certain that she had displeased him, Anne began to cry.

CHAPTER 6

THERE WAS A knock at the door. Hunter rolled over in the bed; he saw the open window, and sunlight pouring through. "Go away," he muttered. Alongside him, the girl shifted her position restlessly but did not awake.

The knock came again.

"Go away, damn your eyes."

The door opened, and Mrs. Denby poked her head around. "Begging your pardon, Captain Hunter, but there's a messenger here from the Governor's Mansion. The governor requests your presence at dinner, Captain Hunter. What shall I say?"

Hunter rubbed his eyes. He blinked sleepily in the daylight. "What is the hour?"

"Five o'clock, Captain."

"Tell the governor I will be there."

"Yes, Captain Hunter. And Captain?"

"What is it?"

"That Frenchman with the scar is downstairs looking for you."

Hunter grunted. "All right, Mrs. Denby."

The door closed. Hunter got out of bed. The girl still slept, snoring loudly. He looked around his room, which was small and cramped—a bed, a sea chest with his belongings in one corner, a chamber pot under the bed, a basin of water nearby. He coughed, started to dress, and paused to urinate out of the window onto the street below. A shouted curse drifted up to him. Hunter smiled, and continued to dress, selecting his only good doublet from the sea chest, and his remaining pair of hose that had only a few snags. He finished by putting on his gold belt with the short dagger, and then, as a kind of afterthought, took one pistol, primed it, rammed home the ball with the wadding to hold it in the barrel, and slipped it under his belt.

This was Captain Charles Hunter's normal toilet, performed each evening when he arose at sunset. It took only a few minutes, for Hunter was not a fastidious man. Nor, he reflected, was he much of a Puritan; he looked again at the girl in the bed, then closed the door behind her and went down the narrow creaking wood stairs to the main room of Mrs. Denby's Inn.

The main room was a broad, low-ceilinged space with a dirt floor and several heavy wooden tables in long rows.

Hunter paused. As Mrs. Denby had said, Levasseur was there, sitting in a corner, hunched over a tankard of grog.

Hunter crossed to the door.

"Hunter!" Levasseur croaked, in a thick drunken voice.

Hunter turned, showing apparent surprise. "Why, Levasseur. I didn't see you."

"Hunter, you son of an English mongrel bitch."

"Levasseur," he replied, stepping out of the light, "you son of a French farmer and his favorite sheep, what brings you here?"

Levasseur stood behind the table. He had picked a dark spot; Hunter could not see him well. But the two men were separated by a distance of perhaps thirty feet—too far for a pistol shot.

"Hunter, I want my money."

"I owe you no money," Hunter said. And, in truth, he did not. Among the privateers of Port Royal, debts were paid fully and promptly. There was no more damaging reputation a man could have than one who failed to pay his debts, or to divide spoils equally. On a privateering raid, any man who tried to conceal a part of the general booty was always put to death. Hunter himself had shot more than one thieving seaman through the heart and kicked the corpse overboard without a second thought.

"You cheated me at cards," Levasseur said.

"You were too drunk to know the difference."

"You cheated me. You took fifty pounds. I want it back."

Hunter looked around the room. There were no witnesses, which was unfortunate. He did not want to kill Levasseur without witnesses. He had too many enemies. "How did I cheat you at cards?" he asked. As he spoke, he moved slightly closer to Levasseur.

"How? Who cares a damn for how? God's blood, you cheated me." Levasseur raised the tankard to his lips.

Hunter chose that moment to lunge. He pushed his palm flat against the upturned tankard, ramming it back against Levasseur's face, which thudded against the back wall. Levasseur gurgled and collapsed, blood dripping from his mouth. Hunter grabbed the tankard and crashed it down on Levasseur's skull. The Frenchman lay unconscious.

Hunter shook his hand free of the wine on his fingers, turned, and walked out of Mrs. Denby's Inn. He stepped ankle-deep into the mud of the street, but paid no attention. He was thinking of Levasseur's drunkenness. It was sloppy of him to be so drunk while waiting for someone.

It was time for another raid, Hunter thought. They were all getting soft. He himself had spent one night too many in his cups, or with the women of the port. They should go to sea again.

Hunter walked through the mud, smiling and waving

to the whores who yelled to him from high windows, and made his way to the Governor's Mansion.

"ALL HAVE REMARKED upon the comet, seen over London on the eve of the plague," said Captain Morton, sipping his wine. "There was a comet before the plague of '56, as well."

"So there was," Almont said. "And what of that? There was a comet in '59, and no plague that I recall."

"An outbreak of the pox in Ireland," said Mr. Hacklett, "in that very year."

"There is always an outbreak of the pox in Ireland," Almont said. "In every year."

Hunter said nothing. Indeed, he had said little during the dinner, which he found as dreary as any he had ever attended at the Governor's Mansion. For a time, he had been intrigued by the new faces—Morton, the captain of the *Godspeed*, and Hacklett, the new secretary, a silly pinch-faced prig of a man. And Mrs. Hacklett, who looked to have French blood in her slender darkness, and a certain lascivious animal quality.

For Hunter, the most interesting moment in the evening had been the arrival of a new serving girl, a delicious pale blond child who came and went from time to time. He kept trying to catch her eye. Hacklett noticed, and gave Hunter a disapproving stare. It was not the first disapproving stare he had given Hunter that evening.

When the girl came round to refill the glasses, Hacklett said, "Does your taste run to servants, Mr. Hunter?"

"When they are pretty," Hunter said casually. "And how does your taste run?"

"The mutton is excellent," Hacklett said, coloring deeply, staring at his plate.

With a grunt, Almont turned the conversation to the Atlantic passage his guests had just made. There was a description of a tropical storm, told in exciting and over-wrought detail by Morton, who acted as if he were the first person in human history to face a little white water. Hacklett added a few frightening touches, and Mrs. Hacklett allowed that she had been quite ill.

Hunter grew increasingly bored. He drained his wineglass.

"Well then," Morton continued, "after two days of this most dreadful storm, the third day dawned perfectly clear, a magnificent morning. One could see for miles and the wind was fair from the north. But we did not know our position, having been blown for forty-eight hours. We sighted land to port, and made for it."

A mistake, Hunter thought. Obviously Morton was grossly inexperienced. In the Spanish waters, an English vessel never made for land without knowing exactly whose land it was. The odds were, the Don held it.

"We came round the island, and to our astonishment we saw a warship anchored in the harbor. Small island, but there it was, a Spanish warship and no doubt of it. We felt certain it would give chase."

"And what happened?" Hunter asked, not very interested.

"It remained in the harbor," Morton said, and laughed. "I should like to have a more exciting conclusion to the tale, but the truth is it did not come after us. The warship remained in the harbor."

"The Don saw you, of course?" Hunter said, growing more interested.

"Well, they must have done. We were under full canvas."

"How close by were you?"

"No more than two or three miles offshore. The island wasn't on our charts, you know. I suppose it was too small to be charted. It had a single harbor, with a fortress to one side. I must say we all felt we had a narrow escape."

Hunter turned slowly to look at Almont. Almont was staring at him, with a slight smile.

"Does the episode amuse you, Captain Hunter?"

Hunter turned back to Morton. "You say there was a fortress by the harbor?"

"Indeed, a rather imposing fortress, it seemed."

"On the north or south shore of the harbor?"

"Let me recollect—north shore. Why?"

"How long ago did you see this ship?" Hunter asked.

"Three or four days past. Make it three days. As soon as we had our bearings, we ran straight for Port Royal."

Hunter drummed his fingers on the table. He frowned at his empty wineglass. There was a short silence.

Almont cleared his throat. "Captain Hunter, you seem preoccupied by this story."

"Intrigued," Hunter said. "I am sure the governor is equally intrigued."

"I believe," Almont said, "that it is fair to say the interests of the Crown have been aroused."

Hacklett sat stiffly in his chair. "Sir James," he said, "would you edify the rest of us as to the import of all this?"

"Just a moment," Almont said, with an impatient wave of the hand. He was looking fixedly at Hunter. "What terms do you make?"

"Equal division, first," Hunter said.

"My dear Hunter, equal division is most unattractive to the Crown."

"My dear Governor, anything less would make the expedition most unattractive to the seamen."

Almont smiled. "You recognize, of course, that the prize is enormous."

"Indeed. I also recognize that the island is impregnable. You sent Edmunds with three hundred men against it last year. Only one returned."

"You yourself have expressed the opinion that Edmunds was not a resourceful man."

"But Cazalla is certainly resourceful."

"Indeed. And yet it seems to me that Cazalla is a man you should like to meet."

"Not unless there was an equal division."

"But," Sir James said, smiling in an easy way, "if you expect the Crown to outfit the expedition, that cost must be returned before any division. Fair?"

"Here, now," Hacklett said. "Sir James, are you bargaining with this man?"

"Not at all. I am coming to a gentleman's agreement with him."

"For what purpose?"

"For the purpose of arranging a privateering expedition on the Spanish outpost at Matanceros."

"Matanceros?" Morton said.

"That is the name of the island you passed, Captain Morton. Matanceros. The Don built a fortress there two years ago, under the command of an unsavory gentleman named Cazalla. Perhaps you've heard of him. No? Well, he has a considerable reputation in the Indies. He is said to find the screams of his dying victims restful and relaxing." Almont looked at the faces of his dinner guests. Mrs. Hacklett was quite pale. "Cazalla commands the fortress of Matanceros, built for the sole purpose of being the farthest eastward outpost of Spanish dominion along the homeward route of the Treasure Fleet."

There was a long silence. The guests looked uneasy.

"I see you do not comprehend the economics of this region," Almont said. "Each year, Philip sends a fleet of treasure galleons here from Cádiz. They cross to the Spanish Main, sighting first land to the south, off the coast of New Spain. There the fleet disperses, traveling to various ports—Cartagena, Vera Cruz, Portobello—to collect treasure. The fleet regroups in Havana, then travels east back to Spain. The purpose of traveling together is protection against privateering raids. Am I clear?"

They all nodded.

"Now," Almont continued, "the Armada sails in late summer, which is the onset of the hurricane season. From time to time, it has happened that ships have been separated from the convoy early in the voyage. The Don wanted a strong harbor to protect such ships. They built Matanceros for this reason alone."

"Surely that is not sufficient reason," Hacklett said. "I cannot imagine . . ."

"It is ample reason," Almont said abruptly. "Now then. As luck would have it, two treasure *naos* were lost in a storm some weeks ago. We know because they were sighted by a privateer vessel, which attacked them unsuccessfully. They were last seen beating southward, making for Matanceros. One was badly damaged. What you, Captain Morton, called a Spanish warship was obviously one of these treasure galleons. If it had been a genuine warship, it would surely have given chase at a two-mile range, and captured you, and even now you would be screaming your lungs out for Cazalla's amusement. The ship did not give chase because it dared not leave the protection of the harbor."

"How long will it stay there?" Morton asked.

"It may leave at any time. Or it may wait until the next fleet departs, next year. Or it may wait for a Spanish warship to arrive and escort it home."

"Can it be captured?" Morton asked.

"One would like to think so. In aggregate, the treasure ship probably contains a fortune worth five hundred thousand pounds."

There was a stunned silence around the table.

"I felt," Almont said with amusement, "that this information would interest Captain Hunter."

"You mean this man is a common privateer?" demanded Hacklett.

"Not common in the least," Almont said, chuckling. "Captain Hunter?"

"Not common, I would say."

"But this levity is outrageous!"

"You forget your manners," Almont said. "Captain Hunter is the second son of Major Edward Hunter, of the Massachusetts Bay Colony. He was, in fact, born in the New World and educated at that institution, what is it called—"

"Harvard," Hunter said.

"Umm, yes, Harvard. Captain Hunter has been among us for four years, and as a privateer, he has some standing in our community. Is that a fair summation, Captain Hunter?"

"Only fair," Hunter said, grinning.

"The man is a rogue," Hacklett said, but his wife was looking at Hunter with new interest. "A common rogue."

"You should mind your tongue," Almont said calmly. "Dueling is illegal on this island, yet it happens with monotonous regularity. I regret there is little I can do to stop the practice."

"I've heard of this man," Hacklett said, still more agitated. "He is not the son of Major Edward Hunter at all, at least not the legitimate son."

Hunter scratched his beard. "Is that so?"

"I have heard it," Hacklett said. "Further, I have heard he is a murderer, scoundrel, whoremonger, and pirate."

At the word "pirate," Hunter's arm flicked out across the table with extraordinary speed. It fastened in Hacklett's hair and plunged his face into his half-eaten mutton. Hunter held him there for a long moment.

"Dear me," Almont said. "I warned him about that earlier. You see, Mr. Hacklett, privateering is an honorable occupation. Pirates, on the other hand, are outlaws. Do you seriously suggest that Captain Hunter is an outlaw?"

Hacklett made a muffled sound, his face in his food.

"I didn't hear you, Mr. Hacklett," Almont said.

"I said, 'No,'" Hacklett said.

"Then don't you think it appropriate as a gentleman to apologize to Captain Hunter?"

"I apologize, Captain Hunter. I meant you no disrespect."

Hunter released the man's head. Hacklett sat back, and wiped the gravy from his face with his napkin.

"There now," Almont said. "A moment of unpleasantness has been averted. Shall we take dessert?"

Hunter looked around the table. Hacklett was still wiping his face. Morton was staring at him with open astonishment. And Mrs. Hacklett was looking at Hunter and when she caught his eye, she licked her lip.

AFTER DINNER, HUNTER and Almont sat alone in

the library of the mansion, drinking brandy. Hunter commiserated with the governor over the appointment of the new secretary.

"He makes my life no simpler," Almont agreed, "and I fear it may be the same for you."

"You think he'll send unfavorable dispatches to London?"

"I think he may try."

"The king must surely know what transpires in his Colony."

"That is a matter of opinion," Almont said, with an airy gesture. "One thing is certain; the continued support of privateers will be assured if it repays the king handsomely."

"No less than an equal division," Hunter said quickly. "I tell you, it cannot be otherwise."

"But if the Crown outfits your ships, arms your seamen . . ."

"No," Hunter said. "That will not be necessary."

"Not necessary? My dear Hunter, you know Matanceros. A full Spanish garrison is stationed there."

Hunter shook his head. "A frontal assault will never succeed. We know that from the Edmunds expedition."

"But what alternative is there? The fortress at Matanceros commands the entrance to the harbor. You cannot escape with the treasure ship without first capturing the fortress."

"Indeed."

"Well then?"

"I propose a small raid from the landward side of the fortress."

"Against a full garrison? At least three hundred troops? You cannot succeed."

"On the contrary," Hunter said. "Unless we succeed, Cazalla will turn his guns on the treasure galleon, and sink it at anchor in the harbor."

"I hadn't thought of that," Almont said. He sipped his brandy. "Tell me more of your plan."

CHAPTER 7

LATER, AS HE was leaving the Governor's Mansion, Mrs. Hacklett appeared in the hall, and came over to him. "Captain Hunter."

"Yes, Mrs. Hacklett."

"I want to apologize for the inexcusable conduct of my husband."

"No apology is necessary."

"On the contrary, Captain. I think it entirely necessary. He behaved like a boor and an oaf."

"Madam, your husband apologized as a gentleman on his own behalf, and the matter is concluded." He nodded to her. "Good evening."

"Captain Hunter."

He stopped at the door and turned. "Yes, Madam?"

"You are a most attractive man, Captain."

"Madam, you are very gracious. I look forward to our next meeting."

"I as well, Captain."

Hunter walked away thinking that Mr. Hacklett had best look to his wife. Hunter had seen it happen before—a well-bred woman, reared in a rural gentry setting in England, who found some excitement in the Court—as no doubt Mrs. Hacklett had—if her husband looked away—as no doubt Mr. Hacklett had. Nevertheless, on finding herself in the Indies, far from home, far from the restraints of class and custom . . . Hunter had seen it before.

He walked down the cobbled street away from the mansion. He passed the cookhouse, still brightly lit, the servants working inside. All houses in Port Royal had separate cookhouses, a necessity in the hot climate. Through the open windows, he saw the figure of the blond girl who had served dinner. He waved to her.

She waved back and turned away to her work.

THEY WERE BAITING a bear outside Mrs. Denby's Inn. Hunter watched the children pelt the helpless animal with rocks; they laughed and giggled and shouted as the bear growled and tugged at its stout chain. A couple of whores beat the bear with sticks. Hunter walked past, and entered the inn.

Trencher was there, sitting in a corner, drinking with his one good arm. Hunter called to him, and drew him aside.

"What is it, Captain?" Trencher asked eagerly.

"I want you to find some mates for me."

"Say who they shall be, Captain."

"Lazue, Mr. Enders, Sanson. And the Moor."

Trencher smiled. "You want them here?"

"No. Find where they are, and I'll seek them out. Now, where is Whisper?"

"In the Blue Goat," Trencher said. "The back room."

"And Black Eye is in Farrow Street?"

"I think so. You want the Jew, too, do you?"

"I am trusting your tongue," Hunter said. "Keep it still now."

"Will you take me with you, Captain?"

"If you do as you are told."

"I swear by God's wounds, Captain."

"Then look sharp," Hunter said, and left the inn, returning to the muddy street. The night air was warm and still, as it had been during the day. He heard the soft strumming of a guitar, and, somewhere, drunken laughter, and a single gunshot. He set off down Ridge Street for the Blue Goat.

The town of Port Royal was divided into rough sections, oriented around the port itself. Nearest the dockside were located the taverns and brothels and gaming houses. Farther back, away from the brawling activity of the waterfront, the streets were quieter. Here the grocers and bakers, the furniture workers and ships' chandlers, the blacksmiths and goldsmiths could be found. Still farther back, on the south side of the bay, were the handful of respectable inns and private homes. The Blue Goat was a respectable inn.

Hunter entered, nodding to the gentlemen drinking at the tables. He recognized the best landsman's doctor, Mr. Perkins; one of the councilmen, Mr. Pickering; the bailiff of the Bridewell jail; and several other respectable gentlemen.

Ordinarily, a common privateering seaman would not be welcome in the Blue Goat, but Hunter was accepted with good grace. This was a simple recognition of the way the commerce of the port depended upon a steady stream of successful privateering raids. Hunter was a skilled and daring captain, and thus an important member of the community. In the previous year, his three forays had returned more than two hundred thousand *pistoles* and doubloons to Port Royal. Much of this money found its way to the pockets of these gentlemen, and they greeted him accordingly.

Mistress Wickham, who managed the Blue Goat, was less warm. A widow, she had some years before taken up with Whisper, and she knew, when Hunter arrived, that he had come to see him. She jerked her thumb toward a back room. "In there, Captain."

"Thank you, Mistress Wickham."

He crossed directly to the back room, knocked, and opened the door without hearing any answering greeting;

he knew there would be none. The room was dark, lit only by a single candle. Hunter blinked to adjust to the light. He heard a rhythmic creaking. Finally, he was able to see Whisper, sitting in a corner, in a rocking chair. Whisper held a primed pistol, aimed at Hunter's belly.

"A good evening, Whisper."

The reply was low, a rasping hiss. "A good evening, Captain Hunter. You are alone?"

"I am."

"Then come in" came the hissing reply. "A touch of kill-devil?" Whisper pointed to a barrel beside him, which served as a table. There were glasses and a small crock of rum.

"With thanks, Whisper."

Hunter watched as Whisper poured two glasses of dark brown liquid. As his eyes adjusted to the light, he could see his companion better.

Whisper—no one knew his real name—was a large, heavyset man with oversized, pale hands. He had once been a successful privateering captain in his own right. Then he had gone on the Matanceros raid with Edmunds. Whisper was the sole survivor, after Cazalla had captured him, cut his throat, and left him for dead. Somehow Whisper lived, but not without the loss of his voice. This and the large, white arcing scar beneath his chin were obvious proofs of his past.

Since his return to Port Royal, Whisper had hidden in this back room, a strong, vigorous man but one without courage—the steel gone out of him. He was frightened; he was never without a weapon in his hands and another at his side. Now, as he rocked in his chair, Hunter saw the gleam of a cutlass on the floor within easy reach.

"What brings you, Captain? Matanceros?"

Hunter must have looked startled. Whisper broke into laughter. Whisper's laughter was a horrifying sound, a high-pitched wheezing sizzle, like a steam kettle. He threw his head back to laugh, revealing the white scar plainly.

"I startle you, Captain? You are surprised I know?"

"Whisper," Hunter said. "Do others know?"

"Some," Whisper hissed. "Or they suspect. But they do not understand. I heard the story of Morton's voyage."

"Ah."

"You are going, Captain?"

"Tell me about Matanceros, Whisper."

"You wish a map?"

"Yes."

"Fifteen shillings?"

"Done," Hunter said. He knew he would pay Whisper twenty, to ensure his friendship and his silence to any later visitors. And for his part, Whisper would know the obligation conferred by the extra five shillings. And he would know that Hunter would kill him if he spoke to anyone else about Matanceros.

Whisper produced a scrap of oilcloth and a bit of

charcoal. Placing the oilcloth on his knee, he sketched rapidly.

"The island of Matanceros, it means slaughter in the Donnish tongue," he whispered. "It has the shape of a U, so. The mouth of the harbor faces to the east, to the ocean. This point"—he tapped the left-hand side of the U—"is Punta Matanceros. That is where Cazalla has built the fortress. It is low land here. The fortress is no more than fifty paces above the level of the water."

Hunter nodded, and waited while Whisper gurgled a sip of kill-devil.

"The fortress is eight-sided. The walls are stone, thirty feet high. Inside there is a Spanish militia garrison."

"Of what strength?"

"Some say two hundred. Some say three hundred. I have even heard four hundred but do not believe it."

Hunter nodded. He should count on three hundred troops. "And the guns?"

"On two sides of the fortress only," Whisper rasped. "One battery to the ocean, due east. One battery across the mouth of the harbor, due south."

"What guns are they?"

Whisper gave his chilling laugh. "Most interesting, Captain Hunter. They are *culebrinas*, twenty-four-pounders, cast bronze."

"How many?"

"Ten, perhaps twelve."

It was interesting, Hunter thought. The *culebrinas*—what the English called culverins—were not the most powerful class of armament, and were no longer favored for shipboard use. Instead, the stubby cannon had become standard on warships of every nationality.

The culverin was an older gun. Culverins weighed more than two tons, with barrels as long as fifteen feet. Such long barrels made them deadly accurate at long range. They could fire heavy shot, and were quick to load. In the hands of trained gun crews, culverins could be fired as often as once a minute.

"So it is well made," Hunter nodded. "Who is the gunnery master?"

"Bosquet."

"I have heard of him," Hunter said. "He is the man who sank the *Renown*?"

"The same," Whisper hissed.

So the gun crews would be well drilled. Hunter frowned.

"Whisper," he said, "do you know if the culverins are fix-mounted?"

Whisper rocked back and forth for a long moment. "You are insane, Captain Hunter."

"How so?"

"You are planning a landward attack."

Hunter nodded.

"It will never succeed," Whisper said. He tapped the map on his knees. "Edmunds thought of it, but when he saw the island, he gave up the attempt. Look here, if you beach on the west"—he pointed to the curve of the U—"there is a small harbor which you can use. But to cross to the main harbor of Matanceros by land, you must scale the Leres ridge, to get to the other side."

Hunter made an impatient gesture. "Is it difficult to scale the ridge?"

"It is impossible," Whisper said. "The ordinary man cannot do it. Starting here, from the western cove, the land gently slopes up for five hundred feet or more. But it is a hot, dense jungle, with many swamps. There is no fresh water. There will be patrols. If the patrols do not find you and you do not die of fevers, you emerge at the base of the ridge. The western face of Leres ridge is vertical rock for three hundred feet. A bird cannot perch there. The wind is incessant with the force of a gale."

"If I did scale it," Hunter said. "What then?"

"The eastern slope is gentle, and presents no difficulty," Whisper said. "But you will never reach the eastern face, I promise you."

"If I did," Hunter said, "what of the Matanceros batteries?"

Whisper gave a little shrug. "They face the water, Captain Hunter. Cazalla is no fool. He knows he cannot be attacked from the land."

"There is always a way."

Whisper rocked in his chair, in silence, for a long time. "Not always," he said finally. "Not always."

DON DIEGO DE RAMANO, known also as Black Eye or simply as the Jew, sat hunched over his workbench in the shop on Farrow Street. He blinked nearsightedly at the pearl, which he held between the thumb and forefinger of his left hand. They were the only remaining fingers on that hand. "It is of excellent quality," he said. He handed the pearl back to Hunter. "I advise you to keep it."

Black Eye blinked rapidly. His eyes were weak, and pink, like a rabbit's. Tears ran almost continuously from them; from time to time, he brushed them away. His right eye had a large black spot near the pupil—hence his name. "You did not need me to tell you this, Hunter."

"No, Don Diego."

The Jew nodded, and got up from his bench. He crossed his narrow shop and closed the door to the street. Then he closed the shutters to the window, and turned back to Hunter. "Well?"

"How is your health, Don Diego?"

"My health, my health," Don Diego said, pushing his hands deep into the pockets of his loose robe. He was sensitive about his injured left hand. "My health is indifferent as always. You did not need me to tell you this, either."

"Is the shop successful?" Hunter asked, looking around the room. On rude tables, gold jewelry was displayed. The Jew had been selling from this shop for nearly two years now.

Don Diego sat down. He looked at Hunter, and stroked his beard, and wiped away his tears. "Hunter," he said, "you are vexing. Speak your mind."

"I was wondering," Hunter said, "if you still worked in powder."

"Powder? Powder?" The Jew stared across the room, frowning as if he did not know the meaning of the word. "No," he said. "I do not work in powder. Not after this"— he pointed to his blackened eye—"and after this." He raised his fingerless left hand. "No longer do I work in powder."

"Can your will be changed?"

"Never."

"Never is a long time."

"Never is what I mean, Hunter."

"Not even to attack Cazalla?"

The Jew grunted. "Cazalla," he said heavily. "Cazalla is in Matanceros and cannot be attacked."

"I am going to attack him," Hunter said quietly.

"So did Captain Edmunds, this year past." Don Diego grimaced at the memory. He had been a partial backer of that expedition. His investment—fifty pounds—had been lost. "Matanceros is invulnerable, Hunter. Do not let vanity obscure your sense. The fortress cannot be overcome." He wiped the tears from his cheek. "Besides, there is nothing there."

"Nothing in the fortress," Hunter said. "But in the harbor?"

"The harbor? The harbor?" Black Eye stared into space again. "What is in the harbor? Ah. It must be the treasure *naos* lost in the August storm, yes?"

"One of them."

"How do you know this?"

"I know."

"One *nao*?" The Jew blinked even more rapidly. He scratched his nose with the forefinger of his injured left hand—a sure sign he was lost in thought. "It is probably filled with tobacco and cinnamon," he said gloomily.

"It is probably filled with gold and pearls," Hunter said. "Otherwise it would have made straight for Spain, and risked capture. It went to Matanceros only because the treasure is so great it dared not risk a seizure."

"Perhaps, perhaps . . ."

Hunter watched the Jew carefully. The Jew was a great actor.

"Suppose you are right," he said finally. "It is of no interest to me. A *nao* in Matanceros harbor is as safe as if it were moored in Cádiz itself. It is protected by the fortress and the fortress cannot be taken."

"True," Hunter said. "But the gun batteries which guard the harbor can be destroyed—if your health is good, and if you will work in powder once again."

"You flatter me."

"Most assuredly I do not."

"What has my health to do with this?"

"My plan," Hunter said, "is not without its rigors."

Don Diego frowned. "You are saying I must come with you?"

"Of course. What did you think?"

"I thought you wanted money. You want me to come?"

"It is essential, Don Diego."

The Jew stood up abruptly. "To attack Cazalla," he said, suddenly excited. He began to pace back and forth.

"I have dreamt of his death each night for ten years, Hunter. I have dreamt . . ." He stopped pacing, and looked at Hunter. "You also have your reasons."

"I do." Hunter nodded.

"But can it be done? Truly?"

"Truly, Don Diego."

"Then I wish to hear the plan," the Jew said, very excited. "And I wish to know what powder you need."

"I need an invention," Hunter said. "You must fabricate something which does not exist."

The Jew wiped tears from his eyes. "Tell me," he said. "Tell me."

MR. ENDERS, THE barber-surgeon and sea artist, delicately applied the leech to his patient's neck. The man, leaning back in the chair, his face covered with a towel, groaned as the sluglike creature touched his flesh. Immediately, the leech began to swell with blood.

Mr. Enders hummed quietly to himself. "There now," he said. "A few moments and you will feel much better. Mark me, you will breathe easier, and show the ladies a thing or two, as well." He patted the cheek that was under the towel. "I shall just step outside for a breath of air, and return in a moment."

With that, Mr. Enders left the shop, for he had seen Hunter beckoning to him outside. Mr. Enders was a short man with quick, delicate movements; he seemed to dance rather than walk. He did a modest business in the port, because many of his patients survived his ministrations, unlike those of other surgeons. But his greatest skill, and his true love, was piloting a vessel under sail. Enders, a genuine sea artist, was that rare creature, a perfect helmsman, a man who seemed to find communion between himself and the ship he guided.

"Are you needing a shave, Captain?" he asked Hunter.

"A crew."

"Then you have found your surgeon," Enders said. "And what's the nature of the voyage?"

"Logwood cutting," Hunter said, and grinned.

"I am always pleased to cut logwood," Enders said. "And whose logwood might it be?"

"Cazalla's."

Immediately, Enders dropped his bantering mood. "Cazalla? You are going to Matanceros?"

"Softly," Hunter said, glancing around the street.

"Captain, Captain, suicide is an offense against God."

"You know that I need you," Hunter said.

"But life is sweet, Captain."

"So is gold," Hunter said.

Enders was silent, frowning. He knew, as the Jew knew, as everyone knew in Port Royal, that there was no gold in the fortress of Matanceros. "Perhaps you will explain?"

"It is better that I do not."

"When do you sail?"

"In two days' time."

"And we will hear the reasons in Bull Bay?"

"You have my word."

Enders silently extended his hand, and Hunter shook it. There was a writhing and grunting from the patient in the shop. "Oh dear, the poor fellow," Enders said, and ran back into the room. The leech was fat with blood, and dripping red drops onto the wooden floor. Enders lifted the leech away and the patient screamed. "Now, now, do be calm, Your Excellency."

"You are nothing but a damned pirate and rascal," said Sir James Almont, whipping the cloth off his face and daubing his bitten neck with it.

LAZUE WAS IN a bawdy house on Lime Road, surrounded by giggling women. Lazue was French; the name was a bastardization of Les Yeux, for this sailor's eyes were large, and bright, and legendary. Lazue could see better than anyone in the dark of night; many times, Hunter had gotten his ships through reefs and shoal water with the help of Lazue on the forecastle. It was also true that this slender, catlike person was an extraordinary marksman.

"Hunter," Lazue growled, with an arm around a buxom

girl. "Hunter, join us." The girls giggled and played with their hair.

"A word in private, Lazue."

"You are so tedious," Lazue said, and kissed each of the girls in turn. "I shall return, my sweets," Lazue said, and crossed with Hunter to a far corner. A girl brought them a crock of kill-devil, and each a glass.

Hunter looked at Lazue's shoulder-length tangled hair and beardless face. "Are you drunk, Lazue?"

"Not too drunk, Captain," Lazue said, with a raucous laugh. "Speak your mind."

"I am making a voyage in two days."

"Yes?" Lazue seemed to become suddenly sober. The large, watchful eyes focused intently on Hunter. "A voyage to what end?"

"Matanceros."

Lazue laughed, a deep, rumbling growl of a laugh. It was an odd sound to come from so slight a body.

"Matanceros means slaughter, and it is well-named, from all that I hear."

"Nonetheless," Hunter said.

"Your reasons must be good."

"They are."

Lazue nodded, not expecting to hear more. A clever captain did not reveal much about a raid until the crew was under way.

"Are the reasons as good as the dangers are great?"

"They are."

Lazue searched Hunter's face. "You want a woman on this voyage?"

"That is why I am here."

Lazue laughed again. She scratched her small breasts absently. Though she dressed and acted and fought like a man, Lazue was a woman. Her story was known to few, but Hunter was one.

Lazue was the daughter of a Brittany seaman's wife. Her husband was at sea when the wife found she was pregnant and subsequently delivered a son. However, the husband never returned—indeed, he was never heard from again—and after some months, the woman found herself pregnant a second time. Fearing scandal, she moved to another village in the province, where she delivered a daughter, Lazue.

A year passed and the son died. Meanwhile, the mother ran out of funds, and found it necessary to return to her native village to live with her parents. To avoid dishonor, she dressed her daughter as her son and the deception was so complete that no one in the village, including the child's grandparents, ever suspected the truth. Lazue grew up as a boy, and at thirteen was made a coachman for a local nobleman; later she joined the French army, and lived for several years among troops without ever being discovered. Finally—at least as she told the story—she fell in love with a handsome young cavalry officer and revealed her secret to him. They had a passionate affair but he never married her, and when it ended, she chose to come to the West Indies, where she again resumed her masculine role.

In a town like Port Royal, such a secret could not be kept long, and indeed everyone knew that Lazue was a woman. In any case, during privateering raids, she was in the habit of baring her breasts in order to confuse and terrify the enemy. But in the port, she was customarily treated like a man, and no one made any great cause over it.

Now, Lazue laughed. "You are mad, Hunter, to attack Matanceros."

"Will you come?"

She laughed again. "Only because I have nothing better to do." And she went back to the giggling whores at the far table.

HUNTER FOUND THE Moor, in the early-morning hours, playing a hand of gleek with two Dutch corsairs at a gaming house called The Yellow Scamp.

The Moor, also called Bassa, was a huge man with a giant head, flat slabs of muscle on his shoulders and chest, heavy arms, and thick hands, which curled around the playing cards and made them seem tiny. He was called the Moor for reasons long since forgotten; and even if he were inclined to tell of his origins, he could not do so, for his tongue had been cut out by a Spanish plantation-owner on Hispañola. It was generally agreed that the Moor was not Moorish at all but had come from the region of Africa called Nubia, a desert land along the Nile, populated by enormous black men.

His given name, Bassa, was a port on the Guinea coast, where slavers sometimes stopped, but all agreed that the Moor could not have come from that land, since the natives were sickly and much paler in color.

The fact that the Moor was mute and had to communicate with gestures increased the physical impression that he made. On occasion, newly arrived visitors to the port assumed that Bassa was stupid as well as mute, and as Hunter watched the card game in progress, he suspected that this was happening again. He took a tankard of wine to a side table and sat back to enjoy the spectacle.

The Dutchmen were dandies, elegantly dressed in fine hose and embroidered silk tunics. They were drinking heavily. The Moor did not drink at all; indeed, he never drank. There was a story that he could not tolerate liquor, and that once he had gotten drunk and killed five men with his bare hands before he came to his senses. Whether this was true or not, it was certainly true that the Moor had murdered the plantation owner who had cut out his tongue, then murdered his wife and half the household before making his escape to the pirate ports on the western side of Hispaniola, and from there, to Port Royal.

Hunter watched the Dutchmen as they bet. They were gambling recklessly, joking and laughing in high spirits. The Moor sat impassively, with a stack of gold coins in front of him. Gleek was a swift game that did not warrant casual betting, and indeed, as Hunter watched, the Moor drew three cards alike, showed them, and scooped up the Dutchmen's money.

They stared in silence a moment, and then both shouted "Cheat!" in several languages. The Moor shook his enormous head calmly, and pocketed the money.

The Dutchmen insisted that they play another hand, but in a gesture, the Moor indicated that they had no money left to bet.

At this, the Dutchmen became quarrelsome, shouting and pointing to the Moor. Bassa remained impassive, but a serving boy came over, and he handed the boy a single gold doubloon.

The Dutchmen apparently did not understand that the Moor was paying, in advance, for any damage that he might cause the gaming house. The serving boy took the coin and fled to a safe distance.

The Dutchmen were now standing, and shouting curses at the Moor, who remained seated at the table. His face was bland, but his eyes flicked back and forth from one man to the other. The Dutchmen became more quarrelsome, holding out their hands and demanding the return of their money.

The Moor shook his head.

Then one of the Dutchmen pulled a dagger from his belt, and brandished it in front of the Moor, just inches from his nose. Still the Moor remained impassive. He sat very still, with both hands folded in front of him on the table.

The other Dutchman started to tug a pistol out of his belt, and with that, the Moor sprang into action. His large black hand flicked out, gripped the dagger in the Dutchman's hand, and swung the blade down, burying it three inches deep in the tabletop. Then he struck the second Dutchman in the stomach; the man dropped his pistol and bent over, coughing. The Moor kicked him in the face and sent him sprawling across the room. He then turned back to the first Dutchman, whose eyes were wide with terror. The Moor picked him up bodily, held him high over his head, walked to the door, and flung the man through the air, out into the street, where he landed spread-eagled on his face in the mud.

The Moor returned to the room, plucked the knife out of the table, slipped it into his own belt, and crossed the room to sit next to Hunter. Only then did he allow himself a smile.

"New men," Hunter said.

The Moor nodded, grinning. Then he frowned and pointed to Hunter. His face was questioning.

"I came to see you."

The Moor shrugged.

"We sail in two days."

The Moor pursed his lips, mouthing a single word: *Ou?*

"Matanceros," Hunter said. The Moor looked disgusted.

"You're not interested?"

The Moor smirked, and drew a forefinger across his throat.

"I tell you, it can be done," Hunter said. "Are you afraid of heights?"

The Moor made a hand-over-hand gesture, and shook his head.

"I don't mean a ship's rigging," Hunter said. "I mean a cliff. A high cliff—three or four hundred feet."

The Moor scratched his forehead. He looked at the ceiling, apparently imagining the height of the cliff. Finally, he nodded.

"You can do it?"

He nodded again.

"Even in a high wind? Good. Then you'll go with us."

Hunter started to get up, but the Moor pushed him back into his chair. The Moor jangled the coins in his pocket, and pointed a questioning finger at Hunter.

"Don't worry," Hunter said. "It's worth it."

The Moor smiled. Hunter left.

HE FOUND SANSON in a second-floor room of the Queen's Arms. Hunter knocked on the door and waited. He heard a giggle and a sigh, then knocked again.

A surprisingly high voice called, "Damn you to hell and be gone."

Hunter hesitated, and knocked again.

"God's blood, who is it now?" came the voice from inside.

"Hunter."

"Damn me. Come in, Hunter."

Hunter opened the door, letting it swing wide, but he did not enter; a moment later, the chamber pot and its contents came flying through the open door.

Hunter heard a soft chuckle from inside the room. "Cautious as ever, Hunter. You will outlive us all. Enter."

Hunter entered the room. By the light of a single candle, he saw Sanson sitting up in bed, next to a blond girl.

"You have interrupted us, my son," Sanson said. "Let us pray that you have good reason."

"I do," Hunter said.

There was a moment of awkward silence, as the two men stared at each other. Sanson scratched his heavy black beard. "Am I to guess the reason for your coming?"

"No," Hunter said, glancing at the girl.

"Ah," Sanson said. He turned to the girl. "My delicate peach . . ." He kissed the tips of her fingers and pointed with his hand across the room.

The girl immediately scrambled naked out of bed, hastily grabbed up her clothes, and bolted from the room.

"Such a delightful creature," Sanson said.

Hunter closed the door.

"She is French, you know," Sanson said. "French women make the best lovers, don't you agree?"

"They certainly make the best whores."

Sanson laughed. He was a large, heavy man who gave the impression of brooding darkness—dark hair, dark eyebrows that met over the nose, dark beard, dark skin. But his voice was surprisingly high, especially when he laughed. "Can I not entice you to agree that French women are superior to English women?"

"Only in the prevalence of disease."

Sanson laughed heartily. "Hunter, your sense of humor

is most unusual. Will you take a glass of wine with me?"

"With pleasure."

Sanson poured from the bottle on his bedside table. Hunter took the glass and raised it in a toast. "Your health."

"And yours," Sanson said, and they drank. Neither man took his eyes off the other.

For his part, Hunter plainly did not trust Sanson. He did not, in fact, wish to take Sanson on the expedition, but the Frenchman was necessary to the success of the undertaking. For Sanson, despite his pride, his vanity, and his boasting, was the most ruthless killer in all the Caribbean. He came, in fact, from a family of French executioners.

Indeed, his very name—Sanson, meaning "without sound"—was an ironic comment on the stealthy way that he worked. He was known and feared everywhere. It was said that his father, Charles Sanson, was the king's executioner in Dieppe. It was rumored that Sanson himself had been a priest in Liège for a short time, until his indiscretions with the nuns of a nearby convent made it advantageous for him to leave the country.

But Port Royal was not a town where much attention was paid to past histories. Here Sanson was known for his skill with the saber, the pistol, and his favorite weapon, the crossbow.

Sanson laughed again. "Well, my son. Tell me what troubles you."

"I am leaving in two days' time. For Matanceros."

Sanson did not laugh. "You want me to go with you to Matanceros?"

"Yes."

Sanson poured more wine. "I do not want to go there," he said. "No sane man wants to go to Matanceros. Why do you want to go to Matanceros?"

Hunter said nothing.

Sanson frowned at his feet at the bottom of the bed. He wiggled his toes, still frowning. "It must be the galleons," he said finally. "The galleons lost in the storm have made Matanceros. Is that it?"

Hunter shrugged.

"Cautious, cautious," Sanson said. "Well then, what terms do you make for this madman's expedition?"

"I will give you four shares."

"Four shares? You are a stingy man, Captain Hunter. My pride is injured, you think me worth only four shares—"

"Five shares," Hunter said, with the air of a man giving in.

"Five? Let us say eight, and be done with it."

"Let us say five, and be done with it."

"Hunter. The hour is late and I am not patient. Shall we say seven?"

"Six."

"God's blood, you are stingy."

"Six," Hunter repeated.

"Seven. Have another glass of wine."

Hunter looked at him and decided that the argument was not important. Sanson would be easier to control if he felt he had bargained well; he would be difficult and without humor if he believed he had been unjustly treated.

"Seven, then," Hunter said.

"My friend, you have great reason." Sanson extended his hand. "Now tell me the manner of your attack."

Sanson listened to the plan without saying a word, and finally, when Hunter was finished, he slapped his thigh. "It is true what they say," he said, "about Spanish sloth, French elegance—and English craft."

"I think it will work," Hunter said.

"I do not doubt it for a heartbeat," Sanson said.

When Hunter left the small room, dawn was breaking over the streets of Port Royal.

CHAPTER 8

I T WAS, OF COURSE, impossible to keep the expedition secret. Too many seamen were eager for a berth on any privateering expedition, and too many merchants and farmers were needed to fit out Hunter's sloop *Cassandra*. By early morning, all of Port Royal was talking of Hunter's coming foray.

It was said that Hunter was attacking Campeche. It was said that he would sack Maricaibo. It was even said that he dared to attack Panama, as Drake had done some seventy years before. But such a long sea voyage implied heavy provisioning, and Hunter was laying in so few supplies that most gossips believed the target of the raid was Havana itself. Havana had never been attacked by privateers; the very idea struck most people as mad.

Other puzzling information came to light. Black Eye, the Jew, was buying rats from children and scamps around the docks. Why the Jew should want rats was a question beyond the imagining of any seaman. It was also known that Black Eye had purchased the entrails of a pig—which might be used for divination, but surely not by a Jew.

Meanwhile, the Jew's gold shop was locked and boarded.

The Jew was off somewhere in the hills of the mainland. He had gone off before dawn, with a quantity of sulfur, saltpeter, and charcoal.

The provisioning of the *Cassandra* was equally strange. Only a limited supply of salt pork was ordered, but a large quantity of water was required—including several small casks, which the barrel-maker, Mr. Longley, had been asked to fabricate specially. The hemp shop of Mr. Whitstall had received an order for more than a thousand feet of stout rope—rope too stout for use in a sloop's rigging. The sailmaker, Mr. Nedley, had been told to sew several large canvas bags with grommet fasteners at the top. And Carver, the blacksmith, was forging grappling hooks of peculiar design—the prongs were hinged, so the hooks could be folded small and flat.

There was also an omen: during the morning, fishermen caught a giant hammerhead shark, and hauled it onto the docks near Chocolata Hole, where the turtle crawls were located. The shark was more than twelve feet long, and with its broad snout, with eyes placed at each flattened protuberance, it was remarkably ugly. Fishermen and passers-by discharged their pistols into the animal, with no discernible effect. The shark flopped and writhed on the dockside planking until well into midday.

Then the shark was slit open at the underbelly, and the slimy coils of intestine spilled forth. A glint of metal was perceived and when the innards were cut open, the metal was seen to be the full suit of armor of a Spanish soldier— breastplate, ridged helmet, knee guards. From this it was deduced that the flathead shark had consumed the unfortunate soldier whole, digesting the flesh but retaining the armor, which the shark was unable to pass. This was variously taken as an omen of an impending Spanish attack on Port Royal, or as proof that Hunter was himself going to attack the Spanish.

SIR JAMES ALMONT had no time for omens. That morning, he was engaged in questioning a French rascal named L'Olonnais, who had arrived in port that morning with a Spanish brig as his prize. L'Olonnais had no letters of marque, and in any case, England and Spain were nominally at peace. Worse than that was the fact that the brig contained, at the time it arrived in port, nothing of particular value. Some hides and tobacco were all that were to be found in its hold.

Although renowned as a corsair, L'Olonnais was a stupid, brutal man. It did not take much intelligence, of course, to be a privateer. One had only to wait in the proper latitudes until a likely vessel happened along, and then attack it. Standing with his hat in his hands in the governor's office, L'Olonnais now recited his unlikely tale with childish innocence. He had happened upon the prize vessel, he said, and found it deserted. There were no passengers aboard, and the ship was drifting aimlessly.

"Faith, some plague or calamity must have fallen it," L'Olonnais said. "But 'twas a goodly ship, sire, and I felt a service to the Crown to bring it back to port, sire."

"You found no passengers at all?"

"Not a living thing."

"No dead aboard the ship?"

"Nay, sire."

"And no clue as to its misfortune?"

"Nary a one, sire."

"And the cargo—"

"As your own inspectors found it, sire. We'd not touch it, sire. You know that."

Sir James wondered how many innocent people L'Olonnais had murdered to clear the decks of that merchantman. And he wondered where the pirate had landed to hide the valuables of the cargo. There were a thousand islands and small brackish cays throughout the Carib sea that could serve his purposes.

Sir James rapped his fingers on his desk. The man was obviously lying but he needed proof. Even in the rough environment of Port Royal, English law prevailed.

"Very well," he said at last. "I shall formally state to you that the Crown is much displeased with this capture. The king therefore shall take a fifth—"

"A fifth!" Normally the king took a tenth, or even a fifteenth.

"Indeed," Sir James said evenly. "His Majesty shall have a fifth, and I shall formally state to you further that if any evidence reaches my ears of dastardly conduct on your part, you shall be brought to trial and hanged as a pirate and murderer."

"Sire, I swear to you that—"

"Enough," Sir James said, raising his hand. "You are free to go for the moment, but bear my words in mind."

L'Olonnais bowed elaborately and backed out of the room. Almont rang for his aide.

"John," he said, "find some of the seamen of L'Olonnais and see that their tongues are well oiled with wine. I want to know how he came to take that vessel and I want substantial proofs against him."

"Very good, Your Excellency."

"And John: set aside the tenth for the king, and a tenth for the governor."

"Yes, Your Excellency."

"That will be all."

John bowed. "Your Excellency, Captain Hunter is here for his papers."

"Then show him in."

Hunter strode in a moment later. Almont stood and shook his hand.

"You seem in good spirits, Captain."

"I am, Sir James."

"The preparations go well?"

"They do, Sir James."

"At what cost?"

"Five hundred doubloons, Sir James."

Almont had anticipated the sum. He produced a sack of coin from his desk. "This will suffice."

Hunter bowed as he took the money.

"Now then," Sir James said. "I have caused to be drawn up the paper of marque for the cutting of logwood at any location you deem proper and fitting." He handed the letter to Hunter.

In 1665, logwood cutting was considered legitimate commerce by the English, though the Spanish claimed a monopoly on that trade. The wood of the logwood,

Hematoxylin campaechium, was used in making red dye as well as certain medicines. It was a substance as valuable as tobacco.

"I must advise you," Sir James said slowly, "that we cannot countenance any attack upon any Spanish settlement, in the absence of provocation."

"I understand," Hunter said.

"Do you suppose there shall be any provocation?"

"I doubt it, Sir James."

"Then of course your attack on Matanceros will be piratical."

"Sir James, our poor sloop *Cassandra*, lightly armed and by the proofs of your papers engaged in commerce, may suffer to be fired upon by the Matanceros guns. In that instance, are we not forced to retaliate? An unwarranted shelling of an innocent vessel cannot be countenanced."

"Indeed not," Sir James said. "I am sure I can trust you to act as a soldier and a gentleman."

"I will not betray your confidence."

Hunter turned to go. "One last thing," Sir James said. "Cazalla is a favorite of Philip. Cazalla's daughter is married to Philip's vice chancellor. Any message from Cazalla describing the events at Matanceros differently from your account would be most embarrassing to His Majesty King Charles."

"I doubt," Hunter said, "that there will be dispatches from Cazalla."

"It is important that there not be."

"Dispatches are not received from the depths of the sea."

"Indeed not," Sir James said. The two men shook hands.

As Hunter was leaving the Governor's Mansion, a black womanservant handed him a letter, then wordlessly turned and walked away. Hunter descended the steps of the mansion, reading the letter, which was drafted in a feminine hand.

My dear Captain—

I am lately informed that a beautiful fresh spring can be found on the main portion of the Jamaican island, at the place called Crawford's Valley. To acquaint myself with the delights of my new residence, I shall make an excursion to this spot in the latter part of the day, and I hope that it is as exquisite as I am led to believe.

Fondly, I am,
Emily
Hacklett

Hunter slipped the letter into his pocket. He would not, under ordinary circumstances, pay heed to the invitation implicit in Mrs. Hacklett's words. There was much to do in this last day before the *Cassandra* set sail. But he was required to go to the inland anyway, to see Black Eye. If there was time . . . He shrugged, and went to the stables to get his horse.

CHAPTER 9

THE JEW WAS ensconced in Sutter's Bay, to the east of the port. Even from a distance, Hunter could determine his location by the acrid smoke rising above the green trees, and the occasional report of explosive charges.

He rode into a small clearing and found the Jew in the midst of a bizarre scene: dead animals of all sorts lay everywhere, stinking in the hot midday sun. Three wooden casks, containing saltpeter, charcoal, and sulfur, stood to one side. Fragments of broken glass lay glinting in the tall grass. The Jew himself was working feverishly, his clothing and face smeared with blood and the dust of exploded powder.

Hunter dismounted and looked around him. "What in God's name have you been doing?"

"What you asked," Black Eye said. He smiled. "You will not be disappointed. Here, I will show you. First, you gave me the task of a long and slow-burning fuse. Yes?"

Hunter nodded.

"The usual fuses are of no use," the Jew said judiciously. "One could employ a powder trail, but it burns with great swiftness. Or contrariwise, one could employ a slow match." A slow match was a piece of cord or twine soaked in saltpeter. "But that is very slow indeed, and the flame is often too weak to ignite the final materials. You take my meaning?"

"I do."

"Well then. An intermediate flame and speed of burning is provided by increasing the proportion of sulfur in the powder. But such a mixture is notorious for its unreliability. One does not wish the flame to sputter and die."

"No."

"I tried many soaked strings and wicks and cloths, to no avail. None can be counted on. Therefore I searched for a container to hold the charge. I have found this." He held up a thin, white, stringy substance. "The entrails of a rat," he said, smiling happily. "Lightly dried over warm coals, to remove humors and juices yet retaining flexibility. So, now when a quantity of powder is introduced to the intestine, a serviceable fuse results. Let me show you."

He took one length of intestine, perhaps ten feet long, whitish, with the faint dark appearance of the powder inside. He set it down on the ground and lit one end.

The fuse burned quietly, with little sputtering, and it

was slow—consuming no more than an inch or two in the space of a minute.

The Jew smiled broadly. "You see?"

"You have reason to be proud," Hunter said. "Can you transport this fuse?"

"With safety," the Jew said. "The only problem is time. If the intestine becomes too dry, it is brittle and may crack. This will happen after a day or so."

"Then we must carry a quantity of rats with us."

"I believe as much," the Jew said. "Now I have a further surprise, something you did not request. Perhaps you cannot find a use for it, though it seems to me a most admirable device." He paused. "You have heard of the French weapon which is called the *grenadoe*?"

"No," Hunter shook his head. "A poisoned fruit?" *Grenadoe* was the French word for pomegranate, and poisoning was lately very popular in the Court of Louis.

"In a sense," the Jew said, with a slight smile. "It is so called because of the seeds within the pomegranate fruit. I have heard this device exists, but was dangerous to manufacture. Yet I have done so. The trick is the proportion of saltpeter. Let me show you."

The Jew held up an empty, small-necked glass bottle. As Hunter watched, the Jew poured in a handful of birdshot and a few fragments of metal. While he worked, the

Jew said, "I do not wish you to think ill of me. Do you know of the *Complicidad Grande?*"

"Only a little."

"It began with my son," the Jew said, grimacing as he prepared the *grenadoe*. "In August of the year 1639, my son had long renounced the faith of a Jew. He lived in Lima, in Peru, in New Spain. His family prospered. He had enemies.

"He was arrested on the eleventh of August"—the Jew poured more shot into the glass—"and charged with being a secret Jew. It was said he would not make a sale on a Saturday, and also that he would not eat bacon for his breakfast. He was branded a Judaiser. He was tortured. His bare feet were locked into red-hot iron shoes and his flesh sizzled. He confessed." The Jew packed the glass with powder, and sealed it with dripping wax.

"He was imprisoned for six months," he continued. "In 1640, in January, eleven men were burned at the stake. Seven were alive. One of them was my son. Cazalla was the garrison commander who supervised the execution of the *auto*. My son's property was seized. His wife and children . . . disappeared."

The Jew glanced briefly at Hunter and wiped away the tears in his eyes. "I do not grieve," he said. "But perhaps you will understand this." He raised the *grenadoe*, and inserted a short fuse.

"You had best take cover behind those bushes," the Jew

said. Hunter hid, and watched as the Jew set the bottle on a rock, lit the fuse, and ran madly to join him. Both men watched the bottle.

"What is to happen?" Hunter said.

"Watch," the Jew said, smiling for the first time.

A moment later, the bottle exploded. Flying glass and metal blasted out in all directions. Hunter and the Jew ducked to the ground, hearing the fragments tear through the foliage above them.

When Hunter raised his head again, he was pale. "Good God," he said.

"Not a gentleman's apparatus," the Jew said. "It causes little damage to anything more solid than flesh."

Hunter looked at the Jew curiously.

"The Don has earned such attentions," the Jew said. "What is your opinion of the *grenadoe*?"

Hunter paused. His every instinct rebelled against a weapon so inhumane. Yet he was taking sixty men to capture a treasure galleon in an enemy stronghold: sixty men against a fortress with three hundred soldiers and the crew ashore, making another two or three hundred.

"Build me a dozen," he said. "Box them for the voyage, and tell no one. They shall be our secret."

The Jew smiled.

"You shall have your revenge, Don Diego," Hunter said. Then he mounted his horse and rode off.

CHAPTER 10

CRAWFORD'S VALLEY WAS a pleasant half-hour ride to the north, through the lush green foliage at the foot of the Blue Mountains. Hunter arrived at a high ridge overlooking the valley, and saw the horses of Mrs. Hacklett and her two slaves, tied alongside the gurgling stream, which ran out from the rocky pool at the east edge of the valley. He also saw a picnic cloth spread, and food laid out.

He rode down to the horses, and tied up his own. It took only a moment for him to bribe the two black women, pressing a finger to his lips and tossing them a shilling. Giggling to themselves, the two women slipped away. This was not the first time either of them had been bribed to keep silent about a clandestine meeting, and Hunter had no concern they might tell anyone what they had seen.

Nor did he think they would not soon be peering through the bushes at the two white people, and cackling to themselves. He moved quietly along the rocks by the edge of the pool, at the base of a gentle waterfall. Mrs. Hacklett was splashing about in the waters of the spring. She had not noticed Hunter yet.

"Sarah," Mrs. Hacklett said, speaking to the slave she still thought was nearby, "do you know that Captain Hunter, in the port?"

"Umm-hmmm," Hunter said, in a high-pitched voice. He sat down next to her clothes.

"Robert says he is nought but a common rogue and pirate," she said. "But Robert pays me so little attention. I was the favorite of the king—now there is a merry man and no mistake. But this Captain Hunter, he is so handsome. Does he have the favors of many women in the town, do you know?"

Hunter did not answer. He watched Mrs. Hacklett splashing.

"I expect he must do. He has that look in his eye which melts the hardest heart. And he is obviously strong and brave; no woman could fail to notice that. And his fingers and nose are of goodly length, which bodes well for his attentions. Does he have a favorite in the town, Sarah?"

Hunter did not answer.

"His Majesty has long fingers, and he is wonderfully well-suited for the bedroom." She giggled. "I should not be saying this, Sarah."

Hunter still said nothing.

"Sarah?" she said, turning. And she saw Hunter, sitting there grinning at her.

"Don't you know it is unhealthy to bathe?" Hunter said.

She splashed about angrily. "All that has been spoken of you is true," she complained. "You are a dastardly, uncouth, utterly foul man and truly no gentleman."

"Were you expecting a gentleman today?"

She splashed more. "Certainly I expected more than a common sneak and thief. Leave this spot now, so that I may dress myself."

"I find this spot most amiable," Hunter said.

"You refuse to leave?"

She was very angry. In the clear water, Hunter could see that she was rather too thin for his taste, a small-breasted, bony woman with a pinched face. But her anger aroused him.

"Indeed, I fear I do refuse."

"Then sir, I have misjudged you. I thought you would extend common courtesy and ordinary good manners to a woman at a disadvantage."

"What is your disadvantage?" Hunter asked.

"I am plainly naked, sir."

"So I see."

"And this spring is cold."

"Is it?"

"It is indeed."

"You have just perceived this?"

"Sir, I shall ask you once more to cease this impertinence and allow me a moment's privacy to dry and clothe myself."

In reply, Hunter walked down to the edge of the water, took her hand, and hauled her onto the rock, where she stood dripping and shivering, despite the warmth of the sun. She glared at him.

"You'll catch your death of chill," he said, grinning at her discomfiture.

"Then let us be equal," she said, and abruptly pushed him, fully clothed, into the water.

He landed with a splash, and felt a shock as the icy water touched his body. It made him gasp for breath. He floundered about, while she stood on the rock, laughing at him.

"Madam," he said, struggling. "Madam, I beseech you."

She continued to laugh.

"Madam," he said, "I cannot swim. I pray you to help—" And his head bobbed underwater a moment.

"A seafaring man who cannot swim?" And she laughed more.

"Madam . . ." was all he could say as he came to the surface then sank again. A moment later, he struggled up, splashing and kicking with no coordination, and she looked at him with concern. She reached out her hand, and he kicked and sputtered toward her.

He took her hand and pulled hard, flinging her high over his head. She screamed loudly, and landed flat on her back, with a stinging slap; she shrieked again as she went under. He laughed when she came to the surface. And helped her out onto the warm rock.

"You are nothing," she sputtered, "but a bastard, a rogue, a cutthroat vicious rascally whoreson scoundrel."

"At your service," Hunter said, and kissed her.

She broke away. "And forward."

"And forward," he agreed, and kissed her again.

"I suppose you intend to rape me like a common street woman."

"I doubt," Hunter said, stripping off his wet clothing, "that it will be necessary."

And it was not.

"In daylight?" she said, in a horrified voice, and those were her last intelligible words.

CHAPTER 11

IN THE MIDDLE of the day, Mr. Robert Hacklett confronted Sir James Almont with disturbing news. "The town is rife with rumor," he said, "that Captain Hunter, the same man with whom we supped yesterday past, is now organizing a piratical expedition against a Spanish dominion, perhaps even Havana."

"You place credence in these tales?" Almont asked calmly.

"Your Excellency," Hacklett said, "it is a simple fact that Captain Hunter has caused to have provisions for a sea voyage put aboard his sloop *Cassandra*."

"Probably," Almont said. "What proof is that of crime?"

"Your Excellency," Hacklett said, "with the greatest respect I must inform you that, by rumor, you have countenanced this excursion, and indeed may have made pecuniary gestures of support."

"Do you mean I paid for the expedition?" Almont said, a little irritably.

"In words to that effect, Sir James."

Sir James sighed. "Mr. Hacklett," he said, "when you have resided here a little longer—let us say, perhaps, a week—you will come to know that it is always the rumor that I have countenanced an excursion, and have paid for it."

"Then the rumors are groundless?"

"To this extent: I have given papers to Captain Hunter authorizing him to engage in logwood cutting at any convenient place. That is the extent of my interest in the matter."

"And where shall he cut this logwood?"

"I've no notion," Almont said. "Probably the Mosquito Coast of Honduras. That is the ordinary place."

"Your Excellency," Hacklett persisted, "may I respectfully remind you that in this era of peace between our nation and Spain, the cutting of logwood represents an irritant which might easily be avoided?"

"You may so remind me," Almont said, "but I judge you to be incorrect. Many lands in these parts are claimed by Spain and yet they have no habitation—no town, no colonists, no citizenry on these lands. In the absence of such proofs of dominion, I find the cutting of logwood to be unobjectionable."

"Your Excellency," Hacklett said, "can you not agree that what begins as a logwood-cutting expedition, even granting the wisdom of what you say, may easily turn into a piratical venture?"

"Easily? Not easily, Mr. Hacklett."

TO HIS MOST SACRED MAJESTY CHARLES,
BY THE GRACE OF GOD, OF GREAT BRITAIN
AND IRELAND, KING, DEFENDER OF THE
FAITH, ETC.

THE HUMBLE PETITION OF THE DEPUTY-
GOVERNOR OF HIS MAJESTY'S PLANTATIONS
AND LANDS IN JAMAICA, IN THE WEST
INDIES.

Humbly sheweth
    That I, Your Majesty's most loyal subject,
having been charged by Your Majesty with the
promulgation of the Court's feelings and desires
on the matter of piratical ventures in the West
Indies; and having made known by delivery
of epistle and oral pronouncement to Sir James
Almont, Governor of the aforementioned land
of Jamaica, these same feelings and desires,
I must report that little attention is given to
the cessation and suppression of piracy in these
parts. On the contrary, I must sadly if honestly
state that Sir James himself consorts with all

manner of rogue and villain; that he encourages
by word, deed and coin the continuance of
dastardly and bloody raids on Spanish lands;
that he permits use of Port Royal as a common
meeting place for these cutthroats and knaves,
and for the dispersal of their ill-gotten gains;
that he shows no remorse for these activities
and no evidence of their future cessation; that
he is himself a man unsuited to high capacity
by virtue of poor health and lax moral outlook;
that he abides all manner of corruption and
vice in the name of His Majesty. For all these
reasons and proofs, I most humbly implore and
petition Your Majesty to remove this man from
his position, and to choose, in His Majesty's
great wisdom, a more suitable successor who
shall not daily make a mockery of the Crown.
I most humbly implore Your Majesty's royal
assent to this simple petition, and shall ever
pray. In that continuance, I am, your most
faithful, loyal and obedient servant,

Robert
Hacklett

GOD SAVE THE KING

Hacklett reread the letter once, found it satisfactory, and rang for the servant. Anne Sharpe answered his call.

"Child," he said, "I wish you to see that this letter is dispatched on the next boat to England." And he gave her a coin.

"My lord," she said, with a little curtsey.

"Treat it with care," Hacklett said, frowning at her.

She slipped the coin into her blouse. "Does my lord wish anything else?"

"Eh?" he said, somewhat surprised. The saucy girl was licking her lips, smiling at him. "No," he said tersely. "Be gone now."

She left.

He sighed.

CHAPTER 12

BY TORCHLIGHT, HUNTER supervised the loading of his ship long into the night.

Wharfage fees in Port Royal were high; an ordinary merchant vessel could not afford to dock for more than a few hours to load or unload a cargo, but Hunter's little sloop *Cassandra* spent fully twelve hours drawn up to the pilings, and Hunter was not charged a penny. On the contrary, Cyrus Pitkin, who owned the dock, expressed delight at offering Hunter the space, and, to further encourage the captain to take up the generous offer, provided him with five free casks of water.

Hunter was polite in his acceptance. He knew that Pitkin was not being truly magnanimous; he would expect some gift on the *Cassandra*'s return, and he would get it.

Similarly, he accepted a barrel of salt pork from Mr. Oates, a farmer on the island. And he accepted a keg of powder from Mr. Renfrew, the gunsmith. It was all done with elaborate courtesy, and a sharp eye to value received and expected.

In between these courtly exchanges, Hunter questioned each member of his crew, and he had Mr. Enders examine them for disease, to be sure they were sound of body, before they were allowed to board. Hunter also checked all the provisions, opening each barrel of pork and water, sniffing the contents, then plunging his hand to the bottom, to be certain it was filled all the way down. He tasted each cask of water; and he satisfied himself that the stores of hard biscuit were fresh and without weevils.

On a long ocean voyage, it was not possible for the captain to make such examinations himself. An ocean voyage called for literally tons of food and water for the passengers; and much of the meat was taken on live, squawking and mooing.

But privateers traveled differently. Their small boats were crammed with men, and provisioning was slight. A privateer did not expect to eat well on a voyage; sometimes, in fact, no food at all was taken on, and the vessel set out with the expectation of obtaining provisions by raiding another ship or a town.

Nor were the privateers heavily armed. The *Cassandra*, a sloop of seventy feet, carried four sakers, swivel-mounted guns positioned fore and aft. These were its only armament, and they were hardly suited against even a fifth- or sixth-rate warship. Instead, the privateers relied on speed and maneuverability—and a shallow draft—to elude their more dangerous opponents. They could sail closer to the wind than a larger warship, and they could make for shoal harbors and channels where a bigger ship could not continue pursuit.

In the Caribbean Sea, where they were hardly ever out of sight of some island with its protective ring of shoal coral reefs, they felt safe enough.

Hunter worked at the loading of his ship until nearly dawn. From time to time, whenever curious onlookers gathered, he was careful to send them away. Port Royal was thick with spies; Spanish settlements paid well for advance news of an intended raid. And in any case, Hunter did not want people to see the unusual supplies he was laying in— all the rope, the grappling hooks, and the strange bottles the Jew had provided in cases.

The Jew's cases, in fact, were stored in an oilskin sac, and placed belowdecks, out of view of the seamen themselves. It was, as Hunter explained to Don Diego, "our little secret."

As dawn was breaking, Mr. Enders, still energetic, still bouncing with his lilting walk, came over and said, "Beg pardon, Captain, but there's a one-legged beggar's been lingering by the warehouse for the better part of the night."

Hunter peered at the building, still dark in the early-morning light. The docks were not a profitable place to beg. "You know him?"

"No, Captain."

Hunter frowned. Under other circumstances, he could send the man to the governor and request that the beggar be clapped in Marshallsea jail for a few weeks. But the hour was late; the governor was still sleeping and would not be pleased at a disturbance. "Bassa."

The huge form of the Moor materialized at his side.

"You see the beggar with the wooden leg?"

Bassa nodded.

"Kill him."

Bassa walked away. Hunter turned to Enders, who sighed. "It's best, I think, Captain." He repeated the old proverb. "Better a voyage begin in blood than end in blood."

"I fear we may have plenty of both," Hunter said, and turned back to his work.

When the *Cassandra* set sail a half hour later, with Lazue forward to watch for the shoals of Pelican Point in the dim morning light, Hunter looked back once at the docks and the port. The town slept peacefully. The lamplighters were extinguishing the torches at the dock. A few well-wishers were turning away, having said their good-byes.

Then, floating facedown in the water, he saw the body of the one-legged beggar. In the tide, the body rocked back and forth, the wooden leg knocking softly against a piling.

It was, he thought, either a good omen or a bad one. He could not be certain which.

CHAPTER 13

CONSORTS WITH ALL manner of rogue and villain,'" sputtered Sir James. "'Encourages . . . the continuance of dastardly and bloody raids on Spanish lands'—good God, 'dastardly and bloody,' the man is mad—'permits use of Port Royal as a common meeting place for these cutthroats and knaves . . . unsuited to high capacity . . . abides all manner of corruption . . .' Damn the man."

Sir James Almont, still in his dressing gown, waved the letter in his hand. "Damn the rogue and villain," he said. "When did he give you this?"

"Yesterday, Your Excellency," Anne Sharpe said. "I thought you would want it, Your Excellency."

"Indeed I do," Almont said, giving her a coin for her trouble. "And if there is more of the same, you shall be further rewarded, Anne." He thought to himself that she was proving an exceedingly clever child. "Has he made advances?"

"No, Your Excellency."

"As I thought," Almont said. "Well, we shall devise a way to settle Mr. Hacklett's games of intrigue, once and finally."

He walked to the window of his bedchamber and looked out. In the early dawn light, the *Cassandra*, now rounding the point of Lime Cay, raised her mainsail and headed east, gaining speed.

THE *CASSANDRA*, LIKE all privateering vessels, made first for Bull Bay, a little inlet a few miles east of Port Royal. There, Mr. Enders put the ship into irons, and with sails luffing and fluttering in the light breeze, Captain Hunter made his speech.

These formalities were known to everyone aboard. First, Hunter called for a vote on himself as captain of the vessel; a chorus of ayes greeted him. Then he stated the rules of the voyage—no drink, nor fornication, and no looting without his order; a penalty of death for breaking the rules. These were the usual rules, and the aye vote was perfunctory.

Next, he explained the division of the booty. Hunter, as captain, would take thirteen shares. Sanson would have seven—there was some grumbling at this figure—and Mr. Enders would have one and a half shares. Lazue would take one and a quarter. Black Eye would take one and a quarter. The rest would be equally distributed among the crew.

One crewmember stood. "Captain, are you taking us to Matanceros? It is dangerous."

"Indeed it is," Hunter said, "but the booty is great. There will be plenty for every man. Any man who sees the danger as over-much will be put ashore here, in this bay, and none the worse in my estimation. But he must go before I tell you the treasure that is there."

He waited. No one moved or spoke.

"All right," Hunter said. "Matanceros harbor holds a Donnish treasure *nao*. We are going to take her." At this there was an enormous uproar among the crew. It was several minutes before Hunter could get them silent again. And when they looked back at him, he saw the glint in their eyes, fed by visions of gold. "Are you with me?" Hunter shouted. They responded with a shout.

"Then, on to Matanceros."

Part II

THE BLACK SHIP

CHAPTER 14

SEEN FROM A distance, the *Cassandra* presented a pretty spectacle. Her sails were taut in the morning breeze; she was heeled over a few degrees, and cut a swift, hissing path through the clear blue water.

On board the ship, however, it was cramped and uncomfortable. Sixty fighting men, grizzled and smelly, jostled for space to sit, game, or sleep in the sun. They relieved themselves over the side, without ceremony, and their captain was often presented with the spectacle of a half-dozen bare buttocks leaning over the leeward gunwale.

No food was parceled out, and no water. None was given for the first day at all, and the crew, expecting this, had eaten and drunk their fill on their last night in the port.

Nor did Hunter anchor that evening. It was customary for the privateers to put into some protected cove, to allow the crew to sleep ashore. But Hunter sailed straight through the first night. He had two reasons for haste. First, he feared spies who might make for Matanceros to warn the garrison there. And second, he did not wish to allow extra time, since the treasure *nao* might depart the harbor of Matanceros at any time.

At the end of the second day, they were beating northeast, through the dangerous passage between Hispañola and Cuba. His crew knew this region well, for they were within a day's sail of Tortuga, long a pirate stronghold.

He continued into the third day, and then landed for the night, to rest his weary crew. The following day, he knew, would begin the long ocean run past Inagua, and then to Matanceros itself. There would be no safe landing in the future. Once they crossed Latitude 20, they were in dangerous Spanish waters.

His crew was in good spirits, laughing and joking around the campfires. During the past three days, only one man had been seized by visions of the crawling devils, which sometimes accompanied the absence of rum; that man was now calmer, no longer trembling and shaking.

Satisfied, Hunter stared into the fire before him. Sanson came over, and sat next to him.

"What are your thoughts?"

"None special."

"Do you brood on Cazalla?"

"No." Hunter shook his head.

"I know that he killed your brother," Sanson said.

"He caused him to be killed, yes."

"And this does not anger you?"

Hunter sighed. "Not anymore."

Sanson stared at him in the flickering firelight. "What was the manner of his dying?"

"It is not important," Hunter said evenly.

Sanson sat quietly for some moments. "I have heard," he said, "that your brother was captured on a merchant ship by Cazalla. I have heard that Cazalla strung him up by his arms, cut off his testicles and stuffed them into his mouth until he choked and died."

Hunter did not answer for some time. "That is the story," he said finally.

"And do you believe it?"

"Yes."

Sanson scanned his face. "The crafty English. Where is your anger, Hunter?"

"I have it," Hunter said.

Sanson nodded. He stood. "When you find Cazalla, kill him quickly. Do not let this hatred cloud your brain."

"My brain is not clouded."

"No. I see it is not."

Sanson left. Hunter remained staring into the fire for a long time.

∞

IN THE MORNING, they entered the dangerous Windward Passage, between Cuba and Hispañola. Winds were unpredictable, and the water was rough, but the *Cassandra* made excellent time. Sometime during the night they passed the dark promontory of Le Mole—the westward tip of Hispañola—to starboard. And near dawn, the profile of the land split to reveal Tortuga Island, along the north coast.

They continued on.

THEY WERE IN open water for all of the fifth day, but the weather was good, with only a light chop on the sea. By late afternoon they sighted Inagua Island to port, and soon after, Lazue spotted the crust on the horizon that meant Les Caiques, dead ahead. This was important, for south of Les Caiques was a treacherous shallow bank for several miles.

Hunter gave orders to turn eastward, toward the still-unseen Turk Isles. The weather remained good. The crew sang and dozed in the sun.

The sun was dropping lower in the sky when Lazue electrified the sleepy crew with the shout, "Sail ho!"

Hunter leapt to his feet. He squinted at the horizon, but saw nothing. Enders, the sea artist, had the glass to his eye, scanning in all directions. "Damn me," he said, and handed the glass to Hunter. "She's hard abeam, Captain."

Hunter looked through the spyglass. Through the curving rainbow rings of color, he saw a white rectangle low on the horizon. Even as he watched, the white rectangle took on another corner, becoming two overlapping rectangles.

"How do you make it?" Enders asked.

Hunter shook his head. "You know as well as I." From this distance, there was no way to determine the nationality of the approaching vessel, but these were undisputed Spanish waters. He glanced around the horizon. Inagua was far behind them; it would be a five-hour sail, and that island offered few protections. To the north, Les Caiques were inviting, but the wind was out of the northeast, and they would have to be too close-hauled to make good speed. To the east, Turk Isle was still not visible—and it was in the direction of the approaching sails.

He had to make a decision; none of the alternatives were inviting. "Change course," he said finally. "Make for Les Caiques."

Enders bit his lip and nodded. "Ready about!" he shouted, and the crew jumped to the halyards. The *Cassandra* came through the wind, and tacked north.

"Come off it," Hunter said, eyeing the sails. "Make speed."

"Aye, Captain," Enders said. The sea artist was frowning

unhappily, as indeed he might, for the sails on the horizon were now clearly visible to the naked eye. The other ship was gaining on them; the topgallants had now cleared the horizon, and the foresails were coming into view.

With the glass to his eye, Hunter saw three corners to the topgallants. A three-masted ship almost certainly meant a warship of some nationality.

"Damn!"

As he watched, the three sails merged into one square, then separated once more.

"She's come about," Hunter said. "On a long reach now for us."

Enders's feet did a little nervous dance while his hand gripped the tiller. "We'll not outrun her on this tack, Captain."

"Or any tack," Hunter said gloomily. "Pray for a calm."

The other ship was less than five miles away. In a steady wind, it would inexorably gain on the *Cassandra*. Their only hope now was a drop in the wind; then the *Cassandra*'s lighter weight would let her pull away.

It sometimes happened that the wind died around sunset, but just as commonly it freshened. Soon enough, Hunter felt the breeze more strongly on his cheeks.

"We've no luck today," Enders said.

They could now see the mainsails of the pursuing craft, pink in the sunset and billowing full in the freshened breeze.

Les Caiques were still far away, a safe haven madden-ingly distant, beyond their reach.

"Shall we turn and run, Captain?" Enders asked.

Hunter shook his head. The *Cassandra* might do better in a run before the wind, but that could only be postponing the inevitable. Unable to do anything, Hunter clenched his fists with impotent rage and watched the sails of the pursu-ing ship grow larger. They could see the edge of the hull now.

"She's a ship of the line, all right," Enders said. "I can't make out the bow."

The shape of the bow was the most likely way to tell nationality. Spanish warships tended to have a blunter bowline than English or Dutch ships.

Sanson came back to the tiller. "Are you going to fight?" he said.

In answer, Hunter just pointed to the ship. The hull was now clear of the horizon. She was more than a hun-dred and thirty feet at the waterline, and she had two gun decks. The gunports were opened, the blunt snouts of the cannon protruding. Hunter did not bother to count them; there were at least twenty, perhaps thirty, on the starboard side that he could see.

"She's Donnish to my eye," Sanson said.

"So she is," Hunter agreed.

"Will you fight?"

"Fight that?" Hunter said. Even as he spoke, the warship came around and fired an opening volley at the *Cassandra*. The guns were still too far away; the shot splashed harmlessly off the port side, but the warning was clear. Another thousand yards and the warship would be within range.

Hunter sighed. "Come into the wind," he said softly.

"Beg pardon, Captain," Enders said.

"I said, come into the wind and release all halyards."

"Aye, Captain," Enders said.

Sanson glared at Hunter, and stomped off forward. Hunter paid no attention. He watched as his little sloop nosed into the wind, and the lines were let out. The sails luffed noisily in the breeze; the boat came to a standstill. Hunter's crew lined the port rail, watching as the warship came closer. The hull of the ship was painted entirely black, with gilt trim, and the arms of Philip—prancing lions—shone on the aft castle. It was Spanish all right.

"We could make a fair show," Enders said, "when they move in to take us. You've only to give us the word, Captain."

"No," Hunter said. On a ship of that size, there would be at least two hundred sailors, and as many armed soldiers on deck. Sixty men in an open sloop against four hundred in a larger craft? In the face of the least resistance, the warship would simply move off a distance and fire broadsides at the *Cassandra* until she sank.

"Better to die with a sword in your hands than a Popish rope around your neck, or the Don's damned fire curling your toes," Enders said.

"We will wait," Hunter said.

"Wait for what?"

Hunter had no answer. He watched as the warship came so close that the shadow of the *Cassandra*'s mainsail fell across her side. Spanish voices shouted staccato commands in the growing darkness.

He looked at his own ship. Sanson was hurriedly priming pistols, jamming them into his belt. Hunter went over to him.

"I am going to fight," Sanson said. "You may give yourselves up like timid women, but I will fight."

Hunter had a sudden idea. "Then do this," he said, and whispered into Sanson's ear. A moment later, the Frenchman crept away.

The Spanish shouts continued. Ropes were thrown to the *Cassandra*. An unbroken line of soldiers with muskets stood high above them on the warship's main deck, aiming down into the little sloop. The first of the Spanish soldiers climbed down to *Cassandra*. One by one, Hunter and his crew were prodded with muskets and forced to climb the rope ladder to the enemy vessel.

CHAPTER 15

AFTER THEY HAD spent so many days cramped aboard the *Cassandra*, the warship seemed enormous. Its main deck was so vast it appeared like a plain, stretched out before them. Hunter's crew, hustled together by soldiers around the mainmast—the same crew that filled the sloop to overflowing—looked puny and insignificant here. Hunter looked at the faces of his men; they averted their eyes, not returning the gaze; their expressions were angry, frustrated, disappointed.

High above, the enormous sails fluttered in the breeze, making a noise so great that the dark Spanish officer confronting him had to shout to be heard.

"You are captain?" he bellowed.

Hunter nodded.

"What is called?"

"Hunter," he shouted back.

"English?"

"Yes."

"You go to this captain," the man said, and two armed soldiers hustled Hunter below. Apparently, he was to be taken to the captain of the warship. Hunter looked over his shoulder, and had a last glimpse of his forlorn crew around the mast. Already, their hands were being bound behind their backs. The warship's crew was efficient.

He stumbled down the narrow stairs to the gun deck. He had a brief glimpse of the long line of cannon, their crews standing ready, before he was roughly shoved aft. As he passed the open gunports to aft, he could look down at his little sloop, tied alongside the warship. Spanish soldiers were swarming over it, and the Spanish sailors of the prize crew were examining its fittings and lines, preparing to sail it.

He was not allowed to linger; a musket at his back prodded him along. They came to a door with two heavily armed, evil-looking men standing guard. Hunter noticed that these men wore no uniforms and assumed an air of peculiar superiority; they glanced at him with pitying disdain. One of them knocked on the door and said a few quick words in Spanish; there was an answering grunt, and they opened the door, and pushed Hunter in. One of the guards went inside as well, and closed the door.

The captain's cabin was remarkably large, and ornately fitted. There was evidence of space and luxury everywhere. There was a dining table with a fine linen cloth, and gold plates set out for the evening meal by candlelight. There was a comfortable bed with a brocade bedcover laced in gold. A richly colored oil painting depicting Christ on the cross hung in a corner, above a cannon with an open porthole. In another corner, a lantern cast a warm golden light over the room.

There was another table at the rear of the cabin; maps covered it. Behind that table, in a plush red velvet chair, sat the captain himself.

His back was turned to Hunter as he poured wine from a cut-crystal decanter. Hunter could see only that the man was very large; his back was broad as a bull's.

"Well now," the captain said, in very good English, "can I persuade you to join me in a glass of this excellent claret?"

Before Hunter could reply, the captain turned. Hunter found himself staring into glowering eyes set in a heavy face with a strong nose and jet-black beard. Without his wishing, the word sprang from his lips:

"Cazalla!"

The Spaniard laughed heartily. "Did you expect King Charles?"

Hunter was speechless. He was vaguely aware that his lips worked, but no sound came out. At the same time, a thousand questions sprang to mind. Why was Cazalla here, and not in Matanceros? Did that mean the galleon was gone? Or had he left the fortress in command of some capable lieutenant?

Or perhaps he was ordered away by a higher authority—this warship might be bound for Havana.

Even as these questions flooded his mind, he was overcome by a cold fear. It was all he could do to keep his body from shaking as he stood and looked at Cazalla.

"Englishman," Cazalla said, "your discomfort flatters me. I am embarrassed I do not know your name in turn. Sit down, be at ease."

Hunter did not move. The soldier roughly shoved him into a chair facing Cazalla.

"Much better," Cazalla said. "Will you take your claret now?" He passed Hunter the glass.

With the strongest effort of will, Hunter kept his hand from trembling as he took the proffered glass. But he did not drink; he set it immediately on the table. Cazalla smiled.

"Your health, Englishman," he said, and drank. "I must drink to your health while it is still possible to do so. You are not joining me? No? Come now, Englishman. Even His Excellency the Commander of the Havana Garrison does not have claret so fine as this. It is French, called Haut-Brion. Drink." He paused. "Drink."

Hunter took the glass, and drank a little. He felt mesmerized, almost in a trance. But the taste of the claret broke the spell of the moment; the ordinary gesture of lifting the glass to his lips and swallowing brought him back to himself. His shock passed away, and he began to notice a thousand tiny details. He heard the breathing of the soldier behind him; probably two paces behind, he thought. He saw the irregularity of Cazalla's beard and guessed the man had been some days at sea. He smelled the garlic on Cazalla's breath as he leaned forward and said, "Now, Englishman. Tell me: what is your name?"

"Charles Hunter," he said, in a voice that was stronger and more confident than he had dared hope.

"Yes? Then I have heard of you. You are the same Hunter who took the *Conception* one season ago?"

"I am," Hunter said.

"The same Hunter who led the raid on Monte Cristo in Hispañola and held the plantation owner Ramona for ransom?"

"I am."

"He is a pig, Ramona, do you not think?" Cazalla laughed. "And you are also the same Hunter who captured the slave ship of de Ruyters while it was at anchor in Guadeloupe, and made off with all his cargoes?"

"I am."

"Then I am most pleased to be acquainted with you, Englishman. Do you know your value? No? Well, it has gone up each passing year, and perhaps it has been raised again. When last I heard, King Philip offered two hundred gold doubloons for you, and eight hundred more for your crew to any who effected a capture. Perhaps it is more now. The decrees change, so many details. Formerly we sent pirates back to Seville, where the Inquisition could encourage you to repent your sins and your heresy in the same breath. But that is so tedious. Now we send only the heads, and reserve our cargo space for more profitable wares."

Hunter said nothing.

"Perhaps you are thinking," Cazalla continued, "that two hundred doubloons is too modest a sum. As you may imagine, at this very moment I agree with you. But you enjoy the distinction of knowing that you are the most valued pirate in all these waters. Does that please you?"

"I take it," Hunter said, "in the spirit it was intended."

Cazalla smiled. "I can see that you are born a gentleman," he said. "And I wish to assure you that you shall be hanged with all the dignity of a gentleman. You have my word on that."

Hunter gave a small bow from his chair. He watched as Cazalla reached across his desk for a small glass bowl with a fitted lid. Inside the bowl were broad green leaves. Cazalla removed one of these leaves and chewed it thoughtfully.

"You look puzzled, Englishman. This practice is unfamiliar to you? The Indians of New Spain called this leaf coca. It grows in the high country. To chew it brings energy, and strength. For women it provokes great ardor," he added, chuckling. "You wish to taste for yourself? No? You are reluctant to accept my hospitality, Englishman."

He chewed a moment in silence, staring at Hunter. Finally, he said, "Have we not met before?"

"No."

"Your face is strangely familiar. Perhaps in the past, when you were younger?"

Hunter felt his heart pound. "I do not think so."

"No doubt you are right," Cazalla said. He stared thoughtfully at the painting on the far wall. "All Englishmen look alike to me. I cannot tell one from the next." He looked back at Hunter. "And yet you recognized me. How can that be?"

"Your visage and manner are much known in the English colonies."

Cazalla chewed a bit of lime with his leaves. He smiled, then chuckled. "No doubt," he said. "No doubt."

He abruptly wheeled around in his chair and slapped the table. "Enough: we have business to discuss. What is the name of your vessel?"

"*Cassandra*," Hunter said.

"And who is her owner?"

"I am myself owner and captain."

"And whence put you to sea?"

"Port Royal."

"And for what reason did you make a sea voyage?"

Hunter paused here. If he could have conjured up a plausible reason, he would have immediately said it. But it was not easy to explain the presence of his ship in these waters. Finally, he said, "We were advised a slaver from Guinea would be found in these waters."

Cazalla made a clucking sound, and shook his head. "Englishman, Englishman."

Hunter made his best show of reluctance. Then he said, "We were making for Augustine." That was the most settled town in the Spanish colony of Florida. It had no particular riches, but it was at least conceivable that English privateers would attack it.

"You chose an odd course. And a slow one." Cazalla drummed his fingers on the tabletop. "Why did you not sail west around Cuba, into the Bahama Passage?"

Hunter shrugged. "We had reason to believe there were Spanish warships in the passage."

"And not here?"

"The risk was better here."

Cazalla considered this for a long moment. He chewed noisily, and sipped his wine. "There is nothing in Augustine but swamps and snakes," he said. "And no reason to risk the Windward Passage. And in this vicinity . . ." He shrugged. "No settlement which is not strongly defended, too strongly for your little boat and your puny crew." He frowned. "Englishman, *why are you here?*"

"I have spoken the truth," Hunter said. "We were making for Augustine."

"This truth does not satisfy me," Cazalla said.

At that moment, there was a knock at the door, and a seaman stuck his head into the cabin. He spoke rapidly in Spanish. Hunter knew no Spanish, but he had a little command of French, and with this knowledge he was able to deduce that the seaman was telling Cazalla the sloop was manned with its prize crew and ready to sail. Cazalla nodded and stood.

"We sail now," he said. "You come with me to the deck. Perhaps there are others in your crew who do not share your reluctance to speak."

CHAPTER 16

THE PRIVATEERS HAD been formed up in two ragged lines, their hands bound. Cazalla paced up and down in front of the men. He held a knife in one hand, and slapped the flat of the blade against the palm of his other hand. For a moment, there was complete silence except for the rhythmic slap of steel on his fingers.

Hunter looked away, to the rigging of the warship. She was making an easterly course—probably heading for the protection of Hawk's Nest anchorage, south of Turk Isle. He could see, in the twilight, the *Cassandra* following on the same course a short distance behind the larger ship.

Cazalla interrupted his thoughts.

"Your captain," he said loudly, "will not tell me your destination. He says it is Augustine," he said, with heavy sarcasm. "Augustine: a child could lie more convincingly. But I tell you: I will know your purpose. Which man of you will step forward and say?"

Cazalla looked at the two lines of men. The men stared back at him with blank faces.

"Must I encourage you? Eh?" Cazalla stepped close to one seaman. "You. Will you speak?"

The seaman did not move, did not speak, did not even blink. After a moment, Cazalla resumed his pacing.

"Your silence means nothing," he said. "You are all heretics and brigands, and you will swing at the end of a rope in good time. Until that day, a man can either live comfortably, or not. Any man who speaks shall live at his ease until the appointed day, and for that he has my solemn word."

Still no one moved. Cazalla stopped pacing. "You are fools. You mistake my determination."

He was standing now in front of Trencher, clearly the youngest member of the privateer crew. Trencher trembled, but he held his head high.

"You, lad," Cazalla said, his voice softening. You do not belong in this rough company. Speak up, and tell me the purpose of your voyage."

Trencher opened his mouth, then closed it again. His lip trembled.

"Speak," Cazalla said softly. "Speak, speak . . ."

But the moment had passed. Trencher's lips were firm and tight together.

Cazalla watched him for a moment, and then with a single, swift gesture slit his throat with the knife in his hand. It happened so quickly Hunter hardly saw it. Blood poured in a broad red sheet down the boy's shirt. His eyes were wide with horror and he shook his head slowly in a kind of disbelief. Trencher sank to his knees and remained there a moment, head bowed, watching his own blood drip onto the wood decking, and onto the toes of Cazalla's boots. The Spaniard stepped back with a curse.

Trencher remained kneeling for what seemed an eternity. Then he looked up, and gazed for an agonizing moment into Hunter's eyes. His look was pleading, and confused, and afraid. And then his eyes rolled upward and his body pitched flat onto the deck, and he gave a violent shiver.

All the seamen were watching Trencher die, and yet no man moved. His body convulsed, his shoes making a scrabbling sound on the wood of the deck. Blood ran in a large pool around his face. And then finally he was still.

Cazalla had watched the death throes with utter absorption. Now he stepped forward, placed his foot on the dead boy's neck, and stamped hard. There was the crunch of breaking bones.

He looked at the two lines of seamen. "I shall know the truth," he said. "I swear to you, I shall know it." He spun to his first mate. "Take them below and lock them," he said. He nodded to Hunter. "Take him with them."

And he strode off to the aft castle. Hunter was bound and taken below with the others.

The Spanish warship had five decks. The upper two decks were gun decks; some of the crew slept here, in hammocks stretched between the cannon. Next were quarters for the soldiers. The fourth deck was given over to storage of shot, food, block and tackle, fittings, provisions, and livestock. The fifth and lowest deck was hardly a deck at all: it was barely four feet from the floor to the heavy-beamed ceiling, and because this deck was below the waterline, there was no ventilation. The heavy air stank of feces and bilge.

The *Cassandra*'s crew was taken here. The men were made to sit on the rough floors, a little apart from each other. Twenty soldiers were stationed as guards in corners of the room, and from time to time one would walk around with a lantern, examining each man's bonds to be certain they were not loosened.

Talking was not permitted, nor was sleep, and any man who tried either was treated to a rough kick from a soldier's boot. The men were not allowed to move, and if they had to relieve themselves, they did so where they sat. With sixty men and twenty guards, the narrow airless space soon became suffocating, hot, and fetid. Even the guards were soaked in sweat.

There was no indicator of the passage of time. The only sounds were the heavy thumping movements of the livestock on the deck above, and the endless, monotonous hiss of water as the warship sailed forward. Hunter sat in the corner, trying to concentrate on the sound of the water, waiting for it to cease. He tried to ignore the true desperateness of his condition—he and his crew were buried deep in the bowels of a mighty warship, surrounded by hundreds of enemy soldiers, utterly at their mercy. Unless Cazalla anchored for the night, they were all doomed. Hunter's sole chance depended on the warship halting overnight.

Time passed: he waited.

Eventually, he was aware of a change in the gurgle of the water, and a shift in the creaking of the rigging. He sat up, listening carefully. There was no doubt of it—the ship was slowing.

The soldiers, huddled together and speaking quietly, noticed it too, and commented among themselves. A moment later, the sound of the water ceased entirely, and Hunter heard the rattle of the anchor chain being let out. The anchor splashed loudly; somewhere in his mind, Hunter made a note that he was near the bow of the ship. Otherwise the sound would not be so distinct.

More time passed. The warship rocked gently at anchor. They must be in some protected cove, for the water to be so calm. Yet the ship had a deep draft, and Cazalla would not bring his ship into any harbor at night unless he knew it well.

He wondered where they were, and hoped it was in a cove near Turk Isle. There were several leeward coves deep enough for a ship this size.

The rocking of the warship at anchor was restful. More than once he felt himself dozing off. The soldiers kept busy kicking the seamen, keeping them awake. The gloomy semidarkness of the low deck was frequently punctuated by the grunts and groans of the crew as they were kicked.

Hunter wondered about his plan. What was happening?

After a further passage of time, a Spanish soldier came down and barked, "Every man to stand! Orders of Cazalla! All stand to feet!" Encouraged by the boots of the soldiers, the seamen stood, one by one, bent over in the narrow deck. It was an aching, agonizingly uncomfortable posture.

More time passed. The guard was changed. The new soldiers entered holding their noses and making jokes about the smell. Hunter looked at them oddly; he had long since ceased to be aware of any odor.

The new guards were younger and more casual about their duties. Apparently, the Spaniards were convinced the pirates could give them no trouble. The new guards quickly turned to playing cards. Hunter looked away, and watched drops of his own sweat fall to the floor. He thought of poor Trencher, but he could not work up anger, or indignation, or even fear. He was numb.

A new soldier arrived. He was some sort of officer and apparently he was displeased with the relaxed attitude of the young men. He barked out sharp orders and the men hastily put aside their cards.

The new officer went around the room, examining the faces of the privateers. Finally, he plucked one fellow out of the group, and led him away. The man collapsed on rubbery legs when ordered to walk; the soldiers picked him up and dragged him out.

The door closed. The guards made a brief display of attentiveness, and then relaxed again. But they did not play cards. After a while, two of them decided to engage in a contest to see who could urinate the farthest. The target was a seaman in the corner. This game was considered fine sport by the guards, who laughed and pretended to bet enormous sums of money on the outcome.

Hunter was only dimly aware of these events. He was very tired; his legs burned with fatigue and his back ached. He began to wonder why he had refused to tell Cazalla the purpose of the voyage. It seemed a meaningless gesture.

At that moment, Hunter's thoughts were interrupted by the arrival of another officer, who barked: "Captain Hunter!" And Hunter was led away, out of the room.

As he was pushed and prodded through the decks of sleeping seamen, rocking in their hammocks, he distinctly heard, from somewhere in the ship, an odd and plaintive sound.

It was the sound of a woman crying.

CHAPTER 17

HUNTER HAD NO opportunity to reflect on the meaning of that strange sound, for he was pushed hastily onto the main deck. There, beneath the stars and the reefed sails, he noticed that the moon was low—which meant that dawn could not be more than a few hours away.

He felt a sharp pain of despair.

"Englishman, come here!"

Hunter looked around and saw Cazalla, standing near the mainmast, in the center of a ring of torches. At his feet, the seaman previously taken from the room lay spread-eagled on his back, firmly lashed to the deck. A number of Spanish soldiers stood about, and all were grinning broadly.

Cazalla himself seemed highly excited; he was breathing rapidly and shallowly. Hunter noticed that he was chewing more coca leaf.

"Englishman, Englishman," he said, speaking rapidly. "You are just in time to witness our little sport. Do you know we searched your ship? No? Well, we did, and we found many interesting things."

Oh God, Hunter thought. No . . .

"You have much rope, Englishman, and you have funny iron hooks that fold up, and you have other strange things of canvas which we do not understand. But most of all, Englishman, we do not understand this."

Hunter's heart pounded: if they had found the *grenadoes*, then it would all be finished.

But Cazalla held out a case with four rats. The rats scampered back and forth and squeaked nervously.

"Can you imagine, Englishman, how amazed we were to find that you bring rats on your ship? We say to ourselves, why is this? Why does the Englishman carry rats to Augustine? Augustine has rats of its own, Florida rats, very good ones. Yes? So I wonder, how do I explain this?"

Hunter watched as a soldier did something to the face of the seaman lashed to the deck. At first he could not see what was being done; the man's face was being rubbed or stroked. Then Hunter realized: they were smearing cheese on his face.

"So," Cazalla said, waving the cage in the air, "then I see that you are not kind to your friends, the rats. They are hungry, Englishman. They want food. You see how excited they are? They smell food. That is why they are excited. I think we should feed them, yes?"

Cazalla set the cage down within inches of the seaman's face. The rats flung themselves at the bars, trying to get to the cheese.

"Do you see what I mean, Englishman? Your rats are very hungry. Do you not think we should feed them?"

Hunter stared at the rats, and at the frightened eyes of the immobile seaman.

"I am wondering if your friend here will talk," Cazalla said.

The seaman could not take his eyes off the rats.

"Or perhaps, Englishman, you will talk for him?"

"No," Hunter said wearily.

Cazalla bent over the seaman and tapped him on the chest. "And you, will you talk?" With his other hand, Cazalla touched the latch to the cage door.

The seaman focused on the latch, watching as Cazalla raised the bar slowly, a fraction of an inch at a time. Finally, the latch was released; Cazalla held the door closed with a single finger.

"Your last chance, my friend . . ."

"*Non!*" the seaman shrieked. "*Je parle! Je parle!*"

"Good," Cazalla said, switching smoothly to French.

"Matanceros," the seaman said.

Cazalla turned livid with rage. "Matanceros! You idiot, you expect me to believe that? To attack Matanceros!" And, abruptly, he released the door to the cage.

The seaman shrieked hideously as the rats leapt to his face. He shook his head, the four furry bodies clinging to the flesh of his cheeks and scalp and chin. The rats chattered and squeaked; one was flung off but instantly scrambled back across the man's heaving chest and bit into the neck. The seaman screamed over and over in terror, a monotonous, repeated sound. Finally, the man collapsed from shock, and lay unmoving while the rats, chattering, continued to feed on his face.

Cazalla stood. "Why do you all think me so stupid?" he said. "Englishman, I swear. I will have the truth of your voyage."

He turned to the guards. "Take him below."

Hunter was hustled off the deck. As he was pushed down the narrow stairway, he had a brief glimpse over the rail of the *Cassandra*, lying at anchor some yards away from the warship.

Chapter 18

THE SLOOP *CASSANDRA* was essentially an open boat, with a single main deck exposed to the elements, and small storage lockers located fore and aft. These had been searched by the soldiers and the prize crew, when the ship was taken during the afternoon. The crew had found all the provisions and special fittings that Cazalla considered so perplexing.

Soldiers swarming over the boat had searched it with great thoroughness. They had even peeked through the fore and aft hatches, which opened down into the keelson; with lanterns, they saw bilge water rising almost to the decking itself, and they made sarcastic comments about the laziness of the pirates in emptying the bilge.

When the *Cassandra* made for the protected cove, and hove to in the shadow of the warship, its prize crew of ten spent several hours drinking and laughing by torchlight. When they finally slept in the early hours of the morning, lying on the deck on blankets in the warm night air, their sleep was heavy with rum. Although they had been ordered to post a watch, they did not bother to do so; the nearby warship offered protection enough.

Thus, no member of the crew, lying on the deck, was aware of a soft gurgle from the bilge compartment and no one saw a man with a reed in his mouth rise out of the oily, stinking water.

Sanson, shivering with cold, had lain for hours with his head alongside the oilskin sac, which contained the precious *grenadoes*. Neither he nor the sac had been noticed. Now, he was just able to lift his chin above the level of the bilge water before he struck the top of his head on the decking. He was surrounded by darkness, with no sense of orientation. Using his hands and feet, he pressed his back down against the hull, feeling its curved shape. He decided he was on the port side of the ship, and moved slowly, quietly, toward the centerline. Then, with exquisite slowness, he eased himself aft, until his head softly bumped the rectangular indentation of the aft hatch. Looking up, he saw slats of lights from the grating of the hatch. Stars above. No sounds, except a snoring seaman.

He took a breath, and raised his head. The hatch moved up a few inches. He could see the deck. He was staring directly into the face of a sleeping seaman, not more than a foot away. The man snored loudly.

Sanson lowered the hatch again, and moved forward through the bilge compartment. It took him nearly a quarter of an hour, lying on his back, pushing along with his hands, to traverse the fifty feet between the aft and fore hatches of the *Cassandra*. He raised the new hatch cover, and looked around again. There was no sleeping seaman within ten feet.

Gently, slowly, Sanson removed the hatch cover, and set it on the deck. He lifted himself out of the water, and stood breathing the fresh night air. His drenched body was chilled by the breeze, but he paid no attention. All of his mind was focused on the sleeping prize crew on deck.

Sanson counted ten men. That would be about right, he thought. In a pinch, three men could sail the *Cassandra*; five could handle her comfortably; ten men would be more than ample.

He surveyed the positions of the men on the deck, trying to decide in which order to kill them. It was easy to kill a man quietly, but to kill one in absolute silence was not so simple. Of the ten men, the first four or five were most crucial, for if any of them made a noise, they would raise a general alarm.

Sanson removed the thin cord that served as his belt. He twisted the rope in his hands and tugged it taut between his fists. Satisfied with its strength, he picked up a belaying pin of carved hardwood, and moved forward.

The first soldier was not snoring. Sanson raised the man to sitting position and he grumbled sleepily at the interruption for a moment before Sanson brought the pin crashing down on his head. The blow was fierce, but made only a dull thud as it contacted the scalp. Sanson eased the seaman back to the deck.

In the darkness, he ran his hands over the skull. There was a deep indentation; probably the blow had killed him, but he took no chances. He slipped the cord around the man's throat and squeezed tightly. Simultaneously, he laid his other hand flat on the man's chest to feel the heartbeat. A minute later, there was no pulsation.

Sanson moved to the next man, crossing like a shadow over the deck. He repeated the process. It took him no more than ten minutes to kill every man on the ship. He left them lying in positions of sleep on the deck.

The last man to die was the sentry, slumped aft in a drunken stupor over the tiller. Sanson cut the man's throat and pushed him over the side. He fell into the water with a soft splash, but it was noticed by a guard on the warship deck. The guard leaned over and looked at the sloop.

"*Questa sta bene?*" he called.

Sanson, taking up the sentry's position aft, waved to the

guard. Although he was dripping wet and wearing no uniform, he knew it was too dark for the warship's guard to see.

"Sta bene," he said sleepily.

"Bassera," the guard said, and turned away.

Sanson waited a moment, then turned his attention to the warship. It was some hundred yards away—far enough off that if the big ship turned at anchor with a change of wind or tides, she would not strike the *Cassandra*. Sanson was pleased to see that the Spaniards had neglected to batten down the gunports, which were still open. If he entered through an open port on the lower gun deck, he would be able to avoid sentries on the main deck.

He slipped over the side and swam quickly across to the warship, thinking briefly that he hoped the Spanish had not dumped garbage in the cove during the night. Garbage would draw sharks, and the shark was one of the few creatures in the world Sanson feared. But he made the crossing uneventfully, and soon found himself bobbing in the water alongside the hull of the warship.

The lowest gunports were twelve feet above him. He heard the joking of the sentries on the main deck. A rope ladder was still over the side, but he dared not use it. Once he put his weight to it, it would creak and move, and the sentries on deck might hear that.

Instead, he slipped forward, to the anchor line, and

climbed that to the runners moving back from the bow-sprit. These runners protruded only four inches from the hull surface, but Sanson managed to get a footing, and maneuver back to the foresail rigging. From there, it was easy to hang and look into one of the forward gunports.

Listening intently, he soon heard the steady, measured pacing of the watch. By the footsteps, it sounded like a single sentry, circling the perimeter of the deck endlessly. Sanson waited until the watch passed him, and then eased in through the porthole, and dropped down in the shadow of a cannon, gasping with exertion and excitement. Even for Sanson, to be alone in the midst of four hundred of the enemy—half of them swinging gently in their hammocks before him—was an exhilarating sensation. He waited, and planned his next move.

HUNTER WAITED IN the fetid hold of the ship, stand-ing crouched in the narrow space. He was desperately exhausted. If Sanson did not arrive soon, his men would be too fatigued to make an escape. The guards, now yawn-ing and playing cards again, showed a total indifference to the prisoners, which was tempting and infuriating. If only he could get his men free while the ship still slept around him, then there might be a chance. But when the guard changed—as it might at any time—or when the ship's crew arose at dawn, then there would be no opportunity.

He felt a moment of crushing defeat as a Spanish soldier entered the room.

The watch was changing, and all was lost. A moment later, he realized he was wrong: this was just a single man, not an officer, and the guards who greeted him did so in desultory fashion. The new man assumed an air of considerable strutting self-importance, and went around the room checking the bonds of the privateers. Hunter felt the tug of fingers feeling the ropes on his own hands—and then something cool—the blade of a knife—and his ropes were cut.

Behind him, the man whispered softly: "This will cost you two more shares."

It was Sanson.

"Swear it," Sanson hissed.

Hunter nodded, feeling anger and elation at the same moment. But he said nothing; he just watched as Sanson moved around the room and then stopped at the door to block it.

Sanson faced the seamen and said, in English, very quietly, "Do it softly, softly."

The Spanish guards looked up in stunned surprise as the privateers leapt at them. They were overpowered three to one. It took only a moment. Immediately, the seamen began to strip off the uniforms and to dress in them. Sanson moved over to Hunter.

"I did not hear you swear it."

Hunter nodded, rubbing his wrists. "I swear. Two shares to you."

"Good," Sanson said. He opened the door, put his finger to his lips, and led the seamen out of the hold.

CHAPTER 19

CAZALLA DRANK WINE and brooded on the face of the dying Lord, thinking of the suffering, the agony of the body. From his earliest youth, Cazalla had seen images of that agony, the torment of the flesh, the sagging muscles and the hollow eyes, the blood that poured from the wound in the side, the blood that dripped from the spikes in the hands and feet.

This painting, in his cabin, had come as a gift from Philip himself. It was the work of His Majesty's favorite court painter, a man named Velázquez, now deceased. To be given the painting was a mark of considerable esteem, and Cazalla had been overpowered to receive it; he never traveled unless it was at his side. It was his most treasured possession.

This man Velázquez had not put a halo around the Lord's visage. And the coloring of the body was deathly gray-white. It was altogether realistic, but Cazalla often wished for a halo. He was surprised that a king so pious as Philip had not insisted that a halo be added. Perhaps

Philip disliked the painting; perhaps that was why he had sent it to one of his military captains in New Spain.

In black moments, another thought occurred to Cazalla. He was only too aware of the gap that separated the niceties of life in Philip's Court from the hard life of the men who sent him the gold and silver from the colonies to support such luxuries. One day he would rejoin the Court, a rich man in his latter years. Sometimes, he thought that the courtiers would laugh at him. Sometimes, in his dreams, he killed them all in bloody, angry duels.

Cazalla's reverie was interrupted by the sway of the ship. The tide must be out, he thought; that meant dawn was not far off; soon they would be under way for the day. It would be time to kill another English pirate. Cazalla intended to kill them, one by one, until someone told him the truth he wanted to know.

The ship continued to move, but there was something wrong with the motion. Cazalla sensed it instinctively; the ship was not swinging around its forward anchor line; it was moving laterally; something was very wrong. And then, at that moment, he heard a soft crunch and the ship shuddered and was still.

With a curse, Cazalla sprinted onto the main deck. There he found himself staring into the fronds of a palm tree, just inches from his face. Several palm trees, all lining the shore of the island. His ship was beached. He screamed in fury. The panicked crew scrambled around him.

The first mate, trembling, ran over. "Captain, they cut the anchor line."

"*They?*" Cazalla shouted. When he was angry, his voice became high and thin, the voice of a woman. He ran to the opposite railing and saw the *Cassandra*, heeled over in a fair breeze, making for the open sea. "*They?*"

"The pirates have escaped," said the mate, pale.

"Escaped! How could they have escaped?"

"I don't know, my Captain. The guards are all dead."

Cazalla struck the man full in the face, sending him sprawling across the deck. He was so furious he could hardly think. He stared across the water at the departing sloop. "How could they escape?" he repeated. "God in damnation, how could they escape?"

The captain of the infantry came over. "Sir, we are hard-beached. Shall I land some men and try to push off?"

"The tide is running," Cazalla said.

"Yes, my Captain."

"Well, fool, we cannot get afloat until the tide is in once more." Cazalla cursed loudly. That would be twelve glasses. Six hours before they could begin to free the massive ship. And even then, if the boat was hard-beached, they might not get free. It was the season of the waning moon; each tide was less full than the last. Unless they got free in the next tide—or the one after—they would be beached for three weeks or more.

"Fools!" he shrieked.

In the distance, the *Cassandra* came smartly around on a southerly tack and disappeared from view. A southerly tack?

"They are going to Matanceros," Cazalla said. And he shook with uncontrollable rage.

HUNTER SAT IN the stern of the *Cassandra* and plotted his course. He was surprised to find that he no longer felt any fatigue at all, though he had not slept for two days. Around him, his crew lay sprawled in attitudes of collapse; nearly all were deeply asleep.

"They are good men," Sanson said, looking at them.

"Indeed," Hunter said.

"Did any one of them talk?"

"One did."

"And Cazalla believed him?"

"Not at that moment," Hunter said, "but he may change his view later."

"We have at least six hours on them," Sanson said.

"Eighteen, if we are lucky."

Hunter nodded. Matanceros was two days sail into the

wind; with such a start, they might beat the warship to the fortress.

"We will sail through all the nights," Hunter said.

Sanson nodded.

"Harden that jib sheet," Enders barked. "Lively there."

The sail tautened, and with a fresh breeze from the east, the *Cassandra* cut through the water into the dawn light.

Part III

MATANCEROS

CHAPTER 20

IN THE AFTERNOON, the sky was streaked with patchy clouds that turned dark and gray as the sun faded. The air was damp and forbidding. It was then that Lazue spotted the first of the timbers.

Sailing on, the *Cassandra* moved among dozens of broken pieces of wood and ship's wreckage. The crew threw out lines and brought some of it aboard.

"Looks English," Sanson said, when a piece of the high transom, painted red and blue, was hauled onto the deck.

Hunter nodded. A good-sized ship had been sunk. "Not long ago," he said. He scanned the horizon for any sign of survivors, but there was none. "Our Donnish friends have been hunting."

Pieces of wood thumped against the hull of the ship for another fifteen minutes. The crew was uneasy; sailors did not like to see the evidence of such destruction. Another cross-brace was brought aboard, and from it, Enders guessed the ship had been a merchantman, probably a brig or frigate, one hundred fifty feet or so.

They never found any sign of the crew.

The air turned increasingly sullen as night fell, and a sea squall blew up. In the darkness, hot rain hammered the wooden decks of the *Cassandra*. The men were soaked and miserable through the night. Yet the dawn was fair and clear, and when it broke, they saw their destination dead ahead on the horizon.

From a distance, the western face of the island of Matanceros is singularly uninviting. Its volcanic contours are sharp and jagged, and except for low vegetation along the shore, the island appears dry and brown and barren, with patches of exposed bare reddish-gray rock. Little rain fell on the island, and because it was so far eastward in the Caribbean, the winds off the Atlantic whipped around its single peak ceaselessly.

The crew of the *Cassandra* watched Matanceros approach without any trace of enthusiasm. Enders, at the helm, frowned. "It's September," he said. "She's as green and welcoming as ever she gets."

"Aye," Hunter said. "It's no haven. But there's a forest on the eastern shore, and plenty of water."

"And plenty of Popish muskets," Enders said.

"And plenty of Popish gold," Hunter said. "How long do you make landfall?"

"Fair wind. Midday at latest, I'd warrant."

"Bear for the cove," Hunter said, pointing. Already they could see the only indentation on the western coast, a narrow inlet called Blind Man's Cove.

Hunter went off to collect the supplies that his small landing party would carry with them. He found Don Diego, the Jew, already setting out the equipment on the deck. The Jew fixed Hunter with a weak eye. "Considerate of the Dons," he said. "They looked, but didn't take anything."

"Except the rats."

"We can make do with anything small, Hunter. Possum, any small creature."

"We'll have to," Hunter said.

Sanson was standing in the bow, looking forward at the peak of Mt. Leres. From a distance, it appeared absolutely sheer, a curving semicircle of naked red rock.

"There's no way around it?" Sanson asked.

Hunter responded, "The only passages around will be guarded. We must go over the top."

Sanson gave a slight smile; Hunter went aft again to Enders. He gave orders that once his party had been beached, the *Cassandra* was to sail south to the next island, Ramonas. A small cove with fresh water could be found there, and the sloop would be safe from attack.

"You know the place?"

"Aye," Enders said. "I know it. Holed up a week in that cove some years back under Captain Lewisham with his one eye. She's fair enough. How long do we wait there?"

"Four days. On the afternoon of the fourth day, move out of the cove and anchor in deep water. Sail at midnight, and bring yourself to Matanceros just before dawn on the fifth day."

"And then?"

"Sail right up into the harbor at dawn, and board the men onto the galleon."

"Passing the guns of the fort?"

"They'll not trouble you on the fifth morning."

"I'm not a praying man," Enders said. "But I'm hoping."

Hunter clapped him on the shoulder. "There's nothing to fear."

Enders looked toward the island and did not smile.

BY NOON, IN the still midday heat, Hunter, Sanson, Lazue, the Moor, and Don Diego stood on the narrow strip of white sand beach and watched the *Cassandra* depart. At their feet was more than a hundred and twenty pounds of equipment—rope, grappling hooks, canvas slings, muskets, water caskets.

They stood in silence for a moment, breathing in lung-fuls of burning air. Then Hunter turned away. "Let's make off," he said. They moved away from the water's edge, toward the shoreline.

Beyond the beach, the shoreline of palm trees and tan-gled mangroves appeared as impenetrable as a stone wall. They knew from bitter experience that they could not hack their way through this barrier; to attempt it was to make no more than a few hundred yards of progress in the course of a day of feverish physical effort. The usual method of entering the interior of an island was to find a stream, and move up it.

They knew there must be such a stream here, for the very existence of a cove implied it. Coves were formed in part because there was a break in the outer reefs, and that break meant fresh water pouring out from the land. They walked along the beach, and after an hour located a sparse trickle of water cutting a muddy track through the foli-age along the shore. The streambed was so narrow that the plants overgrew it, making a sort of cramped, hot tunnel. The passage was obviously not easy.

"Should we look for a better one?" Sanson said.

The Jew shook his head. "There is little rainfall here. I doubt there is a better one."

They all seemed to agree, and set out, moving up the creek, away from the sea. Almost immediately, the heat became unbearable, the air hot and rank. It was, as Lazue said, like breathing cloth.

After the first few minutes, they traveled in silence, wasting no energy on talk. The only sound was the thwack of their cutlasses on the foliage, and the chatter of birds and small animals in the canopy of trees above them. Their progress was slow. Toward the end of the day, when they looked over their shoulders, the blue ocean below seemed discouragingly near.

They pressed on, pausing only to capture food. Sanson was a master of the crossbow, and used it to shoot several birds. They were encouraged to notice the droppings of a wild boar near the streambed. Lazue collected plants that were edible.

Nightfall found them halfway up the strip of jungle between the sea and the bare rock of Mt. Leres. Although the air turned cooler, they were trapped beneath the foliage and it remained almost as hot as before. In addition, the mosquitoes were out.

The mosquitoes were a formidable enemy, coming in thick clouds so dense as to be almost palpable, obscuring each man's vision of those near him. The insects buzzed and whined around them, clinging to every part of their bodies, getting into ears and nose and mouth. They coated themselves liberally with mud and water, but nothing really helped. They dared not light a fire, but ate the caught game raw, and slept the night fitfully, propped up against trees, with the droning buzz of mosquitoes in their ears.

In the morning, they awoke, the caked mud dropping off their stiff bodies, and they looked at each other and laughed. They were all changed, their faces red and swollen and lumpy with mosquito bites. Hunter checked the water; a quarter of their supply was gone, and he announced they would have to consume less. They moved on, hoping to see a wild boar, for they were all hungry. They never sighted one. The monkeys chattering in the overhead canopy of foliage seemed to taunt them. They heard the animals, but Sanson never had a clear shot at one.

Late in the second day, they began to notice the sound of the wind. It was faint at first, a far-off low moan. But as they approached the edge of the jungle, where the trees were thinner and their progress easier, the wind grew louder. Soon they could feel it, and although the breeze was welcome, they looked back at each other with anxiety. They knew the breeze would grow in strength as they approached the cliff face of Mt. Leres.

It was late afternoon when they finally reached the rocky base of the cliff. The wind was now a screaming demon that tugged and whipped their clothing, bruised their faces, shrieked in their ears. They had to shout to be heard.

Hunter looked up at the rock wall before them. It was as sheer as it seemed from a distance, and, if anything, higher than he had thought—four hundred feet of naked rock, lashed by a wind so strong that stone chips and rock fragments fell down on them continually.

He motioned to the Moor, who came over. "Bassa," Hunter shouted, leaning close to the huge man. "Will the wind be less at night?"

Bassa shrugged, and made a pinching gesture with two fingers: a little better.

"Can you make the climb at night?"

He shook his head: no. Then he made a little pillow with his hands, and leaned his head on it.

"You want to climb in the morning?"

Bassa nodded.

"He's right," Sanson said. "We should wait until morning, when we are rested."

"I don't know if we can wait," Hunter said. He was looking to the north. Some miles away, across a placid sea, he saw the broad gray line over the water, and above that, angry black clouds. It was a storm, several miles wide, moving slowly toward them.

"All the more reason," Sanson shouted to Hunter. "We should let it pass."

Hunter turned away. From their position at the base of

the cliff, they were five hundred feet above sea level. Looking south, he could see Ramonas, some thirty miles away.
The *Cassandra* was not in sight; it had long since found the
protection of the cove.

Hunter looked back at the storm. They might wait
out the night, and the storm might pass them by. But if
it were large enough, and slow enough, and they lost even
one day, then their timing would be ruined. And three
days hence, the *Cassandra* would sail into Matanceros carrying fifty men to certain death.

"We climb now," Hunter said.

He turned to the Moor. The Moor nodded, and went to
collect his ropes.

IT WAS AN extraordinary sensation, Hunter thought, as
he held the rope in his hands and felt the occasional jerk
and wiggle as the Moor moved up the cliff face. The rope
between Hunter's fingers was an inch and a half thick, yet
high overhead, it thinned to a wispy thread, and the giant
bulk of the Moor was a speck he could barely discern in the
softening light.

Sanson came over to shout in his ear. "You are insane,"
he yelled. "None of us will survive this."

"Afraid?" Hunter shouted back.

"I fear nothing," Sanson said, thumping his chest. "But look at the others."

Hunter looked. Lazue was trembling. Don Diego was very pale.

"They cannot make it," Sanson shouted. "What will you do without them?"

"They'll make it," Hunter said. "They have to." He looked over at the storm, which was closer. It was now only a mile or two away; they could feel the moisture in the wind. He felt a sudden tug on the rope in his hands, then a second quick jerk.

"He's done it," Hunter said. He looked up, but could not see the Moor at all.

A moment later, another rope dropped to the ground.

"Quick," Hunter said. "The supplies." They tied the provisions, already loaded into canvas bags, onto the rope, and gave a signaling tug. The bags began their bumpy, bouncing ascent up the cliff face. Once or twice, the force of the wind blew them away from the rock a distance of five or ten feet.

"God's blood," Sanson said, seeing it.

Hunter looked at Lazue. Her face was tight. He went over and fitted the canvas sling around her shoulder, and another around her hips.

"Mother of God, Mother of God, Mother of God," Lazue said, over and over in a monotone.

"Now listen," Hunter shouted, as the rope came down again. "Hold the long line, and let Bassa pull you up. Keep your face to the rock, and don't look down."

"Mother of God, Mother of God . . ."

"Did you hear me?" Hunter shouted. "Don't look down!"

She nodded, still muttering. A moment later, she started up the rock, hoisted by the sling. She had a brief period of awkwardness, twisting and clutching for the other line. Then she seemed to get her bearings, and her ascent up the face was uneventful.

The Jew was next. He stared at Hunter with hollow eyes as Hunter gave him the instructions: he did not seem to hear; he was like a man sleepwalking as he stepped into the sling and was hoisted up.

The first drops of rain from the approaching storm began to fall.

"You will go next," Sanson shouted.

"No," Hunter said. "I am last."

By now, it was raining steadily. The winds had increased. When the sling came down the cliff again, the canvas was soaked. Sanson stepped into the sling and jerked the rope, to signal his ascent. As he started up, he shouted to Hunter, "If you die, I will take your shares." And then he laughed, his laughter trailing off in the wind.

With the approach of the storm, a gray fog clung around the top of the cliff. Sanson was soon lost from view. Hunter waited. A very long time seemed to pass, and then he heard the wet slap of the sling on the ground nearby. He walked over, and fitted himself into it. Wind-blown rain slashed against his face and body as he tugged on the line and started up.

He would remember that climb for the rest of his life. He had no sense of position, for he was wrapped in a dark gray world. All he could see was the rocky face just a few inches away. The wind tore at him, often swinging him wide away from the cliff, then slamming him back against the rock. The ropes, the rock, everything was wet and slippery. He held the guideline in his hands, and tried to keep himself facing the cliff. Often he lost his footing and twisted around, banging his back and shoulders into the rock.

It seemed to take forever. He had no idea whether he had traversed half the distance, or only a fraction of it. Or whether he was nearly there. He strained to hear the voices of the others at the top but all he heard was the maniacal shriek of the wind, and the splatter of the rain.

He felt the vibration of the tow-rope as he was pulled up. It was a steady, rhythmic shudder. He moved up a few feet; then a pause; then up a few feet more. Then another pause; then another brief ascent.

Suddenly, there was a break in the pattern. No more ascent. The rope vibration changed; it was transmitted to his body through the canvas sling. At first he thought it was some trick of the senses, but then he knew what it was—the hemp, after five rough passages over the rock, was frayed and now was slowly, agonizingly stretching.

In his mind's eye, he saw it thinning, and at that moment gripped the guide rope tightly. In the same instant the sling rope snapped, and came twisting and snaking down on his head and shoulders, heavy and wet.

His grip on the guide rope loosened, and he fell a few feet—how far, he was not sure. Then he tried to take stock of his situation. He was lying flat on his stomach against the cliff, the wet sling around his legs and hanging from him like a deadweight, straining his already aching arms. He kicked his legs, trying to disentangle himself from the sling, but he could not get free of it. It was awful; with the sling there, he was effectively hobbled. He could not use his feet to get purchase on the rock; he would hang there, he knew, until finally fatigue made him release his grip on the rope and he fell to the bottom. Already his wrists and fingers burned with pain. He felt a slight tug on the guide rope. But they did not pull him up.

He kicked again, desperately, and then a sudden gust of wind swung him out from the cliff. The damned sling was acting as a sail, catching the wind and pulling him away. He watched the rock wall disappear in the fog as he was blown out ten, twenty feet from the cliff.

He kicked again, and suddenly was lighter—the sling had fallen away. His body began to arc back toward the cliff. He braced himself for the impact, and then it came, slamming the breath out of his lungs. He gave an involuntary cry, and hung there, gasping for breath.

And then, with a final great effort, he pulled himself up until his hands, gripping the rope, were pressed to his chest. He locked his feet around the rope a moment, resting his arms. His breath returned. He positioned his feet on the rock surface and went up the rope hand over hand. His feet slipped away; his knees banged against the rock. But he had moved upward a distance.

He did it again.

He did it again.

He did it again.

His mind ceased to function; his body worked automatically, of its own accord. The world around him became silent, no sound of rain, no scream of wind, nothing at all, not even the gasp of his own breath. The world was gray, and he was lost in the grayness.

He was not even aware when strong arms fastened under his shoulders, and he was pulled up and flopped on his belly on the flat surface. He did not hear voices. He saw nothing. Later they told him that even after he had been laid out on the ground, his body continued to crawl forward, hunching and going flat, hunching and going flat, with his bleeding face pressed to the rock, until they forcibly held him still. But for the moment, he knew nothing at all. He did not even know he had survived.

HE AWOKE TO the light chatter of birds, opened his eyes, and saw green leaves in sunlight. He lay very still, only his eyes moving. He saw a rock wall. He was in a cave, near the mouth of a cave. He smelled cooking food, an indescribably delicious smell, and he started to sit up.

Violent streaks of pain shot through every part of his body. With a gasp, he fell back again.

"Slowly, my friend," a voice said. Sanson came around from behind him. "Very slowly." He bent over and helped Hunter sit upright.

The first thing Hunter saw were his clothes. His trousers were shredded almost beyond recognition; through the holes, he could see that his skin was in similar condition.

His arms and chest were the same. He looked at his body as if he were examining a foreign, unfamiliar object.

"Your face is not so pretty, either," Sanson said, and laughed. "Do you think you can eat?"

Hunter started to speak. His face was stiff; it was as if he was wearing a mask. He touched his cheek, and felt a thick crust of blood. He shook his head. "No food? Then water." Sanson produced a cask, and helped Hunter take a drink. He was relieved to find it did not hurt to swallow, but his mouth was numb where the cask touched his lips. "Not too much," Sanson said. "Not too much."

The others came over.

The Jew was grinning broadly. "You should see the view."

Hunter felt a jolt of elation. He wanted to see the view. He raised one painful arm to Sanson, who helped him stand. The first moment on his feet was excruciating. He felt light-headed and electric jolts of pain shot through his legs and back. Then it was better. Leaning on Sanson, he took a step, wincing. He thought suddenly of Governor Almont. He thought of the evening spent bargaining with Almont for this raid on Matanceros. He had been so confident then, so relaxed, so much the intrepid adventurer. He started to smile ruefully at the memory. The smile hurt.

Then he saw the view, and immediately he forgot Almont, and his pains, and his aching body.

They were standing at the mouth of a small cave, high on the eastern rim of Mt. Leres. Curving down below them were the green slopes of the volcano, going down more than a thousand feet into dense tropical rain forest. At the very bottom was a wide river, opening out into the harbor and the fortress of Punta Matanceros. Sunlight sparkled off the still waters of the harbor, glittering brilliantly around the treasure galleon moored there just inside the protection of the fortress. It was all laid out before him, and Hunter thought it was the most beautiful sight in the world.

CHAPTER 21

SANSON GAVE HUNTER another drink of water from the cask, and then Don Diego said, "There is something else you should see, Captain."

The little party climbed up the sloping hill toward the edge of the cliff they had scaled the night before. They moved slowly, in deference to Hunter, who felt pain in every step. And as he looked up at the clear, cloudless blue sky, he felt pain of a different sort. He knew he had made a serious and nearly fatal mistake to force the climb during the storm. They should have waited and made the ascent the next morning. He had been foolish and overeager, and he berated himself for the error.

As they approached the lip of the cliff, Don Diego squatted down and looked over cautiously to the west. The others did the same, Sanson helping Hunter. Hunter did not understand why they were being so careful—until he looked over the sheer precipice, to the jungle foliage, to the bay beyond.

In the bay was Cazalla's warship.

"Damn me," he whispered softly.

Sanson, crouched alongside him, nodded. "Luck is with us, my friend. The ship arrived in the bay at dawn. It has been there ever since." As Hunter watched, he could see a longboat ferrying soldiers to the shore. Along the beach, there were dozens of red-coated Spanish troops searching the shoreline. Cazalla, dressed in a yellow tunic, was clearly visible, gesticulating wildly as he gave orders.

"They are searching the beach," Sanson said. "They have guessed our plan."

"But the storm . . ." Hunter said.

"Yes, the storm will have washed away any trace of our presence there."

Hunter thought of the canvas sling that had fallen from his feet. It would be lying now at the base of the cliff. But the soldiers would probably never find it. To reach the cliff was a full daylong hard journey through the undergrowth. They would not make that journey without evidence a party had landed on the shore.

As Hunter watched, a second longboat loaded with soldiers put out from the warship.

"He has been landing men all morning," Don Diego said. "There must be a hundred on the beach now."

"Then he intends to leave men," Hunter said.

Don Diego nodded.

"All the better for us," Hunter said. Any troops left on the western side of the island would be unable to fight in Matanceros. "Let us hope he leaves a thousand."

BACK IN THE mouth of the cave, Don Diego made a gruel for Hunter to drink while Sanson put out their little fire, and Lazue held the spyglass to her eyes. She described the scene to Hunter, who was sitting alongside her. Hunter himself could see only the basic outlines of the structures by the water below. He relied upon the keenness of Lazue's vision to guide him.

"Tell me first," he said, "about the guns. The guns in the fortress."

Lazue's lips worked silently as she peered through the glass. "Twelve," she said finally. "Two batteries of three each face east, toward the open ocean. Six in a single battery fire across the harbor entrance."

"And they are culverins?"

"They have long barrels. I think they are culverins."

"What can you say of their age?"

She was silent a moment. "We are too distant," she replied. "Perhaps later, when we move down, I will see more."

"And the mountings?"

"Carriages. I think wood, with four wheels."

Hunter nodded. Those would be ordinary shipboard gun carriages, transferred to the shore batteries.

Don Diego came over with the gruel. "I am glad they are wood," he said. "I feared they might be stone-mounted. That would make it more difficult."

Hunter said, "We will blow the carriages?"

"Of course," Don Diego said.

The culverins weighed more than two tons each. If their carriages were destroyed, they would be useless; they could not be aimed or fired. And even if the Matanceros fortress had extra gun carriages, it would take dozens of men many hours to seat each cannon back into a new carriage.

"But first," Don Diego said with a smile, "we will breech them."

The idea had never occurred to Hunter, but he immediately saw its value. The culverins were, like all cannon, muzzle-loaders. The crews first rammed a bag of gunpowder down the mouth of the cannon, followed by a ball of shot. Then, through a touch-hole in the breech, the powder bag was broken with a pointed quill, and a burning fuse inserted. The fuse burned through the touch-hole, ignited the powder, and fired the ball.

This method of firing was reliable enough, so long as the touch-hole remained small. But after repeated firings, the burning fuse and the exploding powder corroded the touch-hole, widening it until it acted as an escape valve for the expanding gases. Once that happened, the range of the cannon was severely reduced; ultimately, the ball would not fire at all. And the cannon was very dangerous for its crews to operate.

Faced with this inevitable deterioration, cannon-makers fitted the breech with a replaceable metal plug, wider at one end than the other, with a touch-hole bored in the center. The plug was fitted from inside the cannon, so that the expanding gases of the gunpowder would tend to ram the plug home more snugly with each firing. Whenever the touch-hole became too large, the metal plug was simply removed and a new one fitted.

But sometimes the whole plug was blown out in a piece, leaving a very large hole at the breech of the cannon. That was true breeching, and it rendered the gun wholly useless until a new plug could be fitted. That process took many hours.

"Believe me," Don Diego said, "when we are finished with those guns, they will be useful for nothing but ballast in a merchant's hold."

Hunter turned back to Lazue. "What can you see inside the fortress itself?"

"Tents. Many tents."

"That will be the garrison," Hunter said. During most of the year, the weather in the New World was so fair that troops did not require more permanent protection, and this was particularly true for an island as rainless as Leres. Although now Hunter could imagine the consternation of the troops, who had slept in mud from the storm of the previous night.

"What about the powder magazine?"

"There is a wood building north, inside the walls. That may be it."

"Good," Hunter said. He did not want to spend time searching for the magazine once they entered the fortress. "Are there defenses outside the walls?"

Lazue scanned the ground below. "I see nothing."

"Good. Now what of the ship?"

"A skeleton crew," she said. "I see five or six men on the longboats tied to the shore, by the town."

Hunter had noticed the town. It was a surprise— a series of rough wood buildings along the shore, some distance from the fort. Obviously, they had been erected to house the galleon's crew on land, proof that the crew intended to stay at Matanceros for a period of time, perhaps until next year's sailing of the treasure fleet.

"Troops in the town?"

"I see a few red jackets."

"Guards at the longboats?"

"None."

"They are making things easy for us," Hunter said.

"So far," Sanson said.

The party collected their gear, obliterating any traces of their time in the cave. They started the long hike down the sloping hill to Matanceros.

On their descent, they faced the opposite problem from their trek two days before. High on the eastern slope of Mt. Leres, there was little foliage and little protection. They were obliged to slip from one dense clump of thorny vegetation to the next, and their progress was slow.

At noon, they had a surprise. Cazalla's black warship appeared in the mouth of the harbor, and, reefing her sails, came to anchor near the fort. A longboat was put out; Lazue, with the glass, said that Cazalla was in the stern.

"This ruins everything," Hunter said, looking at the position of the warship. It was parallel to the shore, so that a full broadside of its cannon would rake the channel.

"What if she stays there?" Sanson said.

Hunter was wondering exactly that, and he could think of only one answer. "We'll fire her," he said. "If she stays at anchor, we'll have to fire her."

"Light a longboat from shore, and set it adrift?"

Hunter nodded.

"A slim chance," Sanson said.

Then Lazue, still watching through the glass, said, "There's a woman."

"What?" Hunter said.

"In the longboat. There's a woman with Cazalla."

"Let me see." Hunter took the glass eagerly. But to his eyes, there was only a white irregular shape seated in the stern next to Cazalla, who stood and faced the fortress. Hunter could discern no details. He returned the glass to Lazue. "Describe her."

"White dress and parasol—or some large hat or covering on her head. Dark face. Could be a Negro."

"His mistress?"

Lazue shook her head. The longboat was now tying up by the fort. "She's getting off. She's struggling—"

"Perhaps she's not got balance."

"No," Lazue said firmly. "She is struggling. Three men are holding her. Forcing her to enter the fortress."

"You say she's dark?" Hunter asked again. That was perplexing. Cazalla might have taken a woman captive, but any woman worth ransoming would certainly be very fair.

"Dark, yes," Lazue said. "But I cannot really see further."

"We will wait," Hunter said.

Puzzled, they continued down the slope.

∞

THREE HOURS LATER, in the hottest part of the afternoon, they paused in a cluster of prickly acara bushes to drink a ration of water. Lazue noticed that the longboat was putting out from the fortress, this time carrying a man she described as "stern, very slender, very proper and erect."

"Bosquet," Hunter said. Bosquet was Cazalla's second in command, a renegade Frenchman, known as a cool and implacable leader. "Is Cazalla with him?"

"No," Lazue said.

The longboat tied up alongside the warship, and Bosquet boarded. Moments later, the ship's crew began to hoist the longboat. That could mean only one thing.

"They're setting off," Sanson said. "Your luck holds, my friend."

"Not quite yet," Hunter said. "Let us see if she will be making for Ramonas," where the *Cassandra* and her crew were hidden. The *Cassandra* was in water too shallow for the warship to attack her, but Bosquet could blockade the pirate sloop in the cove—and without the *Cassandra*, there was no point in attacking Matanceros. They needed the men of the *Cassandra* to sail the treasure galleon out of the harbor.

The warship left the harbor on a southerly reach, but that was necessary to make deep water. Outside the channel, it continued south.

"Damn," Sanson said.

"No, she's just making speed," Hunter said. "Wait."

As he spoke, the warship came into the wind, and took a starboard tack to the north. Hunter shook his head in relief.

"I can feel the gold between my fingers now," Sanson said.

After an hour, the black ship was gone from view.

By nightfall, they were no more than a quarter of a mile from the Spanish encampment. The ground cover was more dense here; they selected a heavy clump of Maya-guana trees in which to spend the night. They lit no fire, and ate only a few raw plants before lying down on the damp earth. They were all tired, but excited by the fact that from their position, they could faintly hear the chatter of Spanish voices, and the drifting smells from Spanish cookfires. As they lay beneath the stars, those sounds and aromas reminded them that the coming battle was very close at hand.

CHAPTER 22

HUNTER AWOKE WITH the instant conviction that something was wrong. He heard Spanish voices, but this time they were close—much too close. And he could hear footsteps, and the rustle of foliage. He sat up, wincing as the pains shot through him; if anything, his body ached more fiercely than it had the day before.

He glanced around at his little group. Sanson was already on his feet, peering through palm fronds in the direction of the Spanish voices. The Moor was quietly rising, his body tense, his movements finely controlled. Don Diego was sitting up on one elbow, eyes wide.

Only Lazue still lay on her back. And she was lying absolutely motionless. Hunter jerked his thumb at her to get up. She shook her head slightly, and mouthed "No." She was not moving at all. Her face was covered with a fine sheen of perspiration. He started to move toward her.

"Careful!" she whispered, her voice tense. He stopped,

and looked at her. Lazue was lying on her back, with her legs slightly apart. Her limbs were oddly rigid. He then saw the red, black, and yellow—striped tail disappear up the leg of her trousers.

It was a coral snake, attracted by the warmth of her body. He looked back at her face. It was taut, as if she were withstanding some extraordinary pain.

Behind him, Hunter heard the Spanish voices growing still louder. He could hear several men clumping and thrashing through the underbrush. He gestured to Lazue to wait, and went over to Sanson.

"Six of them," Sanson whispered.

Hunter saw a party of six Spanish soldiers, carrying bedding and food, armed with muskets, moving up the hillside toward them. The soldiers were all young, and apparently regarded this excursion as a lark; they laughed and joked with each other.

"It's not a patrol," Sanson whispered.

"Let them go," Hunter said.

Sanson looked at him sharply. Hunter pointed back to Lazue, still lying rigidly on the ground. Sanson immediately understood. They waited as the Spanish soldiers passed by, and moved on up the hillside. Then they returned to Lazue.

"Where is it now?" Hunter said.

"Knee," she said softly.

"Moving up?"

"Yes."

Don Diego spoke next. "Tall trees," he said, looking around. "We must find tall trees. There!" He tapped the Moor. "Come with me."

The two men set off into the brush, in the direction of a clump of Mayaguana trees some yards away. Hunter looked at Lazue, and then up at the Spanish soldiers. The soldiers were clearly visible, a hundred yards farther up the hillside. If any of the soldiers chose to look back, they would see the group immediately.

"It is too late in the season for mating," Sanson said. He frowned at Lazue. "But we may be lucky and find a chick." He turned to look at the Moor, who was scrambling up one of the trees, while Diego remained on the ground below.

"Where is it now?" Hunter said.

"Past the knee."

"Try to relax."

She rolled her eyes. "Damn you and your expedition," she said. "Damn all of you."

Hunter looked at the trouser leg. He could just see the slight movement in the fabric the snake made as it crawled upward.

"Mother of God," Lazue said. She closed her eyes.

Sanson whispered to Hunter, "If they find no chick, we may have to stand her and shake her."

"The snake will bite."

They both knew the consequences of that.

The privateers were hard and tough; they regarded the poisonous bite of a scorpion, a black widow, or a water moccasin as no more than an inconvenience. Indeed, it was high good fun for a man to drop a scorpion into a comrade's boot. But two venomous creatures commanded the respect and dread of everyone. The fer-de-lance was no laughing matter— and the little coral snake was the worst of all. No one ever survived its timid bite. Hunter could imagine Lazue's terror as she waited for the tiny pinch on her leg that would signal the fatal bite. They all knew what would inevitably occur: first sweating, then shaking, then a creeping numbness that would spread all over the body. Death would follow before sunset.

"Where now?"

"High, very high." Her voice was so soft he could hardly catch her words.

He looked at her pants and saw a slight ripple of the fabric at the crotch.

"Oh God," Lazue moaned.

And then he heard a low squeak, almost a chirp. He turned and saw Diego and the Moor returning. Both smiled broadly. The Moor held something cupped in his hands. Hunter saw it was a tiny bandybird chick. It squeaked and fluttered its feathery, soft body.

"Quick, some cord," the Jew said. Hunter produced a length of twine, and it was fastened around the chick's legs. The chick was placed by the mouth of Lazue's trouser cuff and tied to the ground, where it remained squeaking and twisting around its bonds.

They waited.

"Do you feel anything?" Hunter said.

"No."

They looked back at the bandybird chick. The little creature struggled piteously, exhausting itself.

Hunter turned to Lazue.

"Nothing," she said. And then her eyes abruptly widened. "Coiling . . ."

They looked at her trousers. There was movement. A slowly forming curve in the cloth, which then dissolved.

"Going down," Lazue said.

They waited. Suddenly, the chick became very agitated, squeaking more loudly than ever before. It had smelled the coral snake.

The Jew produced his pistol, shook out the shot and prime, and gripped the barrel in his fist, holding the butt like a club.

They waited. They could see the progress of the snake now passing the knee, going along the calf, moving by slow inches. It seemed to take forever.

And then suddenly, abruptly, the head appeared in the light, and the tongue flicked out. The chick squealed in a paroxysm of terror. The coral snake advanced, and then Don Diego leapt on it, pounding the head into the ground with the pistol butt, and simultaneously Lazue was on her feet, jumping back with a scream.

Don Diego pounded the snake with repeated blows, crushing its body into the soft earth. Lazue turned and was violently sick. But Hunter paid no attention to that—at her scream, he had immediately turned and looked up the hillside, toward the Spanish soldiers.

Sanson and the Moor had done the same.

"Did they hear?" Hunter said.

"We cannot risk it," Sanson said. There was a long silence, interrupted only by Lazue's retching. "You noticed they carried supplies and bedding."

Hunter nodded. The meaning was clear enough. They had been sent up the slope by Cazalla as a warning party, to watch for pirates on the land—and also to scan the horizon for the approach of the *Cassandra*. A single musket-shot from that group would alert the fort below. From their vantage point, they would see the *Cassandra* many miles away.

"I will do this," Sanson said, smiling slightly.

"Take the Moor," Hunter said.

The two men slipped away, moving up the hillside after the Spanish troops. Hunter turned back to Lazue, who was pale, wiping her mouth.

"I am ready to leave," she said.

Hunter, Don Diego, and Lazue shouldered the equipment, and moved on down the hillside.

NOW THEY FOLLOWED the river that opened into the harbor. When they first met it, the river was only a narrow trickle, and a man could step across it easily. But it quickly broadened, and the jungle growth along its banks became thick and deep.

They encountered the first of the organized patrols in late afternoon—eight Spaniards, all armed, moving silently up the river in a longboat. These men were serious and grim, fighting men prepared for battle. As night fell, the high trees along the river turned blue-green, and the river surface black, unmarred except for an occasional ripple of a crocodile. But the patrols were now everywhere, moving in steady cadences, by torchlight. Three other longboats ferried soldiers up the river, their torches casting long, shimmering points of light.

"Cazalla is not a fool," Sanson said. "We are expected."

They were now just a few hundred yards from the fortress of Matanceros. The stone walls loomed high above them. There was a lot of activity, inside and outside the fort. Armed bands of twenty soldiers paced the perimeter.

"Expected or not," Hunter said, "we must keep to our plan. We attack tonight."

CHAPTER 23

ENDERS, THE BARBER-SURGEON and sea artist, stood at the helm of the *Cassandra* and watched the gentle breakers turn silver as they smashed over the reef of Barton's Cay, a hundred yards to port. Up ahead, he could see the black hulk of Mt. Leres looming larger on the horizon.

A man slipped aft to him. "The glass is turned," he said.

Enders nodded. Fifteen glasses had passed since nightfall, which meant it was nearing two in the morning. The wind was from the east and fresh at ten knots; his ship was on a strong tack, and he would reach the island in an hour.

He squinted at the profile of Mt. Leres. Enders could not discern the harbor of Matanceros. He would have to round the southerly point of the island before he came into view of the fortress and the galleon he hoped was still anchored in the harbor.

By then, he would also be within range of the Matanceros guns, unless Hunter and his party had silenced them.

Enders glanced at his crew, standing on the open deck of the *Cassandra*. No man spoke. Everyone watched silently as the island grew larger before them. They all knew the stakes, and they all knew the risks: within hours, each man would either be unimaginably rich or almost certainly dead.

For the hundredth time that night, Enders wondered what had happened to Hunter and his party, and where they were.

IN THE SHADOW of the stone walls of Matanceros, Sanson bit the gold doubloon, and passed it to Lazue. Lazue bit it, then passed it to the Moor. Hunter watched the silent ritual, which all privateers believed brought them luck before a raid. Finally, the doubloon reached him; he bit it, feeling the softness of the metal. Then, while they watched, he tossed the coin over his right shoulder.

Without a word, the five of them set out in different directions.

Hunter and Don Diego, with ropes and grappling hooks slung over their shoulders, crept northward around the fortress perimeter, pausing frequently to allow patrols to pass. Hunter glanced up at the high stone walls of Matanceros. The upper walls had been constructed smoothly, with a rounded lip to make grappling difficult. But the masonry skills of the Spanish were not sufficient to the conception; Hunter was certain his hooks would find purchase.

When they reached the north wall of the fort, farthest from the sea, they paused. After ten minutes, a patrol passed, armor and weapons clanging in the still night air. They waited until the soldiers disappeared from sight.

Then Hunter ran forward and flung the grappling iron up over the wall. He heard a faint metallic clink as it landed on the inside. He tugged on the rope, and the iron came back, crashing to the ground beside him. He cursed and waited, listening.

There was no sound, no indication that anyone had heard him. He threw the grappling iron again, watching it sail high over the walls. Again he tugged. And he had to dodge as the iron came back.

He threw a third time, and this time the hook held— but almost immediately, he heard the noise of another patrol. Quickly, Hunter scrambled up the wall, panting and gasping, urged onward by the approaching sounds of armored soldiers. He reached the parapet, dropped down, and hauled up the rope. Don Diego had retreated back into the underbrush.

The patrol passed by beneath him.

Hunter dropped the rope, and Don Diego scrambled up, muttering and swearing in Spanish. Don Diego was not strong, and his progress seemed interminable. Yet finally he came over the side, and Hunter pulled him to safety. He hauled in the rope. The two men, crouched down against the cold stone, looked around them.

Matanceros was silent in the darkness, the lines of tents filled with hundreds of sleeping men. There was an odd thrill to be so close to so many of the enemy.

"Guards?" the Jew whispered.

"I see none," Hunter said, "except there." On the opposite side of the fortress, two figures stood by the guns. But they were sea watches, posted to scan the horizon for approaching ships.

Don Diego nodded. "There will be a guard at the magazine."

"Probably."

The two men were almost directly above the wooden building Lazue had thought might be the magazine. From where they crouched, they could not see the door to the structure.

"We must go there first," the Jew said.

They had brought no explosives with them, only fuses. They intended to take their explosives from the fortress's own magazine.

Silently, in the darkness, Hunter slipped to the ground, and Don Diego followed, blinking his eyes in the faint light. They moved around to the magazine entrance.

They saw no guard.

"Inside?" the Jew whispered.

Hunter shrugged, went to the door, listened a moment, slipped off his boots, and gently pushed the door open. Looking back, he saw Don Diego also removing his boots. Then Hunter went inside.

The interior of the magazine was lined in copper sheeting on all sides, and the few carefully protected candles gave the room a warm, reddish glow. It was oddly inviting, despite the rows of gunpowder casks and the stacked bags of cannon charge, all suitably labeled in red. Hunter moved soundlessly across the copper floor. He saw no one, but heard a man snoring from somewhere in the magazine.

Slipping among the casks, he looked for this man, and eventually found a soldier asleep, propped up against a barrel of powder. Hunter struck the man hard on the head; the soldier snorted and lay still.

The Jew padded in, surveyed the room, and whispered, "Excellent." They immediately set to work.

IF THE FORTRESS was silent and sleeping, the rough shanty town that housed the galleon's crew was boisterous. Sanson, the Moor, and Lazue slipped through the town, passing windows through which they could see soldiers drinking and gaming in yellow lantern-light. One drunken soldier stumbled out, bumped into Sanson, apologized, and was sick against a wooden wall. The three moved on, toward the longboat landing at the riverside.

Although the landing had not been guarded during the day, a group of three soldiers were there now, talking quietly and drinking in the darkness. They sat at the end of the landing, hanging their feet over the side into the water, the low sound of their voices blending with the slap of water against the pilings. Their backs were to the privateers, but the wooden slats of the landing made a silent approach impossible.

"I will do this," Lazue said, removing her blouse. Naked to the waist, her dagger held behind her back, she whistled a light tune and walked out onto the dock.

One of the soldiers turned. *"Que pasa ca?"* he demanded, and held up a lantern. His eyes widened in astonishment as he saw what must have seemed to him an apparition—a bare-breasted woman nonchalantly walking toward him. *"Madre de Dios,"* he said, and the woman smiled at him. He answered the smile in the instant before the dagger passed through his ribs into his heart.

The other soldiers looked at the woman with the bloody dagger. They were so astonished they hardly resisted as she killed them, their blood spurting over her bare chest.

Sanson and the Moor ran up, stepping over the bodies of the three men. Lazue pulled her tunic back on. Sanson climbed into one boat and immediately set out toward the stern of the galleon. The Moor cut free the other boats, and pushed them out into the harbor, where they drifted free. Then the Moor got into a boat with Lazue, and made for the bow of the galleon. Nobody spoke at all.

Lazue pulled her tunic tighter around her. The blood of the soldiers soaked through the fabric; she felt a chill. She stood in the longboat and looked at the approaching galleon while the Moor rowed in swift, powerful strokes.

The galleon was large, about one hundred and forty feet, but mostly she was dark, only a few torches demarcating her profile. Lazue looked to the right, where she saw Sanson rowing away from them, toward the galleon's stern. Sanson was silhouetted against the lights of the raucous shanty town on shore. She turned and looked left, at the gray line of the fortress walls. She wondered if Hunter and the Jew were inside yet.

HUNTER WATCHED AS the Jew delicately filled the possum entrails with gunpowder. It seemed an interminable process, but the Jew refused to be hurried. He squatted in the center of the magazine, with an opened bag of powder at his side, and hummed a little as he worked.

"How much longer?" Hunter said.

"Not long, not long," the Jew said. He seemed completely nonchalant. "It will be so pretty," he said. "You wait. It will be very beautiful."

When he had the entrails filled, he cut them into various lengths, and slipped them into his pocket.

"All right," he said. "Now we can begin."

A moment later, the two men emerged from the magazine, bent over with the weight of the powder charges they carried. They crossed the main yard of the fortress stealthily, and paused beneath the heavy stone parapet on which the guns rested. The two lookouts were still there.

While the Jew waited with the gunpowder, Hunter climbed onto the parapet and killed the lookouts. One died in complete silence and the other gave only a quiet groan as he slipped to the ground.

"Diego!" Hunter hissed.

The Jew appeared on the parapet and looked at the guns. He poked down a barrel with a rammer.

"How delightful," he whispered. "They are already powdered and primed. We will make a special treat. Here, help me."

The Jew pushed a second bag of powder down the mouth of one cannon. "Now the shot," he said.

Hunter frowned. "But they will add another ball before they fire."

"Of course. Two charges, and two balls—these guns will breech before their eyes."

Quickly, they moved from one culverin to the next. The Jew added a second charge of powder, and Hunter dropped in a ball. Each ball made a low rumbling sound as it moved down the cannon mouth, but there was nobody to hear it.

When they had finished, the Jew said, "Now I have things to do. You must put sand in each barrel."

Hunter slipped down the parapet to the ground. He took the loose sandy surface of the fortress in his fingers and dropped a handful down each cannon mouth. The Jew was clever: even if, by chance, the guns fired, the sand in the barrels would destroy the aim—and ream the inside so badly that they would never be accurate again.

When he was finished, he saw the Jew bent over one gun carriage, working beneath the barrel. He got to his feet. "That's the last," he said.

"What have you done?"

"Touched the fuses to the barrels. The heat of firing the barrel will ignite the fuses on the undercarriage charge." He smiled in the darkness. "It will be wonderful."

∞

THE WIND CHANGED, and the stern of the galleon swung around toward Sanson. He tied up beneath the gilded transom and began to scale the rear bulkhead toward the captain's cabin. He heard the soft sound of a song in Spanish. He listened to the obscene lyrics but could not locate the source of the song; it seemed to drift in the air, elusive and faint.

He stepped through a cannon porthole into the captain's cabin. It was empty. He moved outside, on the gun deck, and down the companionway to the berth deck. He saw no one. He looked at the empty hammocks, all swinging gently in the motion of the ship. Dozens of hammocks, and no sign of a crew.

Sanson did not like this—an unguarded ship implied a ship without treasure. He now feared what they had all feared but never voiced: that the treasure might have been taken off the ship and stored elsewhere, perhaps in the fortress. If that were true, their plans were all in vain.

Therefore, Sanson found himself hoping for a good-sized skeleton crew and guard. He moved to the aft galley, and here he was encouraged. The galley was deserted, but there was evidence of recent cooking—a bullock stew in a large cauldron, some vegetables, a cut lemon rocking back and forth on the wooden counter.

He left the galley, and moved forward again. In the

distance, he heard shouts from the sentry on deck, greeting Lazue and the Moor as they approached.

Lazue and the Moor tied up alongside the midships ladder of the galleon. The sentry on deck leaned down and waved. *"Questa faire?"* he called.

"We bring rum," Lazue answered in a low voice. "Compliments of the captain."

"The captain?"

"It is his day of birth."

"Bravo, bravo." Smiling, the sentry stepped back as Lazue came aboard. He looked, and had a moment of horror as he saw the blood on her tunic and in her hair. Then the knife flashed through the air and buried itself in his chest. The sentry clutched the handle in surprise. He seemed about to speak. Then he pitched forward onto the deck.

The Moor came aboard, and crept forward, toward a group of four soldiers who sat playing cards. Lazue did not watch what he did; she went below. She found ten soldiers sleeping in a forward compartment; silently, she shut the door and barred it.

Five more soldiers were singing and drinking in an adjacent cabin. She peered in and saw that they had guns. Her own pistols were jammed in her belt; she would not fire a shot unless she had to. She waited outside the room.

After a moment, the Moor crept alongside her.

She pointed into the room. He shook his head. They remained by the door.

After a time, one of the soldiers announced his bladder was bursting, and left the room. As he came out, the Moor crashed a belaying pin down on his skull; the man hit the deck with a thud, just a few steps from the room.

The others inside looked toward the sound. They could see the man's feet in the light from the room.

"Juan?"

The fallen man did not move.

"Too much to drink," somebody said, and they resumed their cards. But soon enough one of the men began to worry about Juan, and came out to investigate. Lazue cut his throat and the Moor leapt into the room, swinging the pin in wide arcs. The men dropped soundlessly.

In the aft quarter of the ship, Sanson left the galley and moved forward, running right into a Spanish soldier. The man was drunk, a crock of rum dangling loosely from one hand, and he laughed at Sanson in the darkness.

"You gave me a fright," the soldier said in Spanish. "I did not expect to see anyone."

Then, up close, he saw Sanson's grim face, and did not recognize it. He had a brief moment of astonishment before Sanson's fingers closed around his throat.

Sanson went down another companionway, below the

berth deck. He came to the aft storerooms, and found them all hard-locked and bolted. There were seals on all the locks; in the darkness, he bent to examine them. Unmistakably, in the yellow wax, he saw the crown-and-anchor seal of the Lima mint. So there was New Spain silver here; his heart jumped.

He returned to the deck, coming up on the aft castle, near the tiller. He again heard the faint sounds of singing. It was still no more possible to locate the sound than before. He paused and listened, and then the singing stopped, and a concerned voice said, *"Que pasa? Que esta vous?"*

Sanson looked up. Of course! There, in the perch above the mainmast spars, a man stood looking down at him.

"Que esta vous?" he demanded.

Sanson knew the man could not see him well. He stepped back into shadows.

"Que?" the man said, confused.

In the darkness, Sanson unsheathed his crossbow, bent the steel spring, fitted the arrow, and raised it to his eye. He looked at the Spaniard coming down the rigging, swearing irritably.

Sanson shot him.

The impact of the arrow knocked him free of the rigging; his body flew a dozen yards out into dark space, and he hit the water with a soft splash. There was no other sound.

Sanson prowled the empty aft deck, and finally, satisfied that he was alone, he gripped the tiller in his hands. A moment later, he saw Lazue and the Moor come above-decks near the bow. They looked back and waved to him; they were grinning.

The ship was theirs.

HUNTER AND DON DIEGO had returned to the magazine, and were setting a long fuse to the powder kegs. They worked swiftly now, for when they had left the cannon, the sky above them was already beginning to lighten to a paler blue.

Don Diego stacked the kegs in small clusters around the room. "It must be this way," he whispered. "Otherwise there will be one explosion, which we do not desire."

He broke two kegs and sprinkled the black grain over the floor. Finally, satisfied, he lit the fuse.

At that moment, there was a shout from outside in the fortress yard, and then another.

"What is that?" Diego said.

Hunter frowned. "Perhaps they have found the dead watch," he said.

A moment later, there was more shouting in the yard, and the sound of running feet. Now they heard one word repeated over and over: "*Pirata! Pirata!*"

"The ship must be in the channel," Hunter said. He glanced over at the fuse, which sputtered and sizzled in the corner of the room.

"Shall I put it out?" Diego said.

"No. Leave it."

"We cannot stay here."

"In a few minutes, there will be panic in the yard. Then we will escape."

"It had better be a very few minutes," Diego said.

The shouting in the courtyard was louder. They heard literally hundreds of running feet, as the garrison was mobilized.

"They will check the magazine," Diego said nervously.

"Eventually," Hunter agreed.

And at that moment, the door was flung open, and Cazalla came into the room, with a sword in his hand. He saw them.

Hunter plucked a sword from the dozens that hung in racks along the wall. "Go, Diego," he whispered. Diego dashed out the door as Cazalla's blade struck Hunter's own. Hunter and Cazalla circled the room.

Hunter was backing away.

"Englishman," Cazalla said, laughing. "I will feed the pieces of your body to my dogs."

Hunter did not reply. He balanced the sword in his hand, feeling the unfamiliar weight, testing the whip of the blade.

"And my mistress," Cazalla said, "shall dine on your testicles."

They circled the room warily. Hunter was leading Cazalla out of the magazine, away from the sputtering fuse, which the Spaniard had not noticed.

"Are you afraid, Englishman?"

Hunter backed away, almost to the door. Cazalla lunged. Hunter parried, still backing. Cazalla lunged again. The movement took him into the yard.

"You are a stinking coward, Englishman."

Now they were both in the yard. Hunter engaged Cazalla fully, and Cazalla laughed with pleasure. For some moments they fought in silence, Hunter always moving farther from the magazine.

All around them, the garrison troops ran and shouted. Any of them could kill Hunter from behind in an instant. His danger was extreme, and Cazalla suddenly realized the reason. He broke, stepped back, and looked at the magazine.

"You son of an English buggered swine . . ."

Cazalla ran toward the magazine, just as the first of the explosions engulfed it in rolling white flame and blasting heat.

The crew aboard the *Cassandra*, now moving up the narrow channel, saw the magazine explode and cheered. But Enders, at the helm, was frowning. The guns of Matanceros were still there; he could see the long barrels protruding through the notchings in the stone wall. In the red light of the magazine fires, the gun crews preparing to fire the cannon were clearly visible.

"God help us," Enders said. The *Cassandra* was now directly off the shore batteries. "Stand by, mates," he shouted. "We're going to eat Donnish shot today."

Lazue and the Moor, on the foredeck of the galleon, also saw the explosion. They saw the *Cassandra* beating up the channel past the fortress.

"Mother of God," Lazue said. "They didn't get the guns. *They didn't get the guns.*"

DIEGO WAS OUTSIDE the fortress, running for the water. He did not stop when the magazine exploded with a frightful roar; he did not wonder if Hunter was still inside; he did not think anything. He ran with screaming, painful lungs for the water.

Hunter was trapped in the fortress. The Spanish patrols from outside were pouring in through the west gate; he could not escape that way. He did not see Cazalla anywhere, but he ran east from the magazine toward a low stone building, intending to climb onto the roof, and from there, jump over the wall.

When he got to the building, four soldiers engaged

him; they backed him with swords to the door of the building and he locked himself in. The door was heavy timber; they pounded on it to no avail.

He turned to look around the room. This was Cazalla's quarters, richly furnished. A dark-haired girl was in the bed. She looked at him in terror, holding the sheets to her chin, as Hunter dashed through the room to the rear windows. He was halfway out the window when he heard her say, in English, "Who are you?"

Hunter paused, astonished. Her accent was crisp and aristocratic. "Who the hell are you?"

"I am Lady Sarah Almont, late of London," she said. "I am being held prisoner here."

Hunter's mouth fell open.

"Well, get on your clothing, madam," he said.

At that moment, another glass window shattered, and Cazalla landed on the floor of the room, his sword in his hand. He was gray and blackened from the powder explosion. The girl screamed.

"Dress, madam," Hunter said, as his blade engaged Cazalla's. He saw her hastily pulling on an elaborate white dress.

Cazalla panted as he fought. He had the desperation of fury and something else, perhaps fear.

"Englishman," he said, starting another taunt. Then Hunter flung his sword across the room. The blade pierced

Cazalla in the throat. He coughed and sat backward, into the chair by his heavy ornate desk. He leaned forward, pulling at the blade, and in his posture, he seemed to be examining charts on the desk. Blood dripped onto the charts. Cazalla made a gurgling sound. Then he collapsed.

"Come on," the woman said.

Hunter led her through the window, out of the room. He did not look back at Cazalla's body.

He stood with the woman on the north face of the parapet. The ground was thirty feet below, hard earth with a few scrubby plants. Lady Sarah clutched him.

"It's too far," she said.

"There's no choice," he said, and pushed her. With a shriek, she fell. He looked back, and saw the *Cassandra* pull into the channel, under the main battery of the fortress. The gun crews were ready to fire. Hunter jumped to the ground. The girl was still lying there, holding her ankle.

"Are you hurt?"

"Not badly, I think."

He got her to her feet, and drew her arm over his shoulder. Supporting her, they ran toward the water. They heard the first guns open fire on the *Cassandra*.

The guns of Matanceros were fired serially, one second apart. Each one breeched one second apart, spitting hot powder and fragments of bronze into the air, sending the crews diving for cover. One by one, the big guns rocked back to their recoil position, and were still.

The crews slowly got to their feet, and approached the guns in astonishment. They examined the blown touch-holes and chattered excitedly among themselves.

And then, one by one, the charges under the carriages blew, sending splinters of wood flying, dropping the guns to the ground. The last of the cannon went rolling along the parapet, with terrified soldiers racing out of its path.

Less than five hundred yards offshore, the *Cassandra* sailed untouched into the harbor.

Don Diego was treading water, shouting at the top of his lungs as the *Cassandra* bore down on him. For a horrified moment he thought no one would see or hear him, and then the bow of the sloop veered to port, and strong hands reached over the side and hauled him, dripping, onto the deck. A flask of kill-devil was thrust into his hands; his back was pounded and there was laughter.

Diego looked around the boat. "Where is Hunter?" he said.

In the early-dawn light, Hunter was running with the girl to the shore at the eastern point of Matanceros. He was now just beneath the fort's walls; directly above him were the barrels of some of the guns, now lying at odd and irregular angles.

They paused by the water to catch their breath.

"Can you swim?" Hunter asked.

The girl shook her head.

"Not at all?"

"No, I swear."

He looked at the *Cassandra*'s stern, as she moved up the channel to the galleon.

"Come on," he said. They ran toward the harbor.

Enders, the sea artist, delicately maneuvered the *Cassandra* alongside the galleon. Immediately, most of the crew jumped to the larger boat. Enders himself went aboard the galleon, where he saw Lazue and the Moor at the railing. Sanson was at the tiller.

"My pleasure, sir," Sanson said with a bow, handing the helm to Enders.

"Don't mind if I do, mate," Enders said. Immediately, he looked aloft, where seamen were scrambling up the rigging. "Hoist the foretop. Smart there with the jib!" The sails were let out. The big ship began to move.

Alongside them, the small crew remaining with the *Cassandra* tied the bow to the stern of the galleon and swung around, sails luffing.

Enders paid no attention to the little ship.

His attention was fixed on the galleon. As she began to move, and the crews worked the capstan to bring up the anchor, he shook his head. "Soggy old bitch," he said. "Moves like a cow."

"But she'll sail," Sanson said.

"Oh, she'll sail, in a manner of speaking."

The galleon was moving east, toward the harbor mouth. Enders now looked toward the shore, for Hunter.

"There he is!" Lazue shouted.

And indeed, there he was, standing at the shore with some woman.

"Can you stop?" Lazue demanded.

Enders shook his head. "We'll go into irons," he said. "Throw a line."

The Moor had already thrown a line. It hit the shore. Hunter grabbed it with the girl, and they were immediately yanked off their feet and dragged into the water.

"Better get them up smartly, before they drown," Enders said, but he was grinning.

The girl nearly drowned, she was coughing for hours afterward. But Hunter was in fine spirits as he took command of the treasure *nao* and sailed, in tandem with the *Cassandra*, out into the open seas.

By eight in the morning, the smoking ruins of Matanceros lay far astern. Hunter, drinking heavily, reflected that he now had the distinction of successfully leading the most extraordinary privateering expedition in the century since Drake attacked Panama.

Chapter 24

THEY WERE STILL in Spanish waters, and they moved southward quickly, under every inch of canvas they could muster. The galleon normally carried as many as a thousand people, and crews of two hundred seamen or more.

Hunter had seventy men, including prisoners. But most of the Spanish prisoners were garrison soldiers, not sailors. Not only were they untrustworthy, they were also unskilled. Hunter's crews had their hands full managing the sails and rigging.

Hunter had interrogated the prisoners in his halting Spanish. By midday, he knew a good deal about the ship he now commanded. She was the *nao Nuestra Señora de los Reyes, San Fernando y San Francisco de Paula*, Captain José del Villar de Andrade, owner the Marques de Canada, a vessel of nine hundred tons, built in Genoa. Like all Spanish galleons—which were invariably cumbersomely christened—this ship had a nickname, *El Trinidad*. The origin of the name was obscure.

El Trinidad had been built to carry fifty cannon, but after formal departure from Havana the previous August, the ship had stopped along the Cuban coast, and most of the cannon offloaded to permit the ship to carry more cargo. She was presently fitted with only thirty-two twelve-pounders. Enders had gone over the ship thoroughly and pronounced her seaworthy but filthy. A party of prisoners were now clearing some of the refuse from the holds.

"She's taking on water, too," Enders said.

"Badly?"

"No, but she's an old ship, and bears watching. Not kept in good repair." Enders's frown seemed to encompass the long tradition of shoddy Spanish seamanship.

"How does she sail?"

"Like a pregnant sow, but we'll make do, with fair weather and no trouble. We're short, is the truth."

Hunter nodded. He paced the deck of the ship and looked at the canvas. Fully rigged, *El Trinidad* carried fourteen separate sails. Even the simplest task—such as letting out a reefed topsail—required almost a dozen strong backs.

"If there's heavy seas, we'll have to ride it out with bare poles," Enders said, shaking his head.

Hunter knew this was true. In a storm, he would have no choice but to reef all his canvas, and ride out the foul weather, but that was a dangerous thing to do on a ship so large.

But even more worrisome was the prospect of an attack. A ship under attack needed maneuverability, and Hunter lacked the crew to handle *El Trinidad* smartly.

And then there was the problem of the guns.

His thirty-two twelve-pounders were Danish cannon, of recent vintage, and all in good repair. Together they represented a reasonable—if not formidable—measure of defense. Thirty-two cannon made *El Trinidad* the equivalent of a third-rate ship of the line, and she could be expected to hold her own against all but the largest enemy warships. At least she could if Hunter had the men to work the guns, and he did not.

An efficient gun crew, a crew capable of loading, running out, aiming, and firing a cannon once a minute during battle consisted of fifteen men, not including the gun captain. To allow for injury, and simple fatigue during battle—the men grew tired pushing around two and a half tons of hot bronze—the crews were usually seventeen to twenty men. Assuming only half the cannon were fired at one time, Hunter really needed more than two hundred and seventy men just to work his guns. Yet he had none to spare. He was already shorthanded topside with his canvas.

The hard facts Hunter faced were these: he commanded a crew one-tenth the size he would need to fight well in a sea engagement, and one-third the size he would need to

survive a heavy storm. The implication was clear enough—
run from a fight, and find shelter before a storm.

It was Enders who voiced the concern. "I wish we could
run out full canvas," he said. He looked aloft. Right now, *El
Trinidad* sailed without mizzens, spritsails, or topgallants.

"What're we making?" Hunter asked.

"No better than eight knots. We should be doing double that."

"Not easy to outrun a ship," Hunter said.

"Or a storm," Enders said. "You thinking of scuttling
the sloop?"

Hunter had considered it already. The ten men aboard
the *Cassandra* would help on the larger ship, but not
much; *El Trinidad* would still be sorely undermanned. Fur-
thermore, the sloop was valuable in itself. If he kept his
own boat, he could auction the Spanish galleon to the merchants and captains of Port Royal, where it would fetch
a considerable sum. Or else it would be included in the
king's tenth, and greatly reduce the amount of bullion or
other treasure that King Charles would take.

"No," he said finally. "I want to keep my ship."

"Well, we could lighten the sow," Enders said. "There's
plenty of deadweight aboard. You've no use for the bronze,
or the longboats."

"I know," Hunter said. "But I hate to see us defenseless."

"But we are defenseless," Enders said.

"I know it," Hunter said. "But for the moment we will take our risks, and trust to Providence that we will have a safe return. Chance is on our side, especially once we are in the southern seas." It was Hunter's plan to sail down the Lesser Antilles, and then west, into the vastness of the Caribbean between Venezuela and Santo Domingo. He would be unlikely to meet Spanish warships in so much open water.

"I'm not one for trusting to Providence," Enders said gloomily. "But so be it."

LADY SARAH ALMONT was in an aft cabin. Hunter found her in the company of Lazue, who, with an air of elaborate innocence, was helping the girl comb her hair.

Hunter asked Lazue to leave, and she did.

"But we were having such a pleasant time!" Lady Sarah protested, as the door closed.

"Madam, I fear that Lazue has designs upon you."

"He seemed such a gentle man," she said. "He had a most delicate touch."

"Well," Hunter said, taking a seat in the cabin, "things are not always as they seem."

"Indeed, I have long since discovered that," she replied.

"I was on board the merchantman *Entrepid*, commanded by Captain Timothy Warner, of whom His Majesty King Charles has a most high opinion, as a fighting man. Imagine my surprise to discover that Captain Warner's knees shook more vigorously than my own, when confronted by the Spanish warship. He was, in brief, a coward."

"What happened to the ship?"

"It was destroyed."

"Cazalla?"

"Yes, the same. I was taken as prize. The crew and the ship were fired upon and sunk by Cazalla."

"All killed?" Hunter asked, raising his eyebrows. He was not really surprised, but this incident gave him the provocation that Sir James would sorely need to justify the attack on Matanceros.

"I did not witness it," said Lady Sarah. "But I presume so. I was locked in a cabin. Then Cazalla captured another ship of Englishmen. What befell them, I do not know."

"I believe," Hunter said, with a slight bow, "that they made good their escape."

"Perhaps so," she said, with no sign of understanding Hunter's meaning. "And now? What will you vagabonds have with me? I presume I am in the clutches of pirates."

"Charles Hunter, freeborn privateer, at your service. We are making our way to Port Royal."

She sighed. "This New World is so tedious. I hardly know whom to believe. You will forgive me if I am suspicious of you."

"Indeed, madam," said Hunter, feeling irritation at this prickly woman whose life he had saved. "I merely came below to inquire after your ankle—"

"It is improved much, thank you."

"—and to ask if you are, ah, otherwise well."

"Ah yes?" Her eyes flashed. "Do you not rather mean, if the Spaniard had his way with me, so that you can freely follow?"

"Madam, I did not—"

"Well, I can assure you, the Spaniard took nothing from me that was not already missing." She gave a bitter laugh. "But he did it in his fashion."

Abruptly, she turned in her chair. She wore a dress of Spanish cut—one she found in the ship—and it had a low back. Hunter saw a series of ugly welts across her shoulders.

She spun back to face him, "Now perhaps you understand," she said. "Although probably you do not. I have other trophies of my encounter with the Court of Philip in the New World." She lowered the neckline of her dress a trifle, to reveal a round red mark on one breast. She did it so quickly, so immodestly, that he was taken aback. Hunter could never accustom himself to well-born women from the court of the Merry Monarch who acted like their common counterparts. What must England be like, these days?

She touched the spot. "That is a burn," she said. "I have others. I fear they will scar. Any husband of mine will know the truth of my past soon enough." She glared at him defiantly.

"Madam," he said, "I am pleased to have dispatched the villain on your behalf."

"That is just like a man!" she said, and began to cry. She sobbed for some moments while Hunter stood, not certain what to do.

"Madam . . ." he said.

"My breasts were my best feature," she sniffled, through her tears. "I was the envy of every woman of breeding in London. Don't you understand anything?"

"Madam please . . ." Hunter fumbled for a handkerchief, but he had none. He was still wearing his ragged clothes from the attack. He looked around the cabin, found a table napkin, and handed it to her.

She blew her nose loudly.

"I am marked like a common criminal," she said, still crying. "I shall never be able to wear the fashions of the town again. I am ruined."

Hunter found her inexplicable. She was alive, and safe, and returning to her uncle. Why was she crying? Her lot was better than it had been in many days. Thinking that she was an ungrateful and inexplicable woman, he merely poured her a glass of wine from a decanter. "Lady Sarah, please do not torment yourself thus."

She took the wine, and gulped the entire glass in a single long swallow. She sniffled, and sighed.

"After all," he added, "fashions change."

At this, she burst into fresh tears. "Men, men, men," she moaned. "And all because I made a sojourn to visit my uncle. Oh, my poor fate!"

There was a knock on the door, and a seaman stuck his head in. "Begging pardon, Captain, but Mr. Enders says we have landfall within a glass, and then the sea chests to open."

"I shall be on deck," Hunter said, and he left the cabin. Lady Sarah burst into tears once more, and he heard her sobbing even as he closed the door behind him.

CHAPTER 25

THAT NIGHT, ANCHORED in Constantina Bay, in the shadow of a low and scrubby island, the crew voted six of their company to join Hunter and Sanson in the counting of the treasure. This was a serious and solemn business. Although the rest of the crew took the opportunity to become roaring drunk on Spanish rum, the eight men remained sober until accounting was completed.

There were two treasure vaults on Hunter's ship; the first was opened, and found to contain five chests. The first chest contained pearls, of uneven quality but still extremely valuable. The second chest was heaped with gold escudos, which gleamed dully in the lantern light. The escudos were painstakingly counted, and counted again, before being replaced in the chest. Gold in those days was extremely rare—only one Spanish ship in a hundred carried any—and the privateers were elated. The remaining three chests were filled with silver bars from Mexico. Hunter estimated that the total value of the five chests was more than ten thousand pounds sterling.

In a state of great excitement, the accounting party broke open the second treasure vault. Here they found ten chests, and enthusiasm ran high until the first was opened, to reveal gleaming silver bars with the crown-and-anchor stamp of Peru. But the surface of the bars was multicolored and uneven.

"I don't like the look of this," Sanson said.

The other chests were hastily opened. They were all the same, all multicolored silver ingots.

Hunter said, "Call for the Jew."

Don Diego, squinting in the dark light belowdecks, hiccoughing from Spanish kill-devil, frowned at the silver bars. "This is not good news," he said slowly. He called for a set of scales, and a cask of water, and for a silver bar from the first treasure vault.

When it was all assembled, the accounting group watched as the Jew placed the Mexican silver bar on one side of the scales and tested various bars of Peruvian silver on the other side until he found one that balanced exactly.

"These will do," he said, and set the bars of equal weight to one side. He drew the water cask in front of him and submerged the Mexican silver bar first. The water level inside the cask rose. The Jew marked the new level with his dagger blade, cutting a line in the wood.

He removed the Mexican bar and dropped in the Peruvian silver. The water level went higher than his cut mark.

"What does this mean, Don Diego? Is it silver?"

"In part," the Jew said. "But not entirely. There is some
impurity, some other metal, heavier than silver, but of the
same color."

"Is it *plumbum*?"

"Perhaps. But lead is dull on the surface, and this is
not. I warrant that this silver is mixed with *platina*."

This news was greeted with groans. Platinum was a
worthless metal.

"How much of it is *platina*, Don Diego?"

"I cannot say. To know exactly I need better measures. I
guess as much as half."

"The damned Dons," Sanson said. "Not only do they
steal from the Indians, they steal from each other. Philip is
a poor king to be so openly cheated."

"All kings are cheated," Hunter said. "It is in the
nature of being a king. But these bars are still worth something—at least ten thousand pounds. We have still captured a great treasure."

"Aye," Sanson said. "But think what it might have been."

There was other treasure to be accounted. The holds
of the ships contained household articles, fabrics, logwood,
tobacco, and spices such as chili and cloves. All these could

be auctioned on the docks of Port Royal, and they would amount, in total, to a substantial sum—perhaps two thousand pounds.

The accounting ran long into the night, and then the counting team joined the others in drunken songs and revelry. Neither Hunter nor Sanson participated; instead, they met in Hunter's cabin.

Sanson came directly to the point. "How is the woman?"

"Prickly," Hunter said. "And she cries a good deal."

"But she is unscathed?"

"She is alive."

"She must be accounted a part of the king's tenth," Sanson said. "Or the governor's."

"Sir James will not allow it."

"Surely you can persuade him."

"I doubt it."

"You have rescued his only niece . . ."

"Sir James has a keen business sense. His fingers cling to gold."

"I think you must try, on the part of all the crew," Sanson said, "to show him the correct way of thinking."

Hunter shrugged. He had, in fact, already thought of this, and was planning to argue the case before the governor.

But he did not wish to make any promises to Sanson.

The Frenchman poured wine. "Well," he said heartily.

"We have done great things, my friend. What is your plan for the return?"

Hunter sketched his intention to travel south, then to stay in open water until they could reach northward for Port Royal.

"Do you not think," Sanson said, "that we will be safer if we divide the treasure between the two ships, and separate now, returning by different routes?"

"I think it is better we remain together. Two ships present a formidable obstacle, seen from a distance. Singly, we might be attacked."

"Aye," Sanson said. "But there are a dozen Spanish ships of the line patrolling these waters. If we separate, it is most unlikely we would both encounter warships."

"We need not fear Spanish warriors. We are legitimate Spanish merchantmen. Only the French or the English might attack us."

Sanson smiled. "You do not trust me."

"Of course not," Hunter said, smiling back. "I want you in my sight, and I want the treasure beneath my feet."

"So be it," Sanson said, but there was a dark look in his eyes, and Hunter promised himself he would remember it.

CHAPTER 26

FOUR DAYS LATER, they sighted the monster.

It had been an uneventful sail, down the chain of the Lesser Antilles. The wind was fair and the sea calm; Hunter knew he was now nearly a hundred miles south of Matanceros, and with each passing hour he breathed more easily.

His crew was busy making the galleon as seaworthy as possible. The Spanish crew had kept *El Trinidad* in a lamentable state of repair. Rigging was frayed; sails were thin in places, torn in others; decks were filthy and the holds stank with refuse. There was much to do as they sailed southward, past Guadeloupe and San Marino.

At noon of the fourth day, Enders, ever watchful, noticed the change in the water. He pointed off to starboard. "Look there," he said to Hunter.

Hunter turned. The water was placid, with only a slight chop to mar the glassy surface. But barely a hundred yards away, there was a churning beneath the waves—some large object moving toward them, and at incredible speed.

"What are we making?" he demanded.

"Ten knots," Enders said. "Mother of God . . ."

"If we are making ten, that thing is making twenty," Hunter said.

"At least twenty," Enders said. He glanced around at the crews. No one had noticed it.

"Move to landward," Hunter said. "Get us in shoal water."

"The kraken don't like it shallow," Enders said.

"Let us hope not."

The submerged shape moved closer, and passed by the boat some fifty yards away. Hunter had a glimpse of dead gray-white, a suggestion of tentacles, and then the thing was gone. It moved off, and circled, then came back again.

Enders slapped his cheek. "I'm dreaming," he said. "I must be. Say it is not true."

"It's true," Hunter said.

From the nest of the mainmast, Lazue, the lookout, whistled to Hunter. She had seen the thing. Hunter looked up at her and shook his head, to keep silent.

"Thank God she didn't give out the cry," Enders said, "that's all we'd be needing, isn't it?"

"Shoal water," Hunter said grimly. "And quickly." He watched the churning water approach once more.

Up in the mainmast nest, Lazue was high above the clear blue water, and she could see the approach of the kraken plainly. Her heart was in her throat, for this was a legendary beast, the stuff of sailing songs and stories for the children of seafarers. But few had ever seen such a creature, and Lazue was not glad of the experience. It seemed to her that her heart stopped as she watched the thing approach again, with frightening speed, plowing up the surface as it came toward *El Trinidad*.

When it was very close, she saw the entire animal clearly. Its skin was a dead gray. It had a pointed snout, a bulbous body at least twenty feet long, and trailing behind, a tangle of long tentacles, like a Medusa's head. It passed beneath the ship, not touching the hull, but the waves from the creature's movements rocked the galleon. Then she saw it emerge on the other side and plunge down into the blue depths of the ocean. She wiped her sweating brow.

Lady Sarah Almont came on deck to find Hunter peering over the side. "Good day, Captain," she said. He turned and gave her a slight bow. "Madam."

"Captain, you are quite ashen. Is all well?"

Without replying, Hunter rushed to the other side of the aft deck and peered over the side again.

Enders at the tiller said, "You see it?"

"See what?" asked Lady Sarah.

"No," Hunter said. "It dived."

"We should have thirty fathoms beneath us," Enders said. "That's shoal for the thing."

"What thing?" asked Lady Sarah, pouting prettily.

Hunter came back to her.

Enders said, "It may be back."

"Aye," Hunter said.

She looked from Hunter to Enders. Both men were drenched in cold sweat. Both were very pale.

"Captain, I am no sailor. What is the meaning of this?"

Enders, tense, exploded. "God's blood, woman, we have just seen—"

"—an omen," said Hunter smoothly, with a sharp look to Enders. "An omen, my lady."

"An omen? Are you superstitious, Captain?"

"Aye, he's very superstitious, he is," said Enders, glancing out toward the horizon.

"It is plain," said Lady Sarah, stamping her foot on the deck, "that you will not tell me what is amiss."

"That's right," Hunter said, smiling. He had a charming smile, even through his pallor. He could be most exasperating, she thought.

"I know I am a woman," she began, "but I really must insist—"

And at that moment, Lazue shouted, "Sail ho!"

Straining his eyes to the glass, Hunter saw square canvas directly astern, coming above the line of the horizon. He turned back to Enders, but the sea artist was already barking orders to run out all the canvas *El Trinidad* possessed. The topgallants were unreefed; the foresprit was run up, and the galleon gathered speed.

A warning shot was fired to the *Cassandra*, a quarter of a mile ahead. Soon after, the little sloop also let out her full canvas.

Hunter looked through the glass again. The sails on the horizon had not grown larger—but neither had they diminished in size.

"God's blood, from one monster to another," Enders said. "How do we fare?"

"We're holding," Hunter said.

"We must come off this course soon," Enders said.

Hunter nodded. *El Trinidad* was running free before an easterly wind, but her course carried her too far west, toward the island chain to their right. Soon the water would be too shallow; they would have to alter course. On any ship, a course change meant at least a temporary loss in speed. Short-handed, the galleon would be especially slow.

Hunter said, "Can you wear her?"

Enders shook his head. "I dare not, Captain. We are too short-manned."

Lady Sarah said, "What is the problem?"

"Quiet," Hunter said. "Go below."

"I will not—"

"Go below!" he bellowed.

She backed off, but did not go below. Standing some distance away, she watched what she viewed as a strange spectacle. The man Lazue came down from the rigging with catlike grace, almost feminine in his movements. It was with a shock that Lady Sarah noticed the press of the wind against Lazue's blouse, clearly outlining breasts. So the gentle man was a woman! She had no time to ponder this, however, for Hunter was standing with Lazue and Enders, and all were engaged in fierce conversation. Hunter showed her the pursuing ship, and the island chain to the right. He pointed to the cloudless sky, and the sun, already on its downward arc as afternoon wore on. Lazue was frowning.

"What island will you make for?" she said.

"Cat," Enders said, pointing to a large island down the chain.

"Monkey Bay?" she asked.

"Aye," Enders said. "Monkey Bay."

"Do you know it?" Hunter said.

"Yes, but it was years past, and this is a windward port. How is the moon?"

"Third quarter," Hunter said.

"And there are no clouds," Lazue said. "Pity."

At this, they all nodded and shook their heads very gloomily. Then Lazue said, "Are you a gambler?"

"You know I am," Hunter said.

"Then make your course change, and see if you can outrun the ship. If you do, well and good. If not, we will manage."

"I trust your eyes," Hunter said.

"Do," Lazue said, and she scrambled back up the rigging to her lookout post.

Lady Sarah could make nothing of this conversation, although she recognized the tension and concern well enough. She remained by the railing, looking toward the horizon— where the sails of the pursuing ship were now clearly visible to her naked eye—until Hunter came over to her. Now that the decision was made, he seemed more relaxed.

"I did not understand a word of that," she said.

"It is simple enough," Hunter said. "You see the ship following?"

"I do."

"And you see the island downwind, Cat Island?"

"I do."

"There is a harbor there, called Monkey Bay. It is our first refuge, if we can make it."

She looked from the pursuing ship to the island. "But

surely you are close to the island, and there will be no problem."

"You see the sun?"

"Yes . . ."

"The sun is setting to the west. In another hour, it will gleam off the water with a brightness to cause pain to the eye. And we cannot see the obstructions beneath, as we make for that bay. In these waters, a ship cannot sail into the sun unless you risk tearing out the bottom on coral."

"But Lazue has entered the port before."

"Aye, but it is a windward port. Windward ports are exposed to the storms and strong currents of the open ocean, and they change. A sand bar can shift in days, weeks. Monkey Bay may not be as Lazue remembers it."

"Oh." She was silent a moment. "Then why make for port? You have not stopped these three nights past. Sail on into the night, and lose the ship in darkness." She felt very pleased with this solution.

"There is a moon," Hunter said gloomily. "Third quarter, it will not be up until midnight. But it will be enough for the ship to follow us—we will have only four hours of true darkness. We cannot lose her in so short a time."

"Then what will you do?"

Hunter picked up the glass and scanned the horizon. The pursuing ship was slowly gaining on them.

"I will make for Monkey Bay. Into the sun."

"Ready about!" Enders shouted, and the ship came around into the wind, slowly, cumbersomely changing course. It took a full quarter of an hour before they were cutting through the water again, and during that interval, the sails of the pursuing craft had grown much larger.

As Hunter peered through the glass, he felt something about those sails was depressingly familiar. "You don't suppose . . ."

"What, sir?"

"Lazue!" Hunter shouted, and pointed to the horizon.

Up above, Lazue put the glass to her eye.

"What do you make it to be?"

She shouted down: "Our old friend!"

Enders groaned. "Cazalla's warship? The black ship?"

"None other."

"Who commands her now?" Enders said.

"Bosquet, the Frenchy," Hunter said, recalling the slim, composed man he had seen board the ship at Matanceros.

"I know of him," Enders said. "Steady and competent seaman, he knows his trade." He sighed. "Too bad it's not a Don at the helm, we might have better luck." The Spaniards were notoriously bad seamen.

"How long to landfall now?"

"A full hour," Enders said, "could be more. If the passage is tight, we've got to get in some of this canvas."

That would cut their speed even more, but it could not be helped. If they were to have control over the ship in confined waters, they would have to shorten sail.

Hunter looked back at the pursuing warship. She was changing course, her sails tilting as she wore to leeward. She lost ground a moment, but soon was moving ahead at full speed.

"It will be a very near thing," he said.

"Aye," Enders said.

Lazue up in the rigging stretched her left arm. Enders changed course, watching until she dropped her arm. Then he held steady. A short time later, her right arm was held out, half-bent.

Enders again corrected course, turning slightly to starboard.

Part IV

MONKEY BAY

CHAPTER 27

EL TRINIDAD MADE for the cove of Monkey Bay.

Aboard the *Cassandra*, Sanson watched the larger ship maneuver. "Blood of Louis, they're making for land," he said. "Into the sun!"

"It is madness," moaned the man at the helm.

"Now hear me," Sanson said, spinning on him. "Come about, and fall into the wake of that Donnish hog, and follow it exactly. I mean none else: exactly. Our bows must cut their form, or I will cut your throat."

"How can they do it, into the sun?" moaned the helmsman.

"They have Lazue's eyes," Sanson said. "It may be enough."

LAZUE WAS CAREFUL where she looked. She was also careful what she did with her arms, for the most casual gesture would cause a course change. At this moment, she stared westward, holding her left hand flat under her nose, blocking the reflection of the sun off the water just ahead of the bow. She looked only to the land—the sloping green contours of Cat Island, at this moment a flat outline, without depth.

She knew that somewhere ahead, when they were closer, the island contour would begin to separate, to show definition, and she would see the entrance to Monkey Bay. Until that moment, her job was to hold the fastest course bearing on the point where she expected to find the entrance.

Her elevation helped her; from this vantage point atop the mainmast, she was able to see the color of the water many miles ahead, an intricate pattern of blues and greens of different intensities. In her mind, these registered as depths; she could read them as if they were a chart marked with soundings.

This was no mean skill. The ordinary seaman, knowing the clarity of Caribbean water, naturally assumed that deep blue meant deep water, and green, still deeper. Lazue knew better: if the bottom was sandy, the water might be light blue, though the depth was fifty feet. Or a deep green color could mean a sea grass bottom just ten feet deep. And the shifting sun over the course of the day played odd tricks: in early morning or late afternoon all the colors were richer and darker; one had to compensate.

But for the moment, she had no concern for depth. She scanned the colors at the shoreline, looking for some clue to the entrance to Monkey Bay. She remembered that Monkey Bay was the outflow of a small river of fresh water, as was the case with most usable coves. There were many other Caribbean coves that were not safe for large ships, because there was no gap in the offshore coral reef. To have a gap, one needed a fresh-water outflow, for where there was fresh water, coral did not grow.

Lazue, scanning the water near the shoreline, knew that the gap might not be near the stream itself. Depending on the currents that carried the freshwater out to sea, the actual break in the reef might be a quarter-mile north or south. Wherever it was, currents often produced a brownish turbidity in the water, and a change in the surface appearance.

She scanned carefully, and finally she saw it, south of the ship's present course. She signaled corrections to Enders on the deck below. As *El Trinidad* came closer, she was glad that the sea artist had no idea what he was facing; he would faint if he knew how narrow the gap in the reef really was. There were coral heads awash on both sides, and between them the open space was no more than a dozen yards.

Satisfied with the new course, Lazue closed her eyes for several minutes. She was aware of the pink color of sunlight on her eyelids; she was not aware of the motion of the ship, or the wind in the sails, or the smells of the ocean.

She was focused entirely on her eyes as she rested them. Nothing mattered but her eyes. She breathed deeply and slowly, preparing herself for the coming exertion, gathering her energy, sharpening her concentration.

She knew how it would happen; she knew the inevitable progression—an easy beginning and then the first ache in her eyes, the increasing pain, then tears, stinging, burning. At the end of the hour, she knew she would be wholly exhausted, her entire body limp. She would need sleep as if she had been awake for a week, and would probably collapse as soon as she climbed down to the deck.

It was for this coming, massive exertion that she prepared herself now; breathing in long, slow breaths, with her eyes closed.

FOR ENDERS, AT the helm, his concentration was very different. His eyes were open, but he had little interest in what he saw. Enders felt the tiller in his hands; the pressure it exerted on his palms; the cant of the deck beneath his feet; the rumble of the water slipping by the hull; the wind on his cheeks; the vibration of the rigging; the whole complex of forces and stresses that made up the trim of the ship. Indeed, in his absolute concentration, Enders became part of the ship, joined to it as if physically connected; he was the brain to its body, and he knew its condition to the minutest detail.

He knew its speed to a fraction of a knot; he sensed when any sail was wrongly trimmed; he knew when any cargo shifted in the hold, and he knew where; he felt how much water was in the bilge; he knew when the ship was sailing easy, when she was on her best line; he knew when she was past it, and how long she could hold past it, and how far he could push her.

All this he could have told you with his eyes closed. He could not have said how he knew it, only that he did. Now, working with Lazue, he was worried, precisely because he had to give over part of his control to someone else. Lazue's hand signals meant nothing to him that he could sense directly; yet he followed her directions blindly, knowing that he must trust her. But he was nervous about it; he sweated at the tiller, feeling the wind more strongly on his damp cheeks, and he made more corrections as Lazue stretched out her arms.

She was taking the ship southward. She must have spotted the break in the reef, he thought, and was now making for it. Soon they would pass through the gap. The very idea made him sweat more.

∞

HUNTER'S MIND WAS wholly occupied with other concerns. He raced back and forth, from bow to stern, ignoring both Lazue and Enders. The Spanish warship was closing with each passing minute; the upper edge of the mainsail was now clear of the horizon. She still carried full sail, while *El Trinidad*, now only a mile off the island, had dropped much of her canvas.

Meanwhile, the *Cassandra* had fallen behind the larger ship, dropping back to port to let Hunter's vessel show them the course to harbor. The maneuver was necessary, but Hunter's canvas was eating *Cassandra*'s wind, and the little ship was not making good speed. Indeed, she would not until she was completely astern of *El Trinidad*. At that point, she would be very vulnerable to the Spanish warship unless she stayed close to Hunter.

The trouble would come when making the bay itself. The two ships would have to pass through in close succession; if *El Trinidad* did not make passage smoothly, the *Cassandra* might ram her, injuring both ships. If it happened in the passage itself, it could be a nightmare, both ships sinking on the rocks of the reef. He was sure Sanson was aware of the danger; he was equally sure that Sanson would know that he dared not drop too far back.

It was going to be a very tricky maneuver. He ran forward, and stared through the shimmering glare of the

sunlit water at Monkey Bay. He could see now the curving finger of hilly land, extending out from the island and
forming the protected hook of the bay.

The actual gap in the reef was invisible to him; it lay
somewhere in the sheet of glaring, sparkling water directly
ahead.

He looked up the mainmast to Lazue and saw her make
a signal to Enders—she swung her fist upward to strike the
flat palm of her hand.

Enders immediately barked orders to lower more sail.
Hunter knew that could only mean one thing: they were
very close to the reef passage. He squinted forward into the
glare, but still could see nothing.

"Linemen! Starboard and larboard!" shouted Enders,
and soon after, two men at either side of the bow began
to alternate shouted soundings. The first unnerved Hunter.
"Full five!"

Five fathoms—thirty feet—was already shallow water.
El Trinidad drew three fathoms, so there was not much to
spare. In shoal waters, coral undersea outcroppings could
easily rise a dozen feet from the bottom in irregular patterns.
And the sharp coral would tear the wooden hull like paper.

"*Cinq et demi*" came the next cry. That was better.
Hunter waited.

"Full six and more!"

He breathed a little easier. They must have passed the outer reef—most islands had two, a shallow inner reef and a deeper one offshore. They would have a short space of safe water now, before they reached the dangerous inside reef.

"*Moins six!*" came the cry.

It was already growing more shallow. Hunter turned again to look at Lazue, high on the mainmast. Her body was leaning forward, relaxed, almost indifferent. He could not see her expression.

LAZUE'S BODY WAS indeed relaxed; it was so limp she was in danger of falling from her high post. Her arms gripped the top railing lightly as she leaned forward; her shoulders were slumped; every muscle sagged.

But her face was tight and pinched, her mouth pulled back into a fixed grimace, her teeth clamped together as she squinted into the glare. She held her eyes nearly shut and she had been doing this for so long that her lids fluttered with tension. This might have been distracting, but Lazue was not even aware of it for she had long ago slipped into a kind of trance state.

Her world consisted of two black shapes—the island ahead and the bow of the ship just beneath her. Separating them was a flat expanse of shimmering, excruciatingly bright sunlit water, which fluttered and sparkled in a hypnotic pattern. She could see almost no detail in that surface.

Occasionally, she had a glimpse of coral outcroppings awash. They appeared as brief black spots in the blinding white glare.

At other times, during lulls in the gusting wind, she had a momentary image of eddies and currents, which swirled the uniform pattern of sparkles.

Otherwise, the water was opaque, blinding silver. She guided the ship through this shimmering surface entirely by memory, for she had marked, in her mind, the position of shallow water, coral heads, and sand bars more than half an hour ago, when the ship was farther offshore and the water ahead was clear. She had made a detailed mental image using landmarks on the shore and in the water itself.

Now, by looking directly down at the water passing amidships—which was transparent—she could gauge *El Trinidad*'s position relative to her mental image. Far below, she saw a round head of brain coral, resembling a gargantuan clump of cauliflower, pass on the port side. She knew that meant they would have to bear north; she extended her right arm, and watched as the black silhouette of the bow nosed around, and waited until they were in line with a dead palm tree on the shore. Then she dropped her hand; Enders held the new course.

She squinted ahead. She saw the coral awash, marking the sides of the channel. They were bearing directly for the gap. From memory, she knew that before reaching the gap, they had to veer to starboard slightly to miss another coral head. She extended her right hand. Enders corrected.

She looked straight down. The second coral head went past, dangerously close to the hull; the ship shivered as it scraped the outcropping, but then they were clear.

She held out her left arm, and Enders changed course again. She lined herself on the dead palm again, and waited.

Enders had been electrified by the sound of the coral head on the hull; his nerves, straining to hear exactly that dreaded sound, were raw; he jumped at the tiller, but as the crunching continued, a vibration moving aft, he realized that they were going to kiss the coral, and he breathed a deep sigh.

In the stern, he felt the vibration approaching him down the length of the ship. At the last moment, he released the tiller, knowing that the rudder was the most vulnerable part of the ship below water. A grazing collision that merely scraped the hull of barnacles could snap a hard-turned rudder, so he released tension. Then he took the tiller in his hand again, and followed Lazue's instructions.

"She would break a snake's back," he muttered, as *El Trinidad* twisted and turned toward Monkey Bay.

"Less four!" shouted the lineman.

Hunter, in the bow, flanked on either side by the men with their plumb lines, watched the glaring water ahead. He could see nothing at all forward; looking to the side, he saw coral formations fearsomely close to the surface, but somehow, *El Trinidad* was missing them.

"*Trois et demi!*"

He gritted his teeth. Twenty feet of water. They could not take much less. As he had the thought, the ship struck another coral formation, but this time there was only a single sharp impact, then nothing. The ship had snapped the coral head, then continued on.

"Three and one!"

They had lost another foot. The ship plowed forward into the sparkling sea.

"*Merde!*" yelled the second linesman, and started running aft. Hunter knew what had happened; his line had become snarled in coral, and caught; he was trying to free it.

"Full three!"

Hunter frowned—they should be aground now, according to what his Spanish prisoners had told him. They had sworn *El Trinidad* drew three fathoms of water. Obviously, they were wrong: the ship still sailed smoothly toward the island. He silently damned Spanish seamanship.

Yet he knew the three-fathom draft could not be far wrong; a ship this size must draw very nearly that.

"Full three!"

They were still moving. And then, with frightening suddenness, he saw the gap in the reef, a desperately narrow passage between coral awash on both sides. *El Trinidad* was right in the center of the passage, and a damned fortunate thing, too, for there was no more than five yards to spare on either side as they passed through.

He looked astern to Enders, who saw the coral on both sides of him. Enders was crossing himself.

"Full five!" shouted the linesman hoarsely, and the crew gave a jubilant cheer. They were inside the reef, in deeper water, and moving north now, to the protected cove between the island shore and the curving finger of hilly land, which encircled the seaward side of the bay.

Hunter could now see the full extent of Monkey Bay. He could tell at a glance that it was not an ideal berth for his ships. The water was deep at the mouth of the bay, but it turned rapidly shallow in more protected areas. He would have to anchor the galleon in water that was exposed to the ocean, and, for several reasons, he was unhappy with that prospect.

Looking back, he saw the *Cassandra* make the passage safely, following Hunter's ship so closely he could see the worried expression on the linesman's face in *Cassandra*'s bow. And behind the *Cassandra* was the Spanish warship, no more than two miles distant.

But the sun was falling. The warship would not be able to enter Monkey Bay before nightfall. And if Bosquet chose to enter at dawn, then Hunter would be ready for him.

"Drop anchor!" Enders shouted. "Make fast!"

El Trinidad shuddered to a stop in the twilight. *Cassandra* glided past her, moving deeper into the bay; the smaller ship with her lesser draft could take the shoal water farther in. A moment later, Sanson's anchor splashed into the water and both ships were secured.

They were safe, at least for a time.

CHAPTER 28

AFTER THE TENSION of the reef passage, the crews of both ships were jubilant, shouting and laughing, calling congratulations and mock insults to each other through the twilight. Hunter did not join in the general celebration. He stood on the aft castle of his galleon and watched the warship continue toward them, despite the rapidly growing darkness.

The Spanish man-of-war was now within a half-mile of the bay; she was just outside the reef entrance. Bosquet had great daring, he thought, to come so close in near darkness. He was also taking a considerable and unnecessary risk.

Enders, also watching, asked the unspoken question: "Why?"

Hunter shook his head. He saw the warship drop her anchor line; he saw the splash as it hit the water.

The enemy vessel was so close he could hear the shouted commands in Spanish drifting to him across the water. There was a lot of activity in the stern of the ship; a second anchor was thrown out.

"Makes no sense," Enders said. "He's got miles of deep water to ride out the night, but he puts himself in four fathoms."

Hunter watched. Another stern anchor was thrown over the side, and many hands tugged at the line. The stern of the warship swung around toward the shore.

"Damn me," Enders said. "You don't suppose . . ."

"I do," Hunter said. "She's lining up a broadside. Hoist anchor."

"Hoist anchor!" Enders shouted to his surprised crew. "Ready on the foresprit, there! Lively with the lines!" He turned back to Hunter. "We'll run aground for sure."

"We have no choice," Hunter said.

Bosquet's intent was clear enough. He had anchored in the mouth of the bay, just beyond the reef, but within range of his broadside cannon. He intended to stay there and pound the galleon through the night. Unless Hunter moved out of range, risking the shallow water, his ships would be demolished by morning.

And indeed, they could see the gunports springing open on the Spanish warship, and the muzzles of the cannon as they were fired, the balls smashing through *El Trinidad*'s rigging, and splashing in the water around them.

"Get her moving, Mr. Enders," Hunter barked.

As if in answer, a second broadside blasted from the

Spanish warship. This one was more on target. Several balls struck *El Trinidad*, splintering wood, tearing lines.

"Damn me," Enders said, with as much pain in his voice as if he had himself been injured.

But Hunter's ship was moving now, and she inched out of range so that the next broadside fell harmlessly into the water in a straight line of splashes. That straightness was itself impressive.

"She's well manned," Enders said.

"There are times," Hunter said, "when you are too appreciative of good seamanship."

By now it was quite dark; the fourth broadside came as a pattern of hot red flashes from the black profile of the warship. They heard, but could barely see, the splashes of shot in the water astern.

And then the low offshore hilly curve obliterated the view of the enemy vessel.

"Drop anchor," Enders shouted, but it was too late. At that very moment with a soft, crunching sound, *El Trinidad* ran aground on the sandy bottom of Monkey Bay.

THAT NIGHT, SITTING alone in his cabin, Hunter took stock of his situation. The fact that he was grounded did not bother him in the least; the ship had struck sand at low tide, and he could easily get her afloat in a few hours.

For the moment, the two ships were safe. The harbor was not ideal, but it was serviceable enough; he had fresh water and provisions to last more than two weeks without subjecting his crew to any hardship. If they could find food and water ashore—and they probably could—then he could remain in Monkey Bay for months.

At least he could remain until a storm came up. A storm could be disastrous. Monkey Bay was on the windward side of an ocean island and its waters were shallow. A heavy storm would crush his ships to splinters in a matter of hours. And this was the season for hurricanes; he could not expect too many days to pass without experiencing one, and he could not remain in Monkey Bay when it struck.

Bosquet would know this. If he were a patient man, he could simply blockade the bay, riding in deep water, and wait for the foul weather, which would force the galleon to leave the harbor and be exposed to his attack.

Yet Bosquet did not seem to be a patient man. Quite the opposite: he gave every indication of resource and daring, a man who preferred to take the offensive when he could. And there were good reasons for him to attack before bad weather.

In any naval engagement, foul weather was an equalizer, desired by the weaker force, avoided by the stronger. A storm plagued both ships, but it reduced the effectiveness of the superior ship disproportionately. Bosquet must know that Hunter's ships were short-handed and lightly armed.

Sitting alone in his cabin, Hunter put himself into the mind of a man he had never met, and tried to guess his thoughts. Bosquet would surely attack in the morning, he decided.

That attack would either come from land, or sea, or both. It depended upon how many Spanish soldiers Bosquet had aboard, and how well they trusted their commander. Hunter remembered the soldiers who had guarded him in the hold of the warship; they were young men, not experienced, poorly disciplined.

They could not be relied upon.

No, he decided, Bosquet would first attack from his ship. He would try to enter Monkey Bay, until he was within view of the galleon. He probably suspected that the privateers were in shoal water, which would make maneuvering difficult.

Right now, they were showing the enemy their stern, the most vulnerable part of the ship. Bosquet could sail just inside the mouth of the cove, and fire broadsides until he sank both ships. And he could do that with impunity, because the treasure on the galleon would then lie in shallow water, where it could be salvaged from the sand by native divers.

Hunter called for Enders, and ordered that the Spanish prisoners be locked away safely. Then he ordered that every able-bodied privateer be armed with muskets, and put ashore without delay.

DAWN CAME GENTLY to Monkey Bay. There was only a slight wind; the sky was laced with wispy clouds that caught the pink glow of first light. Aboard the Spanish warship, the crews began their morning's work in lazy and desultory fashion. The sun was well above the horizon before orders were shouted to let out the sails and raise anchor.

At that moment, from all along the shore, on both sides of the passage to the bay, the concealed privateers opened with withering gunfire. It must have astounded the Spanish crews. In the first few moments, all the men winching the main anchor were killed; all the men hoisting the aft anchor were killed or wounded; the officers visible on the decks were shot; and the men in the rigging were picked off with astonishing accuracy, and fell screaming to the deck.

Then, just as abruptly, the firing ceased. Except for an acrid gray haze of powder hanging in the air on the shore, there was no sign of movement, no rustling of foliage, nothing.

Hunter, positioned at the seaward tip of the hilly finger of land, watched the warship through his glass with satisfaction. He heard the confused shouts, and watched the half-unreefed sails snap and flutter in the breeze. Several minutes passed before new crews began to climb the rigging, and work the winches on deck. They began timidly at first, but when there was no further firing from the shore, grew bolder.

Hunter waited.

He had a distinct advantage, he knew. In an era when neither muskets nor musketeers were notably accurate, the privateers were, to a man, superb marksmen. His men could pick off sailors on the deck of a ship while giving chase in the rolling pitch of an open boat. To fire from the shore was child's play to his men.

It was not even good sport.

Hunter waited until he saw the anchor line beginning to move and then he gave the signal to fire again. Another round poured onto the warship, with the same devastating effect. Then, another silence.

Bosquet must surely realize by now that to enter the coral passage—coming closer to shore—would be extremely costly. He could probably make the passage and enter the bay, but dozens, perhaps hundreds of his men would be killed. Far more serious was the risk that key men aloft, or even the helmsman himself, might be shot, leaving the ship rudderless in dangerous waters.

Hunter waited. He heard shouted commands, then more silence. And then he saw the main anchor line plop into the water. They had cut the anchor. A moment later, the stern lines were also cut, and the ship drifted slowly away from the reef.

Once out of musket range, men again appeared on deck and in the rigging. The sails were let out. Hunter waited to see if she turned and made for the shore. The warship did not turn. Instead, she moved north perhaps a hundred yards, and another anchor was dropped in the new position. The sails were taken up; the ship rode gently at anchor, directly off the hills protecting the bay.

"Well," Enders said. "That's it, then. The Don can't get in, and we can't get out."

By midday, Monkey Bay was burning hot and airless. Hunter, pacing the heated decks of his galleon, feeling the sticky ooze of softened pitch beneath his feet, was aware of the irony of his predicament. He had conducted the most daring privateering raid in a century, with complete success—only to become trapped in a stifling, unhealthy cove by a single Donnish ship of the line.

It was a difficult moment for him, and even more difficult for his crew. The privateers looked to their captain for guidance and fresh plans, and it was all too obvious that Hunter had none. Someone broke into the rum, and the crew fell to brawling; one argument evolved into a duel. Enders stopped it at the last minute. Hunter passed the word that any man who killed another would himself be killed by Hunter. The captain wanted his crew intact, and personal disagreements could await landfall in Port Royal.

"Don't know if they'll stand for it," Enders said, gloomy as ever.

"They will," Hunter said.

He was standing on deck in the shadow of the mainmast with Lady Sarah when another pistol shot rang out somewhere belowdecks.

"What's that?" Lady Sarah said, alarmed.

"Hell," Hunter said.

A few moments later, a struggling seaman was brought above, in the grip of the enormous Bassa. Enders trailed disconsolately behind.

Hunter looked at the seaman. He was a grizzled man of twenty-five, named Lockwood. Hunter knew him slightly.

"Winged Perkins in the ear with this," Enders said, handing Hunter a pistol.

The crew was slowly filtering onto the main deck, surly and grim in the hot sun. Hunter took his own pistol from his belt, and checked the prime.

"What are you going to do?" said Lady Sarah, watching.

"This is none of your concern," Hunter said.

"But—"

"Look away," Hunter said. He raised his pistol.

Bassa, the Moor, released the seaman. The man stood there, head bowed, drunk.

"He crossed me," the seaman said.

Hunter shot him in the head. His brains spattered over the gunwale.

"Oh God!" said Lady Sarah Almont.

"Throw him overboard," Hunter said. Bassa picked up the body and dragged it, feet scraping loudly in the midday silence on the deck. A moment later, there was a splash; the body was gone.

Hunter looked at his crew. "Do you want to vote a new captain?" he said loudly.

The crew grumbled, and turned away. No one spoke.

Soon after, the decks were cleared again. The men had gone below, to escape the direct heat of the sun.

Hunter looked at Lady Sarah. She said nothing, but her glance was accusing.

"These are hard men," Hunter said, "and they live by rules we have all accepted."

She said nothing, but turned on her heel and walked away.

Hunter looked at Enders. Enders shrugged.

Later in the afternoon, Hunter was informed by his look-outs that there was new activity aboard the warship; all the longboats had been lowered on the ocean side, out of view of the land. They were apparently tied up to the ship, for none had appeared. Considerable smoke was issuing from the deck of the warship. Some kind of fire was burning, but its purpose was unclear. This situation continued until nightfall.

Nightfall was a blessing. In the cool evening air, Hunter paced the decks of *El Trinidad*, staring at the long rows of his cannon. He walked from one to the next, pausing to touch them, running his fingers over the bronze, which still held the warmth of the day. He examined the equipment neatly stowed by each: the rammer, the bags of powder, the shot clusters, the quill touch-pins, and the slow fuses in the notched water buckets.

It was all ready to use—all this firepower, all this armament. He had everything he needed except the men to fire them. And without the men, the cannon might as well not be there at all.

"You are lost in thought."

He turned, startled. Lady Sarah was there, in a white shift. It looked like an undergarment in the darkness.

"You should not dress like that, with the men about."

"It was too hot to sleep," she said. "Besides, I was restless. What I witnessed today . . ." Her voice trailed off.

"It disturbed you?"

"I have not seen such savagery, even in a monarch. Charles himself is not so ruthless, so arbitrary."

"Charles has his mind on other things. His pleasures."

"You deliberately miss my meaning." Even in the darkness, her eyes glowed with something like anger.

"Madam," Hunter said. "In this society—".

"Society? You call this"—she gestured with a sweeping hand to the ship, and the men sleeping on the deck—"you call this society?"

"Of course. For wherever men gather, there are rules of conduct. These men have different rules from the Court of Charles, or of Louis, or even of Massachusetts Colony, where I was born. And yet there are rules to be upheld, and penalties to pay for breaking them."

"You are a philosopher." Her voice in the darkness was sarcastic.

"I speak what I know. In the Court of Charles, what would befall you if you failed to bow before the monarch?"

She snorted, seeing the direction of his argument.

"It is the same here," Hunter said. "These men are fierce and violent. If I am to rule them, they must obey me. If they are to obey me, they must respect me. If they are to respect me, they must recognize my authority, which is absolute."

"You speak like a king."

"A captain is king, over his crew."

She moved closer to him. "And do you take your pleasure, as a king does?"

He had only a moment to reflect before she threw her arms around him, and kissed him on the mouth, hard. He returned her embrace. When they broke, she said, "I am so frightened. Everything is strange here."

"Madam," he said, "I am obliged to return you safely to your uncle and my friend, Governor Sir James Almont."

"There is no need to be pompous. Are you a Puritan?"

"Only by birth," he said, and kissed her again.

"Perhaps I will see you later," she said.

"Perhaps."

She went below, with a final glance at him in the darkness. Hunter leaned on one of the cannon, and watched her go.

"Spicy one, isn't she."

He turned. It was Enders. He grinned.

"Get a well-born one across the line, and they start to itch, eh?"

"So it appears," Hunter said.

Enders looked down the row of cannon, and slapped one with his hand. It rang dully. "Maddening, isn't it," he said. "All these guns, and we can't use 'em for lack of men."

"You'd best get sleep," Hunter said shortly, and walked off.

But it was true, what Enders had said. As he continued pacing the decks, the woman was forgotten, and his
thoughts returned to the cannon. Some restless part of his
brain churned over the problem, again and again, looking
for a solution. Somehow he was convinced there was a way
to use these guns. Something he had forgotten, something
he knew long ago.

The woman obviously thought he was a barbarian—or,
worse, a Puritan. He smiled in the darkness at the thought.
In fact, Hunter was an educated man. He had been taught
all the main categories of knowledge, as they had been
defined since medieval days. He knew classical history,
Latin and Greek, natural philosophy, religion, and music.
At the time, none of it had interested him.

Even as a young man, he was far more concerned with
practical, empirical knowledge than he was in the opin-
ions of some long-dead thinker. Every schoolboy knew that
the world was much larger than Aristotle had ever dreamt.
Hunter himself had been born on land that the Greeks did
not know existed.

Yet now, certain elements of his formal training tugged
at his mind. He kept thinking of Greece—something about
Greece, or the Greeks—but he did not know what, or why.

Then he thought of the oil painting in Cazalla's cabin,
aboard the Spanish warship. Hunter had hardly noticed it

at the time. Nor did he remember it clearly now. But there was something about a painting aboard a warship that intrigued him. In some way, it was important.

What did it matter? He knew nothing of painting; he regarded it as a very minor talent, suitable only for decoration, and of interest only to those vain and wealthy noblemen who would pay to have their portraits done, with flattering improvements. The painters themselves were, he knew, trivial souls who wandered like gypsies from one country to another in search of some patron who would support their efforts. They were homeless, rootless, frivolous men who lacked the solid attachment of strong feeling for the nation of their birth. Hunter, despite the fact that his parents had fled England for Massachusetts, considered himself wholly English and passionately Protestant. He was at war with a Spanish and Catholic enemy and did not comprehend anyone who was not equally patriotic. To care only for painting: that was a pale allegiance indeed.

And yet the painters wandered. There were Frenchmen in London, Greeks in Spain, and Italians everywhere. Even in times of war, the painters came and went freely, especially the Italians. There were so many Italians.

Why did he care?

He walked along the dark ship, passing from cannon to cannon. He touched one. Stamped on its postern was a motto:

SEMPER VINCIT

The words mocked him. Not always, he thought. Not without men to load and aim and fire. He touched the lettering, running his fingers over the grooves, feeling the fine, smooth curve of the S, the clean lines of the E.

SEMPER VINCIT

There was strength in the crispness of Latin, two tight words, military and hard. The Italians had lost all that; Italians were soft and flowery, and their tongue had changed to reflect the softness. It had been a long time since Caesar had bluntly said: *Veni, vidi, vici.*

VINCIT

That one word seemed to suggest something. He looked at the clean lines of the letters, and then in his mind he saw more lines, lines and angles, and he was back to the Greeks, to his Euclidean geometry, which had been so agonizing to him as a boy. He had never been able to understand why it mattered that two angles were equal to another, or that two lines intersected at one point or another. What difference did it make?

VINCIT

He remembered Cazalla's painting, a work of art on a warship, out of place, serving no purpose. That was the trouble with art, it was not practical. Art conquered nothing.

VINCIT

It conquers. Hunter smiled at the irony of the motto, stamped into a cannon that would conquer nothing. This weapon was as worthless to him as Cazalla's painting. It was as worthless to him as Euclid's postulates. He rubbed his tired eyes.

All this thinking mattered not at all. He was traveling in circles with no sense, no purpose, no destination, only the persistent itch of a frustrated man who was trapped and sought an exit in vain.

And then, he heard the cry that seamen fear more than any other: "Fire!"

CHAPTER 29

HE RUSHED TOPSIDE, in time to see six fireboats bearing down on the galleon. They were the warship's longboats thickly coated with pitch, and now blazing brightly, illuminating the still waters of the bay as they floated forward.

He cursed himself for not anticipating this maneuver; the smoke on the warship's decks had been a clear clue, which Hunter had failed to understand. But he wasted no time in recrimination. Already the seamen of *El Trinidad* were pouring over the side, into the galleon's longboats, tied alongside the ship; the first of the longboats cast off, the men stroking furiously toward the fire ships.

Hunter spun on his heel. "Where are our lookouts?" he demanded of Enders. "How did this happen?"

Enders shook his head. "I don't know, the watch was posted on the sandy point and the shore beyond."

"Damn!"

The men had either fallen asleep at their posts, or else Spaniards had swum ashore in the darkness, surprised the

men, and killed them. He watched the first of his longboats with its complement of seamen battle the flames
of one burning ship. They were trying to fend it off with
their oars, and to overturn it. One seaman caught fire and
jumped screaming into the water.

Then Hunter himself went over the side, dropping into
a boat. As the crew rowed, they drenched themselves with
seawater, as they approached the burning boats. He looked
off and saw that Sanson was leading a longboat from *Cassandra* to join the fight.

"Bend your backs, lads!" Hunter shouted, as he moved
into the inferno. Even at a distance of fifty yards, the heat
from the fire ships was fierce; the flames streaked and
jumped high into the night; burning gobs of pitch crack-
led and spit in all directions, sizzling in the water.

The next hour was a living nightmare. One by one,
the burning ships were beached, or held away in the water
until their hulls burned out and they sank.

When Hunter finally returned to his ship, covered in
soot, his clothes ragged, he immediately fell into a deep sleep.

ENDERS WOKE HIM the next morning with the news
that Sanson was down in the hold of *El Trinidad*. "He says
he has found something," Enders said doubtfully.

Hunter pulled on his clothes and climbed down the four decks of *El Trinidad* to the hold. On the lowest deck, redolent of dung from the cattle above, he found Sanson, grinning broadly.

"It was an accident," Sanson said. "I cannot take credit. Come and see."

Sanson led the way below to the ballast compartment. This narrow, low passage stank of hot air and bilge water, which sloshed back and forth with the gentle motion of the boat. Hunter saw rocks placed there for ballast. And then he frowned—they were not rocks, they were too regular in shape. They were shot.

He picked one up in his hand, hefting it, feeling the weight. It was iron, slippery with slime and bilge water.

"Five pounds or so," Sanson said. "We have nothing on board to fire a five-pound shot."

Still grinning, he led Hunter aft. By the light of a flickering lantern, Hunter saw another shape in the hold, half-submerged by water. He recognized it immediately— it was a saker, a small cannon no longer much used on ships. Sakers had fallen out of popularity thirty years earlier, replaced either by small swivel guns or by very large cannon.

He bent over the gun, running his hands along it, underwater. "Will she fire?"

"She's bronze," Sanson said. "The Jew says she will be serviceable."

Hunter felt the metal. Because it was bronze, it had not corroded much. He looked back at Sanson. "Then we will give the Don a taste of his own delights," he said.

The saker, small though it was, still comprised seven feet of solid bronze weighing sixteen hundred pounds. It took the better part of the morning to wrestle the gun onto *El Trinidad*'s deck. Then the gun had to be lowered over the side, to a waiting longboat.

In the hot sun, the work was excruciating and had to be done with consummate delicacy. Enders shrieked orders and curses until he was hoarse, but finally the saker settled into the longboat as gently as if it were a feather. The longboat sank alarmingly under the weight. Her gunnels clearing the water by no more than inches. Yet she was stable, as she was towed to the far shore.

Hunter intended to set the saker on top of the hill that curved out from Monkey Bay. That would place it within range of the Spanish warship, and allow it to fire on the offshore vessel. The gun emplacement would be safe; the Spaniards could not get enough elevation from their own cannon to make any reply, and Hunter's men could shell them until they ran out of balls.

The real question was when to open fire. Hunter had no

illusions about the strength of this cannon. A five-pound shot was hardly formidable; it would take many rounds to cause significant damage. But if he opened fire at night, the Spanish warship might, in confusion, cast off and try to move out of range. And in shoal water at night, she could easily run aground or even sink.

That was what he hoped for.

The saker, lying in the wallowing longboat, reached the shore, and thirty seamen groaned to haul it onto the beach. There it was placed on rollers, and laboriously dragged, foot by foot, to the edge of the underbrush.

From there, the saker had to be pulled a hundred feet up to the top of the hill, through dense clusters of mangrove and palm trees. Without winches or tackles to help with the weight, it was a forbidding job, yet his crew bent to the task with alacrity.

Other men worked equally hard. The Jew supervised five men who scrubbed the rust from the iron shot, and filled shot-bags with gunpowder. The Moor, a skilled carpenter, built a gun carriage with trunnion notches.

By dusk, the gun was in position, overlooking the warship. Hunter waited until a few minutes before darkness closed in, and then he gave the order to fire. The first round was long, splashing on the seaward side of the Spanish vessel. The second round hit its mark, and so did the third. And then it became almost too dark to see anything.

For the next hour, the saker slammed shot into the Spanish warship and in the gloom they saw white sails unfurl.

"He's going to run for it!" Enders shouted hoarsely.

There were cheers from the gun crew. More volleys were fired as the warship backed and filled, easing away from the mooring. Hunter's men kept up a steady pattern of shots, and even when the warship was no longer visible in the darkness, he gave orders to carry on firing. The crack of the saker continued through the night.

By the first light of dawn, they strained to see the fruits of their labors. The warship was again anchored, perhaps a quarter-mile farther offshore, but the sun rose behind the vessel, making her a black silhouette. They could see no evidence of damage. They knew they had caused some, but it was impossible to judge the extent.

Even in the first moments of light, Hunter was depressed. He could tell from the way the ship rode at anchor that she had not been seriously injured. With great good fortune, she had maneuvered the night waters outside the bay without striking coral or running aground.

One of her topsail spars hung cracked and dangling. Some of her rigging was ragged, and her bowline was chipped and splintered. But these were minor details: Bosquet's warship was safe, riding smoothly in the sunlit waters offshore. Hunter felt enormous fatigue and enormous depression. He watched the ship some moments longer, noticing her motion.

"God's blood," he said softly.

Enders, by his side, had noticed it, too. "Longish chop," he said.

"The wind is fair," Hunter said.

"Aye. For another day or so."

Hunter stared at the long, slow sea swell that rocked the Spanish warship back and forth at anchor. He swore. "Where is it from?"

"I'd guess," Enders said, "that it's straight up from the south, this time of year."

In the late summer months, they all knew to expect hurricanes. And as consummate sailors, they were able to predict the arrival of these frightful storms as much as two days in advance. The early warnings were always found in the ocean surface: the waves, pressed forward by storm winds of a hundred miles an hour, were altered in places far distant.

Hunter looked at the still-cloudless sky. "How much time, do you reckon?"

Enders shook his head. "It will be tomorrow night at the latest."

"Damn!" Hunter said. He turned and looked back at the galleon in Monkey Bay. She rode easily at anchor. The tide was in, and it was abnormally high. "Damn!" he said again, and returned to his ship.

He was in a foul mood, pacing the decks of his ship under the hot midday sun, pacing like a man trapped in a dungeon cell. He was not inclined to polite conversation, and it was unfortunate that Lady Sarah Almont chose this moment to speak with him. She requested a longboat and crew to take her ashore.

"To what end?" he said curtly. In the back of his mind, he wondered that she had made no mention whether he had visited her cabin the night previous.

"What end? Why to gather fruits and vegetables for my diet. You have nothing adequate on board."

"Your request is quite impossible," he said, and turned away from her.

"Captain," she said, stamping her foot, "I shall have you know that this is no mean matter to me. I am a vegetarian, and eat no meat."

He turned back. "Madam," he said, "I care not a whit for your eccentric fancies, and have neither the time nor the patience to oblige them."

"Eccentric fancies?" she said, coloring. "I shall have you know that the greatest minds of history were vegetarian, from Ptolemy to Leonardo da Vinci, and I shall have you know further, sir, that you are a common drip-knuckle and a boor."

Hunter exploded in an anger matching hers. "Madam," he said, pointing to the ocean, "are you aware in your monumental ignorance that the sea has changed?"

She was silent, perplexed, unable to connect the slight chop offshore to Hunter's obvious concern over it. "It seems trivial enough for so large a ship as yours."

"It is. For the moment."

"And the sky is clear."

"For the moment."

"I am no sailor, Captain," she said.

"Madam," Hunter said, "the swells are running long and deep. They can mean only one thing. In less than two days' time, we shall be in the midst of a hurricane. Can you understand that?"

"A hurricane is a fierce storm," she said, as if reciting a lesson.

"A fierce storm," he said. "If we are still in this damnable harbor when the hurricane strikes, we shall be smashed to nothing. Can you understand that?"

Very angry, he looked at her, and saw the truth—that she did not understand. Her face was innocent. She had never witnessed a hurricane, and so she could only imagine that it was somehow greater than other storms at sea.

Hunter knew that a hurricane bore the same relation to a fierce storm that a wild wolf bore to a lapdog.

Before she could reply to his outburst, he turned away, leaning on a pastpin. He knew he was being too harsh; his own concerns were rightly not hers, and he had every reason to indulge her. She had been up all night treating the burned seamen, an act of great eccentricity for a well-born woman. He turned back to face her.

"Forgive me," he said quietly. "Inquire of Enders, and he will make arrangements for you to go ashore, so that you can carry on the noble tradition of Ptolemy and Leonardo."

He stopped.

"Captain?"

He stared into space.

"Captain, are you well?"

Abruptly, he walked away from her. "Don Diego!" he shouted. "Find me Don Diego!"

DON DIEGO ARRIVED in Hunter's cabin to discover the captain drawing furiously on slips of paper. His desk was littered with sketches.

"I do not know if this will succeed," Hunter said. "I have only heard of it. The Florentine, Leonardo, proposed it, but he was not heeded."

"Soldiers do not attend an artist," Don Diego said.

Hunter glowered at him. "Wisely or not," he said.

Don Diego looked at the diagrams. Each showed a ship's hull, drawn in profile from above, with lines running out from the sides of the hull. Hunter drew another.

"The idea is simple," he said. "On an ordinary ship, each cannon has its own gun captain, who is responsible for the firing of that single gun."

"Yes . . ."

"After the gun is loaded and run out, the gun captain crouches behind the barrel and sights the target. He orders his men with handspikes and side tackles to aim the gun as he thinks best. Then he orders his men to slide the wedge to set the elevation—again as his eye thinks best. Then he fires. This is the procedure for each individual gun."

"Yes . . ." the Jew said. Don Diego had never actually seen a large cannon fired, but he was familiar with the general method of operation. Each gun was separately aimed, and a good gun captain, a man who could accurately judge the right angle and elevation of his cannon, was highly regarded. And rare.

"Now then," Hunter said, "the usual method is parallel fire." He drew parallel lines out from the sides of the ship on the paper. "Each gun fires and each captain prays that his shot will find its mark. But in truth, many guns will miss until the two ships are so close that almost any angle or elevation will hit the target. Let us say, when the ships are within five hundred yards. Yes?"

Don Diego nodded slowly.

"Now the Florentine made this proposal," Hunter said, sketching a new ship. "He said, do not trust the gun captains to aim each volley. Instead, aim all the guns in advance of the battle. Look now what you achieve."

He drew from the hull converging lines of fire, which came together at a single point in the water.

"You see? You concentrate the fire at one place. All your balls strike the target at the same point, causing great destruction."

"Yes," Don Diego said, "or all your balls miss the target and fall into the sea at the same point. Or all your balls strike the bowsprit or some other unimportant portion of the ship. I confess I do not see the value of your plan."

"The value," Hunter said, tapping the diagram, "lies in the way these guns are fired. Think: if they are pre-aimed, I can fire a volley with only one man to a gun—perhaps even one man for two guns. And if my target is within range, I know I will score a hit with each gun."

The Jew, aware of Hunter's short crew, clapped his hands together. "Of course," he said. Then he frowned. "But what happens after the first volley?"

"The guns will run back from the recoil. I then collect all the men into a single gun crew, which moves from gun to gun, loading each and running it out again, to the predetermined marks. This can be done relatively quickly. If the men are trained, I could fire a second volley within ten minutes."

"By then the other ship will have changed position."

"Yes," Hunter said. "It will be closer, inside my point. So the fire will be more spread, but still tight. You see?"

"And after the second volley?"

Hunter sighed. "I doubt that we will have more than two chances. If I have not sunk or disabled the warship in those two volleys, we shall surely lose the day."

"Well," the Jew said finally, "it is better than nothing." His tone was not optimistic. In a sea battle, warring ships usually settled a contest with fifty broadsides or more. Two well-matched ships with disciplined crews might fight the better part of a day, exchanging more than a hundred broadsides. Two volleys seemed trivial.

"It is," Hunter said, "unless we can strike the aft castle, or the magazine and shot-hold."

Those were the only truly vulnerable points on a warship. The aft castle carried all the ship's officers, the helmsman, and the rudder. A solid hit there would leave the ship without guidance. The shot-hold and magazine in the bow would explode the warship in a moment.

Neither point was easily hit. To aim far forward or aft increased the likelihood of a harmless miss by all cannon.

"The problem is our aim," the Jew said. "You will set your marks by gunnery practice, here in the harbor?"

Hunter nodded.

"But how will you aim, once at sea?"

"That is exactly why I have sent for you. I must have an instrument for sighting, to line the ship up with the enemy. It is a question of geometry, and I no longer remember my studies."

With his fingerless left hand, the Jew scratched his nose. "Let me think," he said, and left the cabin.

ENDERS, THE UNFLAPPABLE sea artist, had a rare moment of discomposure. "You want what?" he said.

"I want to set all thirty-two cannon on the port side," Hunter repeated.

"She'll list to port like a pregnant sow," Enders said. The very idea seemed to offend his sense of propriety and good seamanship.

"I'm sure she will be ungainly," Hunter said. "Can you still sail her?"

"After a fashion," Enders said. "I could sail the Pope's coffin with m'lady's dinner napkin. After a fashion." He sighed. "Of course," he said, "you'll shift the cannon once we're in open water."

"No," Hunter said. "I'll shift them here, in the bay."

Enders sighed again. "So you want to clear the reef with your pregnant sow?"

"Yes."

"That means cargo topside," Enders said, staring into space. "We'll move those cases in the hold up on the starboard railing and lash them there. It'll help some, but then we are top-heavy as well as off-trim. She'll roll like a cork in a swell. Make the devil's own job to fire those guns."

"I'm only asking if you can sail her."

There was a long silence. "I can sail her," Enders said finally. "I can sail her just as pretty as you wish. But you better get her back in trim before that storm hits. She won't last ten minutes in weather."

"I know that," Hunter said.

The two men looked at each other. While they sat, they heard a reverberating rumble overhead, as the first of the starboard cannon was shifted to the port side.

"You play long odds," Enders said.

"They are the only odds I have," Hunter replied.

Firing commenced in the early afternoon. A piece of white sailcloth was set five hundred yards away, on the shore, and the cannon were fired individually until they struck the target. The positions were marked on the deck with the blade of a knife. It was a long, slow, laborious process continuing on into the night, when the white sail target was replaced by a small fire. But by midnight, they had all thirty-two cannon aimed, loaded, and run out. The cargo had been brought topside and lashed to the starboard railing, partially compensating for the list to port. Enders pronounced himself satisfied with the trim of the boat, but his expression was unhappy.

Hunter ordered all hands to get a few hours sleep, and announced they would sail with the morning tide. Just before he drifted off to sleep, he wondered what Bosquet would make of the day's cannon fire inside the cove. Would he guess the meaning of those shots? And what would he do if he did?

Hunter did not ponder the question. He would know soon enough, he thought, and closed his eyes.

CHAPTER 30

H E WAS ON deck at dawn, pacing back and forth, watching the crew's preparations for battle. Lines and braces were being doubled, so that if some were shot away the others would allow the ship to sail. Bedding and blankets, soaked in water, were lashed along rails and bulkheads to protect against flying splinters. The entire deck was washed down repeatedly, soaking the dry wood to reduce the danger of fire.

In the midst of all this, Enders came up. "Lookout's just reported, Captain. The warship is gone."

Hunter was stunned. "Gone?"

"Aye, Captain. Gone during the night."

"It is not in sight at all?"

"Aye, Captain."

"He cannot have given up," Hunter said. He considered the possibilities a moment. Perhaps the warship had gone to the north or south side of the island to lie in wait. Perhaps Bosquet had some other plan or, perhaps, the pounding by the saker had done more damage than the privateers suspected. "All right, carry on," Hunter said.

The immediate effect of the warship's disappearance was salutary, he knew. It meant that he would be able to make a safe exit from Monkey Bay with his ungainly ship.

That passage had been worrying him.

Across the bay, he saw Sanson directing preparations aboard the *Cassandra*. The sloop sat lower in the water today; during the night, Hunter had transferred half the treasure from his vaults to the hold of the *Cassandra*. There was a good likelihood that at least one of the two ships might be sunk, and he wanted at least part of the treasure to survive.

Sanson waved to him. Hunter waved back, thinking that he did not envy Sanson this coming day. According to their plans, in an attack the smaller ship would run for the nearest safe harbor, while Hunter engaged the Spanish warship. That was not without risk for Sanson, who might find it difficult to escape unmolested. If the Spaniard chose to attack Sanson first, Hunter's ship would be unable to attack. *El Trinidad*'s cannon were prepared only for two volleys of defense.

But if Sanson feared this eventuality, he gave no sign; his wave was cheery enough. A few minutes later, the two ships raised anchor and, under light sail, made for the open sea.

The sea was rough. Once past the coral reefs and shallow water, there were forty-knot winds and twelve-foot swells. In that water, the *Cassandra* bobbed and bounced, but Hunter's galleon wallowed and slopped like a sick animal.

Enders complained bitterly, and then asked Hunter to take the helm for a moment. Hunter watched as the sea artist moved forward in the boat until he was standing clear of all the sails in the bow.

Enders stood with his back to the wind and both arms stretched wide. He remained there a moment, then turned slightly, still keeping his arms wide.

Hunter recognized the old seaman's trick for locating the eye of a hurricane. If you stood with your arms out and your back to the wind, the eye of the storm was always two points forward of the left hand's direction.

Enders came back to the helm, grunting and swearing. "She's south-southwest," he said, "and damn me if we won't feel her strong before nightfall."

Indeed, the sky overhead was already darkening gray, and the winds seemed to strengthen with each passing minute. *El Trinidad* listed unhappily as she cleared Cat Island and felt the full roughness of the open sea.

"Damn me," Enders said. "I don't trust all those cannon, Captain. Can't we shift just two or three to starboard?"

"No," Hunter said.

"Make her sail smarter," Enders said. "You'd like it, Captain."

"So would Bosquet," Hunter said.

"Show me Bosquet," Enders said, "and you can keep your cannon with nary a word from me."

"He's there," Hunter said, pointing astern.

Enders looked, and saw the Spanish warship clear the north shore of Cat Island, in hot pursuit of the galleon.

"Right up our bum hole," Enders said. "God's bones, he's well set."

The warship was bearing down on the most vulnerable part of the galleon, its aft deck. Any ship was weak astern—that was why the treasure was always stowed forward, and why the most spacious cabins were always astern. A ship's captain might have a large compartment, but in time of battle it was assumed he would not be in it.

Hunter had no guns aft at all; every piece of bronze hung on the port side. And their ungainly list deprived Enders of the traditional defense from a rear attack—a twisting, erratic course to make a poor target. Enders had to hold his best course to keep the ship from taking on water, and he was unhappy about it.

"Steady as you go," Hunter said, "and keep land to starboard."

He went forward to the side railing, where Don Diego

was sighting along an odd instrument he had made. It was a wooden contraption, roughly three feet long, mounted to the mainmast. At each end there was a small square frame of wood, with crossed hairs, forming an X.

"It's simple enough," the Jew said. "You sight along here," he said, standing at one end, "and when you have the two sets of hairs matched, you are in the proper position. Whatever part of your target is in the crossing of the hairs is what you will strike."

"What about the range?"

"For that, you need Lazue."

Hunter nodded. Lazue, with her sharp eyes, could estimate distances with remarkable accuracy.

"Range is not the problem," the Jew said. "The problem is timing the swells. Here, look."

Hunter stepped into position behind the crosshairs.

He closed one eye and squinted until the double X overlapped. And then he saw how much the boat pitched and rocked.

One instant the crosshairs were pointing at empty sky; the next, they were pointing into the rolling sea.

In his mind, he pretended to fire a round of shot. Between his shouted command and the moment the gunners tugged on the shot-cords there would be a delay, he knew. He had to estimate that. And the shot itself was slow-moving: another half-second would pass before the target was struck. All together, more than a second between the order to fire and the impact.

In that second, the ship would roll and bounce madly on the ocean. He felt a wave of panic. His desperate plan was impossible in heavy seas. They would never be able to get off two accurately aimed volleys.

"Where timing is paramount," the Jew suggested, "the example of the duel might be useful."

"Good," Hunter said. It was a helpful thought. "Notify the gun crews. The signals will be ready to fire, one, two, three, fire. Yes?"

"I shall tell them," the Jew said. "But in the noise of battle . . ."

Hunter nodded. The Jew was very acute today, and thinking much more clearly than Hunter himself. Once the firing began, verbal signals would be lost, or misunderstood. "I shall call the commands. You stand at my side and give hand signals."

The Jew nodded and went to tell the crews. Hunter called for Lazue, and explained to her the need for accurate ranging. The shot was aimed for five hundred yards; she would have to measure with delicacy. She said she could do it.

He went back to Enders, who was delivering a continuous string of oaths. "We shall taste his bugger's staff soon enough," he said. "I can near feel that prickle upon the flower."

At that moment, the Spanish warship opened fire with its bow cannon. Small shot whistled through the air.

"Hot as an ardent boy," Enders said, shaking his fist in the air.

A second volley splintered wood on the aft castle, but caused no serious damage.

"Steady on," Hunter said. "Let him gain."

"Let him gain. Tell me how I could do other?"

"Keep your wits," Hunter said.

"It's not my wits at risk," Enders said, "but my dearest bunghole."

A third volley passed harmlessly amidships, the small shot whistling through the air. Hunter had been waiting for that.

"Smokepots!" Hunter shouted, and the crew raced to light the caskets of pitch and sulfur on deck. Smoke billowed into the air, and drifted astern. Hunter knew that this would give the appearance of damage. He could well imagine how *El Trinidad* appeared to the Spaniard a listing ship in trouble, now belching dark smoke.

"He's moving east," Enders said. "Coming in for the kill."

"Good," Hunter said.

"Good," Enders repeated, shaking his head. "Dear Judas's ghost, our captain says good."

Hunter watched as the Spanish warship moved to the port side of the galleon. Bosquet had begun the engagement in classic fashion, and was continuing in the same way. He was moving wide of his target, getting himself onto a parallel course just out of cannon range.

Once he had lined up his broadside on the galleon, he would begin to close. As soon as he was within range— starting at about two thousand yards—Bosquet would open fire, and would continue to fire as he came closer and closer. That would be the most difficult period for Hunter and his crew. They would have to weather those broadsides until the Spanish ship was within their range.

Hunter watched as the enemy vessel pulled directly into a parallel course with *El Trinidad*, slightly more than a mile to the port.

"Steady on," Hunter said, and rested a hand on Enders's shoulder.

"You shall have your way with me," Enders grumbled, "and so will the Donnish prickler."

Hunter went forward to Lazue.

"She is just under two thousand yards," Lazue said, squinting at the enemy profile.

"How fast does she close?"

"Fast. She's eager."

"All the better for us," Hunter said.

"She is eighteen hundred yards now," Lazue said.

"Stand by for shot," Hunter said.

Moments later, the first broadside exploded from the warship, and fell splashing into the water off the port side.

The Jew counted. "One Madonna, two Madonna, three Madonna, four Madonna . . ."

"Under seventeen hundred," Lazue said.

The Jew had counted to seventy-five when the second broadside was fired. Iron shot screamed through the air all around them, but none struck the ship.

Immediately, the Jew began to count again. "One Madonna, two Madonna . . ."

"Not as sharp as she could be," Hunter said. "She should have gotten off in sixty seconds."

"Fifteen hundred yards," Lazue muttered.

Another minute went by, and then the third broadside was fired. This found its mark with stunning effect; Hunter was suddenly engulfed in a world of utter confusion—men screaming, splinters whistling through the air, spars and rigging crashing to the deck.

"Damage!" he shouted. "Call damage!" He peered through the smoke at the enemy ship, still closing on them. He was not even aware of the seaman at his feet, writhing and screaming with pain, clutching his hands to his face, blood spurting between his fingers.

The Jew looked down and saw a giant splinter had passed through the seaman's cheek and upward through the roof of his mouth. In the next moment, Lazue calmly bent over and shot the man in the head with her pistol. Pinkish cheesy material was flung all over the wooden deck. With an odd detachment, the Jew realized it was the man's brains. He looked back at Hunter, who was staring at the enemy with fixed gaze.

"Damage report!" Hunter shouted as the next volley from the warship pounded them.

"Foresprit gone."

"Fore sail gone!"

"Number two cannon out."

"Number six cannon out!"

"Mizzen top blown!"

"Out below!" came the cry, as the mizzen top spars came crashing down to the deck, in a rain of heavy wood and rope rigging.

Hunter ducked as spars crashed around him. Canvas covered him and he struggled to his feet. A knife poked through the canvas, just inches from his face. He pulled back and saw daylight; Lazue was cutting him free.

"Almost got my nose," he said.

"You'll never miss it," Lazue said.

Another volley from the Spanish warship whistled overhead.

"They're high," Enders screamed, in insane jubilation. "Blimey, they're high!"

Hunter looked forward, just as a shot smashed into the number five gun crew. The bronze cannon was flung into the air; heavy splinters of wood flew in all directions. One man took a razor-sharp sliver through the neck. He clutched his throat and fell to the ground, writhing in pain.

Nearby, another man took a direct hit from a ball. It cut his body in half, his legs falling out from beneath him. The stump of torso screamed and rolled on the deck for a few moments until shock brought death.

"Damage report!" shouted Hunter. A man standing beside him was struck in the head by a tackle block; it shattered his skull, and he fell in a pool of red, sticky blood.

The fore top spar came down, pinning two men to the deck, crushing their legs; they howled and screamed pitifully.

Still the broadside came from the Spaniard.

To stand in the midst of this injury and destruction and keep a cool head was almost impossible, and yet that was what Hunter tried to do, as one volley after another slammed home into his vessel. It had been twenty minutes since the warship opened fire; the deck was littered with rigging and spars and wooden splinters; the screams of the wounded blended with the sizzling whine of the cannon balls that snapped through the air. For Hunter, the destruction and chaos around him had long ago merged into a steady background so constant he no longer paid attention to it; he knew his ship was being slowly and inexorably destroyed, but he remained fixed on the enemy vessel, which moved closer with each passing second.

His losses were heavy. Seven men were dead, and twelve wounded; two cannon emplacements were destroyed. He had lost his foresprit and all her sail; he had lost his mizzen top and his mainsail rigging on the leeside; he had taken two hits below the waterline, and *El Trinidad* was shipping water fast. Already he sensed she rode lower in the water, and moved less smartly; there was a soggy, heavy quality to her forward progress.

He could not attempt to repair the damage. His little crew was busy just holding the ship on a manageable course. It was now a question of time before she became impossible to control, or sank outright.

He squinted through the smoke and haze at the Spanish ship. It was becoming hard to see. Despite the strong wind, the two ships were surrounded by acrid smoke.

She was closing fast.

"Seven hundred yards," Lazue said tonelessly. She had been injured already; a jagged shaft of wood had creased her forearm on the fifth volley. She had quickly applied a tourniquet near the shoulder, and now continued her sightings, oblivious to the blood that dripped onto the deck at her feet.

Another volley screamed at them, rocking the ship with multiple impacts.

"Six hundred yards."

"Ready to fire!" Hunter shouted, bending to sight along the crosshairs. He was lined up for a midships hit, but as he watched, the Spanish warship moved forward slightly. He was now lined on the aft castle.

So be it, he thought, as he gauged the rocking of *El Trinidad* through the crosshairs, getting a sense of the timing, up and down, up and down, seeing clear sky, then nothing but water, then seeing the warship again. Then clear sky as *El Trinidad* continued her upward roll.

He counted to himself, over and over, silently mouthing the words.

"Five hundred yards," Lazue said.

Hunter watched a moment longer. Then he counted.

"One," he shouted, as the crosshairs pointed into the sky. Then the ship rocked down, quickly passing the outline of the warship.

"Two," he called, as the crosshairs pointed into the boiling sea.

There was a brief hesitation in the motion. He waited.

"Three!" He called, as the upward motion began again.

"Fire!"

The galleon rocked madly, a crazy upward heave as

all thirty of her cannon exploded in a volley. Hunter was thrown back against the mainmast with a force that knocked the breath from him. He hardly noticed it; he was watching for the downward movement, to see what had happened to the enemy.

"You hit her," Lazue said.

Indeed he had. The impact had knocked the Spanish vessel laterally in the water, swinging the stern outward. The profile of the aft castle was now a ragged line, and the entire mizzenmast was falling in a strange, slow motion, sails and all, into the water.

But in the same moment Hunter saw that he had struck too far forward to damage the rudder and not far enough forward to hit the helmsman at the tiller. The warship was still under control.

"Reload and run out!" he shouted.

There was much confusion aboard the Spanish ship. He knew he had bought time. Whether he had bought the ten minutes he needed to prepare a second volley, he could not be sure.

Seamen were everywhere in the aft of the warship, cutting the fallen mizzenmast away, trying to get free. For a moment, it looked like the debris in the water would foul the rudder, but that did not happen.

Hunter heard the rumbling beneath his own decks as,

one after another, his cannon were reloaded and run back to the gunports.

The Spanish warship was closer now, less than four hundred yards to port, but she was angled badly and could not get off a broadside.

One minute passed, then another.

The Spanish ship came under control, her mizzen with its sails and rigging drifting away in the wake of the ship.

The bow swung into the wind. She was coming about, and moving to Hunter's weak starboard side.

"Damn me," Enders said. "I knew he was a clever bastard!"

The Spanish ship lined up for a starboard broadside, and delivered it a moment later. At this closer range, it was miserably effective. Spars and rigging came crashing down around Hunter.

"We cannot take any more," Lazue said softly.

Hunter had been thinking the same thing. "How many cannon run out?" he shouted.

Don Diego, below, peered up onto the deck. "Sixteen ready!"

"We will fire with sixteen," Hunter said.

Another broadside from the Spanish warship hit them with devastating effect. Hunter's ship was shattering around him.

"Mr. Enders!" Hunter bellowed. "Prepare to come about!"

Enders looked at Hunter in disbelief. To come about

now would bring Hunter's ship through the bow of the Spanish ship—and much closer.

"Prepare to come about!" Hunter shouted again.

"Ready about!" Enders yelled. Astounded seamen ran to the lines, furiously working to unsnarl them.

The warship closed.

"Three hundred fifty yards," Lazue said.

Hunter hardly heard her. He no longer cared about the range. He sighted down the crosshairs at the smoky profile of the warship. His eyes stung and blurred with tears. He blinked them away, and fixed on an imaginary point on the Spanish profile. Low, and just behind the bowline.

"Ready about! The helm's a-lee!" Enders bellowed.

"Ready to fire," Hunter shouted.

Enders was astonished. Hunter knew it, without looking at the sea artist's face. He kept his eye to the crosshairs. Hunter was going to fire while the ship was coming about. It was unheard of, an insane thing to do.

"One!" Hunter shouted.

In the crosshairs, he saw his ship swing through the wind, coming around to bear on the Spaniard . . .

"Two!"

His own ship was moving slowly now, the crosshairs inching forward along the warship's hazy profile. Past the forward gunports, onto bare wood . . .

"Three!"

The crosshairs crept forward on the target, but it was too high. He waited for a dip in his own ship, knowing that at the same moment the warship would rise slightly, exposing more flank.

He waited, not daring to breathe, not daring to hope. The warship rode up a little, then—

"Fire!"

Again his ship rocked under the impact of the cannon. It was a ragged volley; Hunter heard it and felt it, but he could see nothing. He waited for the smoke to clear and the ship to right herself. He looked. "Mother of God," Lazue said.

There was no change in the Spanish warship. Hunter had missed her clean.

"Damn me to hell," Hunter said, thinking that there was now an odd truth to the words. They were all damned to hell; the next broadside from the Spaniards would finish them off.

Don Diego said, "It was a noble try. A noble try, and bravely done."

Lazue shook her head. She kissed him on the cheek. "The saints preserve us all," she said. A tear ran down her cheek.

Hunter felt a crushing despair. They had missed their final chance; he had failed them all. There was nothing to do now but run up the white flag and surrender.

"Mr. Enders," he called, "run up the white—"

He stopped cold: Enders was dancing behind the tiller, slapping his thigh, laughing uproariously.

Then he heard a cheer from belowdecks. The gun crews were cheering.

Were they mad?

Alongside him, Lazue gave a shriek of delight, and began to laugh as loudly as Enders. Hunter spun to look at the Spanish warship. He saw the bow lift in a wave—and then he saw the gaping hole running seven or eight feet, wide open, below the waterline. A moment later the bow plunged down again, obscuring the damage.

He hardly had time to recognize the significance of this sight when clouds of smoke billowed out of the forecastle of the warship. They rose with startling suddenness. A moment later, an explosion echoed across the water.

And then the warship disappeared in a giant sphere of exploding flame as the powder-hold went off. There was one rumbling detonation, so powerful that *El Trinidad* shook with the impact. Then another, and a third as the warship dissolved before their eyes in a matter of seconds. Hunter saw only the most fragmentary images of destruction—the masts crashing down; the cannon flung into the air by invisible hands; the whole substance of the ship collapsing in on itself, then blasting outward.

Something crashed into the mainmast over his head, and dropped onto his hair. It slid down to his shoulder and onto the deck. He thought it must be a bird, but, looking down, saw that it was a human hand, severed at the wrist. There was a ring on one finger.

"Good God," he whispered, and when he looked back at the warship, he saw an equally astonishing sight.

The warship was gone.

Literally, gone: one minute it had been there, consumed by fire and hot spheres of explosions, and yet there. Now it was gone. Burning debris, sails, and spars floated on the surface of the water. The bodies of seamen floated with them, and he heard the screams and shouts of the survivors. Yet the warship was gone.

All around him, his crew was laughing and jumping in frenzied celebration. Hunter could only stare at the water where the warship had once been. Amid the burning wreckage, his eye fell on a body floating facedown in the water. The body was that of a Spanish officer; Hunter could tell from the blue uniform on the man's back. The man's trousers had been shredded in the explosions, and his naked buttocks were exposed to view. Hunter stared at the bared flesh, fascinated that the back should be uninjured and yet the clothing below torn away. There was something obscene about the randomness and casualness of the injury. Then, as the body bounced on the waves, Hunter saw that it was headless.

Aboard his own ship, he was distantly aware that the crew was no longer jubilant. They had all fallen silent, and had turned to look at him. He looked around at their faces, weary, smudged, bleeding, the eyes drained and blank with fatigue, and yet oddly expectant.

They were looking at him, and waiting for him to do something. For a moment, he could not imagine what was expected of him. And then he became aware of something on his cheeks.

Rain.

Chapter 31

THE HURRICANE STRUCK with furious intensity. Within minutes, the wind was screaming through the rigging at more than forty knots, lashing them with stinging pellets of rain. The seas were rougher, with fifteen-foot swells, mountains of water that swung the boat crazily. One moment they were high in the air, riding the crest of a swell; seconds later they were plunged into a stomach-wrenching trough, with water looming high all around them.

And each man knew that this was just the beginning. The wind, and the rain, and the seas would become much worse, and the storm would last for hours, perhaps days.

They sprang to work with an energy that belied the fatigue they all felt. They cleared the decks and reefed shredded canvas; they fought to get a sail over the side, and plug the holes in the ship below the waterline. They worked in silence on the slippery, shifting wet decks, each man knowing that at the next instant he might be swept overboard, and that no one would even see it happen.

But the first task—and the worst—was to trim the ship, by moving the cannon back to the starboard side. This was no easy matter on calm seas with dry decking. In a storm, when the ship was taking water over her sides, with the deck pitching to forty-five-degree angles, with every deck surface and line soaked and slippery, it was plainly impossible and a nightmare. Yet it had to be done if they were to survive.

Hunter directed the operation, one cannon at a time. It was a problem of anticipating the pitch, of letting the angles do the work as the men wrestled with the five-thousand-pound weights.

They lost the first cannon; a line snapped, and the gun shot across the slanted deck like a missile, shattering the hull railing on the far side and crashing into the water. The men were terrified by the speed with which it happened. Double lines were lashed around the second cannon, yet it also broke free, crushing a seaman in its path.

For the next five hours, they battled the wind and the rain to get the cannon in position and safely lashed down. When they were finished, every man on *El Trinidad* was exhausted beyond endurance; the sailors clung like drowning animals to stays and railings, exerting every last ounce of energy to keep from being washed over the side.

And yet, Hunter knew, the storm was just beginning.

∞

A HURRICANE, THE most awesome event in nature, was discovered by the voyagers to the New World. The name—hurricane—is an Arawak word for storms that had no counterpart in Europe. Hunter's crew knew of the awful power of these giant cyclonic events, and responded to the terrible physical reality of the storm with the oldest sailor's superstitions and rites.

Enders, at the helm, watched the mountains of water all around him, and muttered every prayer he had ever learned as a boy, while he simultaneously clutched the shark's tooth around his neck and wished he could raise more canvas. *El Trinidad* was struggling with three sails at the moment, and it was unlucky to sail with three.

Belowdecks, the Moor took his dagger and cut his own finger, then drew a triangle on the deck with his blood. He placed a feather in the center of the triangle, and held it there while he whispered an incantation to himself.

Forward, Lazue threw a casket of salt pork over the side, and held three fingers into the air. Hers was the most ancient superstition of all, though she knew only the old seaman's tale that food over the side and three fingers in the air might save a foundering ship. In fact, the three fingers represented the trident of Neptune, and the food was a sacrifice to the god of the oceans.

Hunter himself professed to despise such superstition,

yet he went to his cabin, locked the door, got down on his knees, and prayed. All around him, the furniture of the cabin crashed back and forth from one wall to another, as the ship rocked crazily on the seas.

Outside, the storm screamed with demonic fury, and the ship beneath him creaked and groaned in long, agonizing moans. At first, he did not notice any other sound, and then he heard a woman's scream. And then another.

He left his cabin and found five sailors dragging Lady Sarah Almont forward, to the companionway ladder. She was screaming and wrestling in their grip.

"Hold there," Hunter shouted, and went up to them. Waves crashed over them, smashing against the deck.

The men would not look him in the eye.

"What goes here?" Hunter demanded.

None of the men spoke. It was Lady Sarah who finally shrieked: "They're going to throw me in the ocean!"

The leader of the men seemed to be Edwards, a rough seaman, veteran of dozens of privateering campaigns.

"She's a witch," he said, looking at Hunter defiantly. "That's what it is, Captain. We'll never last this storm if she's on board."

"Don't be ridiculous," Hunter said.

"Mark me," Edwards said. "We'll not last with her on board. Mark me, she's a witch as ever I saw."

"How do you know this?"

"I knew it first I seen her," Edwards said.

"By what proofs?" Hunter persisted.

"The man is mad," Lady Sarah said. "Stark mad."

"What proofs?" Hunter demanded, shouting over the wind.

Edwards hesitated. Finally, he released the girl, and turned away. "No use talking of it," he said. "You mark me, though. Mark me."

He walked away. One by one, the other men backed off. Hunter was alone with Lady Sarah.

"Go to your cabin," Hunter said, "and bolt the door, and stay there. On no account come out, and do not open the door for any reason."

Her eyes were wide with fright. She nodded, and went to her room. Hunter waited until he saw the door to her cabin close, and then, after a moment's hesitation, he went on deck, into the full blast of the storm.

Belowdecks, the storm seemed fearsome, but on the main deck it exceeded all preparation. The wind tore at him like an invisible brute, a thousand strong hands pulling at his arms and legs, wrenching him away from any handhold or support. The rain struck him with such force that at first he cried aloud. He could hardly see in the first few seconds. He made out Enders at the tiller, lashed firmly into his position.

Hunter went over to him, holding to a guideline strung along the deck, finally reaching the shelter of the aft castle. He took an extra line and looped it around himself, leaned closer to Enders, and shouted, "How fare you?"

"No better, no worse," Enders shouted back. "We hold, and we'll hold some while longer, but it's hours. I can feel her start to break."

"How many hours?"

Enders reply was lost in the mountain of water that surged over them and smashed down on the deck.

It was, Hunter thought, as good an answer as any. No ship could take such a pounding for long, especially not a crippled ship.

BACK IN HER CABIN, Lady Sarah Almont surveyed the destruction caused by the storm, and the seamen who had burst in upon her as she had been making her preparations. Carefully, as the boat rocked, she righted her candles on the deck, and lit them one after another, until there were five red candles glowing. Then she scratched a pentagram on the deck, and stepped inside it.

She was very afraid. When the Frenchwoman, Madame de Rochambeau had shown her the latest in the fads of the Court of Louis XIV, she had been amused, even scoffed a little. But they said in France that women killed their newborn babies in order to secure eternal youth. If that was so, perhaps a little spell might preserve her life . . .

What was the harm? She closed her eyes, hearing the storm howl around her. "Greedigut," she whispered, feeling the words on her lips. She caressed herself, kneeling on the deck inside the scratched pentagram. "Greedigut. Greedigut, come to me."

The deck pitched crazily, the candles slid one way, then the next. She had to pause to catch them in their slide. It was all very distracting. How difficult to be a witch! Madame de Rochambeau had told her nothing of spells aboard ship. Perhaps they did not work. Perhaps it was all a lot of French foolishness.

"Greedigut . . ." she moaned. She caressed herself.

And then, she fancied she heard the storm abating.

Or was it just her imagination?

"Greedigut, come to me, have me, dwell in me . . ."

She imagined claws, she felt the wind whipping at her nightdress, she sensed a presence . . .

And the wind died.

Part V

The Mouth of the Dragon

CHAPTER 32

HUNTER AWOKE FROM a restless sleep with an odd sense that something was wrong. He sat up in bed, and realized that everything was quieter: the motion of the ship was less frantic, and the wind had died to a whisper.

He hurried onto the deck, where a light rain was falling. He saw that the seas were calmer, and visibility had increased. Enders, still at the tiller, looked half-dead but he was grinning.

"We weathered her, Captain," he said. "Not much left to her, but we've come through."

Enders pointed to starboard. There was land—the low, gray profile of an island.

"What is it?" Hunter said.

"Dunno," Enders said. "But we'll just make it."

Their ship had been blown for two days and nights, and they had no idea of their position. They approached the little island, which was low, and scrubby, and uninviting. Even from a distance they could see the cactus plants thick along the shore.

"I reckon we're down the Windward Chain," Enders said, squinting judiciously. "Probably near the Boca del Dragon, and there's no respite in those waters." He sighed. "Wish we could see the sun, for a sighting."

The Boca del Dragon—the Dragon's Mouth—was the stretch of water between the Windward Caribbean islands and the coast of South America. It was a famous and feared stretch of water, though at the moment it seemed placid enough.

Despite calm seas, *El Trinidad* rolled and wallowed like a drunkard. Yet they managed with shredded canvas to round the southern tip of the island, and find a fair cove on the western shore. It was protected, and had a sandy bottom suitable for careening. Hunter secured the ship, and his exhausted crew went ashore to rest.

There was no sign of Sanson or the *Cassandra*; whether they had survived the storm was a matter of indifference to Hunter's men, exhausted beyond the point of reasonable fatigue. The men lay sprawled in their wet clothes on the beach and slept with their faces in the sand, their bodies prostrate like corpses. The sun emerged, briefly, from behind thinning clouds. Hunter felt weariness overtake him, and slept as well.

The next three days were fair. The crew worked hard careening the ship, repairing the damage below the waterline, and the spars of the ragged superstructure. A search of the ship disclosed no wood aboard. Normally, a galleon the size of *El Trinidad* carried extra spars and masts in the hold, but these had been removed by the Spanish to allow more cargo. Hunter's men had to make do as best they could.

Enders sighted the sun with his astrolabe and fixed their latitude. They were not far from the Spanish strongholds of Cartagena and Maricaibo, on the South American coast. But aside from this, they had no knowledge of their island, which they called No Name Cay.

Hunter felt a captain's vulnerability with *El Trinidad* hauled over on her side, unseaworthy. Should they be attacked now, they would have a difficult time of it. Still he had no reason to fear anything; the island was obviously uninhabited, as were the two nearest little islands to the south.

But there was something hostile and uninviting about No Name. The land was arid, and thickly overgrown with cactus, in places as dense as any forest. Brightly colored birds chattered high up in the overgrowth, their cries carried by the wind. The wind never stopped; it was a hot, maddening wind that blew at almost ten knots, throughout the day and night, with only a brief respite at dawn. The men grew accustomed to working and sleeping with the whine of the wind in their ears.

Something about this place made Hunter post guards around the ship and the scattered campfires of the crew. He told himself it was the need to reestablish discipline among the men, but in truth it was some other foreboding. On the fourth evening, at dinner, he gave the night's watches. Enders would take the first; he himself would take the midnight watch, and he would be relieved by Bellows. He sent a man off to notify Enders and Bellows. The man returned an hour later.

"Sorry, Captain," he said. "I can't find Bellows."

"What do you mean, can't find him?"

"He's not to be found, Captain."

Hunter scanned the undergrowth around the shore. "He's off sleeping somewhere," he said. "Find him and bring him to me. It will be the worse for him."

"Aye, Captain," the man said.

But a search of the cove did not yield any trace of Bellows. In the growing darkness, Hunter called off the search and collected his men around the fires. He counted thirty-four, including the Spanish prisoners and Lady Sarah. He ordered them to stay close to the fires, and assigned another man to take Bellows's watch.

The night passed uneventfully.

IN THE MORNING, Hunter led a party in search of wood. There was none to be found on No Name, so he set off with ten armed men toward the island nearest to the south. This island was, at least from a distance, similar to their own, and Hunter had no real expectation of finding wood.

But he felt obliged to search.

He beached his boat on the eastern shore, and set off with his party into the interior, moving through dense clumps of cactus that plucked and tore at his clothes. They reached high ground at mid-morning, and from there, made two discoveries.

First, they could clearly see the next island in the chain to the south. Thin gray trickles of smoke from a half-dozen fires drifted into the air; the island was obviously inhabited.

Of more immediate interest, they saw the roofs of a village, along the water on the western coast of the island. From where they stood, the buildings had the crude appearance of a Spanish outpost settlement.

Hunter led his men cautiously forward to the village. With muskets at the ready, they slipped from one clump of cactus to another. When they were very close, one of Hunter's men discharged his musket prematurely; the sound of the report echoed, and was carried by the wind. Hunter swore, and watched for the village to panic.

But there was no activity, no sign of life.

After a short pause, he led his men down into the village. Almost immediately, he could tell the settlement was deserted. The houses were empty; Hunter entered the first but he found nothing save a Bible, printed in Spanish, and a couple of moth-eaten blankets thrown across rude, broken beds. Tarantulas scampered for cover in the darkness.

He went back into the street. His men moved stealthily into one house after another, only to emerge empty-handed, shaking their heads.

"Perhaps they were warned of our coming," a seaman suggested.

Hunter shook his head. "Look at the bay."

In the bay were four small dinghies, all moored in shoal water, rocking gently with the lapping waves. Fleeing villagers would certainly have escaped by water.

It made no sense to leave any boats behind.

"Look here," said a crewman, standing on the beach. Hunter went over. He saw five long deep trenches in the sand, the marks of narrow boats, or perhaps canoes of some sort, pulled up from the beach. There were many footprints of naked feet. And some reddish stains.

"Is it blood?"

"I don't know."

There was a church, as rudely constructed as the other dwellings, at the north end of the town. Hunter and his men entered it. The interior was demolished, and all the walls were covered in blood. Some sort of slaughter had occurred here, but not recently. At least several days past. The stench of dried blood was sickening.

"What's this?"

Hunter went over to a seaman, who was staring at a skin on the ground. It was leathery and scaly. "Looks like a crocodile."

"Aye, but from where?"

"Not here," Hunter said. "There are no crocs here."

He picked it up. The animal had once been large, at least five feet. Few Caribbean crocs grew so large; those in the inland swamps of Jamaica were only three or four feet.

"Skinned some time past," Hunter said. He examined it carefully. There were holes cut around the head, and a string of rawhide passed through, as if it were to be worn on a man's shoulders.

"Damn me, look there, Captain."

Hunter looked toward the next island to the south. The smoke fires, previously visible, had now disappeared. It was then that they heard the faint thumping of drums.

"We had best return to the boat," Hunter said, and, in the afternoon light, his men moved quickly. It took the better part of an hour to return to their longboat, beached on the eastern shore. When they arrived, they found another one of the mysterious canoe-trenches in the sand.

And something else.

Near their boat, an area of sand had been patted smooth and ringed with small stones. In the center, five fingers of a hand protruded into the air.

"It's a buried hand," one of the seamen said. He reached forward and pulled it up by one finger.

The finger came away clean. The man was so startled he dropped it and stepped back. "God's wounds!"

Hunter felt his heart pound. He looked at the seamen, who were cowering.

"Come now," he said, and reached forward, to pluck up all the fingers, one after another. Each came away clean. He held them in his palm. The crew stared with horror.

"What's it mean, Captain?"

He had no idea. He put them into his pocket. "Back to the galleon, and we'll see," he said.

IN THE EVENING firelight, he sat staring at the fingers. It was Lazue who had provided the answer they all sought.

"See the ends," she said, pointing to the rough way the fingers had been cut from the palm. "That's Caribee work, and no mistake."

"Caribee," Hunter repeated, astonished. The Carib Indians, once so warlike on many Caribbean islands, were now a kind of myth, a people lost in the past. All the Indians of the Caribbean had been exterminated by the Spanish in the first hundred years of their domination. A few peaceful Arawaks, living in poverty and filth, could be found in the interior regions of some remote islands. But the blood-thirsty Caribs had long since vanished.

Or so it was said.

"How do you know?" Hunter said.

"It is the ends," Lazue repeated. "No metal made those cuts. They were made by stone blades."

Hunter's brain struggled to accept this new information.

"This must be a Donnish trick, to frighten us off," he said. But even as he said it, he was unconvinced. Everything fit together—the tracks of the canoes, the crocodile skin with pierced rawhide thongs.

"The Caribee are cannibals," Lazue said tonelessly. "But they leave the fingers, as a warning. It is their way."

Enders came up. "Beg pardon, sir, but Miss Almont has not returned."

"What?"

"She's not returned, sir."

"From where?"

"I let her go inland," Enders said miserably, pointing toward the dark cactus, away from the glow of the fires around the ship. "She wanted to gather fruits and berries, seems she's a vegetarian—"

"When did you let her go inland?"

"This afternoon, Captain."

"And she's not back yet?"

"I sent her with two seamen," Enders said. "I never thought—"

He broke off.

In the darkness came the distant pounding of Indian drums.

CHAPTER 33

IN THE FIRST of the three longboats, Hunter listened to the gentle lapping of the water on the sides of the boats, and peered through the night at the approaching island. The drumbeats were louder, and they could see the faint flicker of fire, inland.

Seated alongside him, Lazue said, "They do not eat women."

"Fortunate for you," Hunter said.

"And for Lady Sarah."

"It is said," Lazue said, chuckling in the darkness, "that the Caribee do not eat Spaniards, either. They are too tough. The Dutch are plump but tasteless, the English indifferent, but the French delectable. It is true, do you not think?"

"I want her back," Hunter said grimly. "We need her. How can we tell the governor that we rescued his niece only to lose her to savages for their boucan-barbecue?"

"You have no sense of humor," Lazue said.

"Not tonight."

He looked back at the other boats, following in the

darkness. All together, he had taken twenty-seven men, leaving Enders back on the *El Trinidad*, trying hastily to refit her by the light of fires. Enders was a wizard with ships, but this was asking too much of him. Even if they escaped with Lady Sarah, they could not leave No Name for a day, perhaps more. And in that time the Indians would attack.

He felt his longboat crunch up against the sandy shore. The men jumped out into knee-deep water. Hunter whispered, "Everybody out but the Jew. Careful with the Jew."

Indeed, a moment later, the Jew stepped gingerly onto dry land, his arms cradling a precious cargo.

"Was it dampened?" Hunter whispered.

"I do not think so," Don Diego said. "I was careful." He blinked his weak eyes. "I cannot see well."

"Follow me," Hunter said. He led his group into the interior of the island. Behind him, on the beach, the other two longboats were discharging their armed crews. The men moved stealthily into the cactus ashore. The night was moonless and very dark. Soon they were all deep in the island, moving toward the fires and the pounding drums.

The Caribee village was much larger than he expected: a dozen mud huts with grass roofs, ranged in a semicircle around several blazing fires. Here the warriors, painted a fierce red, danced and howled, their bodies casting long, he was standing alongside a seaman on the beach, helping him to hold down a plank of lumber, when the man slapped his neck.

"Damn mosquitoes," he said.

And then, with an odd look on his face, he collapsed, coughed, and died.

Hunter bent over him. He looked at the neck, and saw only a pinprick, with a single red drop of blood. Yet the man was dead.

From somewhere near the bow, he heard a scream, and another man tumbled to the sand, dead. His crew was in confusion; the posted guards came running back toward the ship; the men working huddled under the hull.

Hunter looked again at the dead man at his feet. Then he saw something in the man's hand. It was a tiny, feathered dart with a needle point.

Poison darts.

"They're coming," shouted the lookouts. The men scrambled behind bits of wood and debris, anything that would afford protection. They waited tensely. Yet no one came; the bushes and cactus clumps along the shore were silent.

Enders crept over to Hunter. "Shall we resume work?"

"How many have I lost?"

"Peters, sir." Enders looked down. "And Maxwell here."

shifting shadows. Several wore crocodile skins over their heads; others raised human skulls into the air. All were naked. They sang an eerie, monotone chant.

The object of their dance could be observed above the fire. There, resting on a lattice of green wood strips, was the armless, legless, gutted torso of a seaman. To one side, a group of women were cleaning the intestines of the man.

Hunter did not see Lady Sarah. Then the Moor pointed. He saw her, lying on the ground to one side. Her hair was matted with blood. She did not move. She was probably dead.

Hunter looked at his men. Their expressions registered shock and rage. He whispered a few words to Lazue, then set out with Bassa and Don Diego, crawling around the periphery of the camp.

The three men entered one hut, knives ready. The hut was deserted. Skulls hung from the ceiling, clinking together in the wind that blew through the encampment. There was a basket of bones in a corner.

"Quickly," Hunter said, ignoring this.

Don Diego set his *grenadoe* in the center of the room, and lit the fuse. The three men slipped back outside, to a far corner of the encampment. Don Diego lit the fuse on a second *grenadoe*, and waited.

The first *grenadoe* exploded with stunning effect. The hut blew apart in a thousand fragments; the stunned lobster-colored warriors howled in frightened surprise. Don Diego lobbed the second *grenadoe* into the fire. It exploded moments later. Warriors screamed as they were riddled with fragments of flying metal and glass.

Simultaneously, Hunter's men opened fire from the underbrush.

Hunter and the Moor crept forward, retrieved the body of Lady Sarah Almont, and moved back into the bushes again. All around them, the Caribee warriors screamed, howled, and died. The grass roofs of the huts caught fire. Hunter's last glimpse of the camp was that of a blazing inferno.

Their retreat was hasty and unplanned. Bassa, with his enormous strength, carried the Englishwoman easily. She moaned.

"She's alive," Hunter said.

She moaned again.

At a brisk trot, the men hurried back to the beach, and their boats. They escaped the island without further incident.

BY DAWN, THEY were all safely back to the ship. Enders, the sea artist, had given over work on the galleon to Hunter, while he attended the woman's injuries. By mid-morning, he was able to report.

"She'll survive," he said. "Nasty blow on the head nothing serious." He looked at the ship. "Wish we wei well off here."

Hunter had been trying to get the careened ship read to sail. But there was still much to do: the mainmast wa still weak, and the maintop missing; the foremast was entirely gone, and there was still a large hole below the waterline. They had torn out much of the deck to obtain lumber for the repairs, and soon they would have to tear up part of the lower gun deck. But progress was slow.

"We can't be off before tomorrow morning," Hunter said.

"I don't fancy the night," Enders said, looking around the island. "Quiet enough now. But I don't fancy staying the night."

"Nor I," Hunter said.

They worked straight through the night, the exhausted men going without sleep in their frantic haste to finish work on the ship. A heavy guard was posted, making the work slower, but Hunter felt it was necessary.

At midnight, the drums began to pound once more and they continued for the better part of an hour. Then there was an ominous silence.

The men were unnerved; they did not want to work, and Hunter had to urge them onward. Toward dawn,

Hunter shook his head. "I can't lose more." His crew was cut to thirty, now. "Wait for the dawn."

"I'll pass the word," Enders said, and crawled away. As he did, there was a whine and a *thwack!* And a small feathered dart buried itself in the wood near Hunter's ear. He ducked down again, and waited.

Nothing further happened until dawn, when, with an unearthly wail, the red-painted men came out from the brush and descended on the beach. Hunter's men answered with a round of musket-fire. A dozen of the savages dropped on the sand, and the others fell back into hiding.

Hunter and his men waited, crouched and uncomfortable, until midday. When nothing occurred, Hunter cautiously gave word to resume work. He led a party of men inland. The savages were gone without a trace.

He returned to the ship. His men were haggard, weary, moving slowly. But Enders was cheerful. "Cross your fingers and praise Providence," he said, "and we'll be off soon."

As the sound of hammering and construction began afresh, he went to see Lady Sarah.

She lay on the sand and stared as Hunter approached.

"Madam," he said, "how do you fare?"

She stared at him, not answering. Her eyes were open, but she did not see him.

"Madam?"

There was no reply.

"Madam?"

He passed a hand in front of her face. She did not blink. She gave no sign of recognition.

He left her, shaking his head.

They floated *El Trinidad* on the evening tide but they could not depart from the cove until dawn. Hunter paced the deck of his ship, keeping an eye toward the shore. The drums had started again. He was very tired, but he did not sleep. At intervals through the night, the air whined with the deadly darts. No man was struck, and Enders, crawling over the ship like a sharp-eyed monkey, pronounced himself satisfied, if not pleased, with the repairs.

At first light, they hauled the stern anchor and backed and filled, making for open water. Hunter watched, expecting to see a fleet of canoes with red warriors attacking. He was able, now, to give them a taste of cannon shot, and he was looking forward to the opportunity.

But the Indians did not attack, and as the sails were raised to catch the wind, and No Name Cay disappeared behind them, the entire episode began to seem like a bad dream. He was very tired. He ordered most of his crew to sleep, leaving Enders at the tiller with a skeleton crew.

Enders was worried.

"By God," Hunter said, "you're eternally worried. We've

just made off from the savages, we have our ship beneath our feet and clear water before us. When will you find it suffices?"

"Aye, the water's clear," Enders said, "but now we are in the Boca del Dragon, and no mistake. And this is no place for a skeleton crew."

"The men must sleep," Hunter said, and he went below. He immediately fell into a tormented, restless sleep in his heated, airless cabin. He dreamt his ship was capsized in the Boca del Dragon, where the waters were deeper than anywhere else in the Western Sea. He was sinking into blue water, then black . . .

He awoke with a start, to the shout of a woman. He ran on deck. It was twilight, and the breeze was very light; the sails of *El Trinidad* billowed and caught the reddish glow of sunset. Lazue was at the helm, having relieved Enders. She pointed out to sea: "Look there."

Hunter looked. To port, there was a churning beneath the surface and a phosphorescent object, blue-green and glowing, came streaking toward them.

"The Dragon," Lazue said. "The Dragon has been following us for an hour."

Hunter watched. The glowing creature came closer, and moved alongside the ship, slowing in speed to match *El Trinidad*. It was enormous, a great bag of glowing flesh with long tentacles stretched out behind.

"No!" shouted Lazue, as the rudder was twisted from her hands. The ship rocked crazily. "It's attacking!"

Hunter grabbed at the rudder, took it in his hands. But some powerful force had taken hold of it and seized control. He was knocked back against the gunwale; the breath went out of him, and he gasped. Seamen ran on deck, drawn by Lazue's shouts. There were terrified cries of "Kraken! Kraken!"

Hunter got to his feet just as a slimy tentacle-arm snaked over the railing and twisted around his waist. Sharp, horny suckers tore at his clothing and dragged him toward the rail. He felt the coldness of the creature's flesh. He overcame his revulsion, and hacked with his dagger at the tentacle that encircled him. It had superhuman strength, lifting him high into the air. He plunged his dagger again and again into its flesh. Greenish blood flowed down his legs.

And then, abruptly, the tentacle released its grip, and he fell to the deck. Getting to his feet, he saw tentacles everywhere, snaking over the stern of the ship, coming up high over the aft deck. A seaman was caught and raised, writhing, into the air. The creature flung him, almost disdainfully, into the water.

Enders shouted: "Get belowdecks! Belowdecks!" Hunter heard musket volleys from somewhere amidships. Men leaned over the side, firing at the thing.

Hunter went to the stern and looked down at the dreadful sight. The bulbous body of the creature was directly astern, and its many tentacles gripped the ship in a dozen places, whipping and snaking this way and that. The entire body of the animal was phosphorescent green in the growing darkness. The creature's green tentacles were snaking into the windows of the aft cabins.

He suddenly remembered Lady Sarah, and rushed below. He found her in her cabin, still stone-faced.

"Come, Madam—"

At that moment, the lead-paned windows shattered, and an enormous tentacle, as thick as a tree trunk, snaked into the cabin. It wrapped itself around a cannon, and hauled at it; the cannon came free of its chock blocks, and rolled across the room. Where the creature's horned suckers had touched it, the gleaming yellow metal was deeply scratched.

Lady Sarah screamed.

Hunter found an ax and hacked at the waving tentacle. Sickening green blood gushed in his face. The suckers brushed against his cheek, tearing his skin. The tentacle backed off, then snaked forward again, wrapping like a glowing green hose around his leg, throwing him to the deck. He was dragged along the floor toward the window. He buried the ax into the decking to hold himself fast;

the ax pulled free, and then Lady Sarah screamed again as Hunter was torn through the already broken glass of the window and outside, over the stern of the ship.

For a moment, he rode in the air, swung back and forth by the tentacle that held his leg, like a doll in the hands of a child. Then he was slammed against the stern of *El Trinidad*; he gripped the railing of the aft cabin, and held on with one painful arm. With the other he used the ax to hack at the tentacle, which finally released him.

He was free, for a moment, and very close to the creature, which churned in the waters below him. He was astounded by its size. It seemed to be eating his ship, holding fast to the stern with its many tentacles. The very air glowed with the greenish light the thing gave off.

Directly beneath him, he saw one huge eye, five feet across, larger than a table. The eye did not blink; it had no expression; the black pupil, surrounded by glowing green flesh, seemed to survey Hunter dispassionately. Further astern, the body of the creature was shaped like a spade with two flat flukes. But it was the tentacles that captured his attention.

Another snaked toward him; he saw suckers the size of dinner plates, rimmed with horns. They tore at his flesh, and he twisted to avoid them, still clinging precariously to the aft cabin railing.

Above him, the seamen were firing down on the animal. Enders shouted, "Hold your fire! It's the Captain!"

And then, in a single swipe, one of the fat tentacles knocked Hunter free of the railing, and he fell into the water, right on top of the animal.

For a moment, he churned and spun in the green glowing water, and then he gained his footing. He was actually standing on the creature! It was slippery and slimy, like standing on a sac of water. The skin of the animal— he felt it whenever he fell to his hands and knees— was gritty and cold. The flesh of the creature pulsed and shifted beneath him.

Hunter crawled forward, splashing in the water, until he came to the eye. Seen so close, the eye was huge, a vast hole in the glowing greenness.

Hunter did not hesitate; he swung his ax, burying it in the curved globe of the eye. The ax bounced off the dome; he swung again, and yet again. Finally the metal cut deep. A gush of clear water spurted upward like a geyser. The flesh around the eye seemed to contract.

And then suddenly the sea turned a milky white, and his footing was lost as the creature sank away, and he was drifting free in the ocean, shouting for help. A rope was thrown to him, and he grabbed it, just as the monster surfaced again. The impact flung him into the air, above the cloudy white water. He crashed back again, landing on the saclike skin of the monster.

Now Enders and the Moor leapt overboard, with lances in hand. They plunged their lances deep into the body of the creature. Columns of greenish blood shot into the air. There was an explosive rush of water—and the animal was gone. It slipped away, down into the depths of the ocean.

Hunter, Enders, and the Moor struggled in the churning water.

"Thanks," Hunter gasped.

"Don't thank me," Enders said, nodding to the Moor. "The black bastard pushed me."

Bassa, tongueless, grinned.

High above them, they saw *El Trinidad* begin to turn, and tack back to retrieve them.

"You know," Enders said, as the three men treaded water, "when we return to Royal, no one will believe this."

Then lines were thrown down to them, and they were hauled, dripping and coughing and exhausted, onto the deck.

Part VI

PORT ROYAL

CHAPTER 34

IN THE EARLY afternoon hours of October 20, 1665, the Spanish galleon *El Trinidad* reached the east channel to Port Royal, outside the scrubby outcropping of South Cay, and Captain Hunter gave orders to drop anchor.

They were two miles from Port Royal itself, and Hunter and his crew stood at the railing of the ship, looking across the channel toward the town. The port was quiet; their arrival had not yet been sighted, but they knew that within moments there would be gunshots and that extraordinary frenzy of celebration that always accompanied the arrival of an enemy prize. The celebration, they knew, often lasted two days or more.

Yet the hours passed, and there was no celebration. On the contrary, the town seemed to grow quieter with each passing minute. There were no gunshots, no bonfires, no shouts of greeting across the still waters.

Enders frowned. "Has the Don attacked?"

Hunter shook his head. "Impossible." Port Royal was the strongest English settlement in the New World. The Spanish might attack St. Kitts, or one of the other outposts. But not Port Royal.

"Something's amiss, sure enough."

"We'll soon know," Hunter said, for as they watched, a longboat put out from Fort Charles, under whose guns they were now anchored.

The longboat tied up alongside *El Trinidad*, and a captain of the king's militia stepped aboard. Hunter knew him; he was Emerson, a rising young officer. Emerson was tense; he spoke too loudly as he said, "Who is the avowed captain of this vessel?"

"I am," Hunter said, coming forward. He smiled. "How are you, Peter?"

Emerson stood stiffly. He gave no sign of recognition. "Identify yourself, sir, if you please."

"Peter, you know full well who I am. What does it mean—"

"Identify yourself, sir, on pain of penalty."

Hunter frowned. "What charade is this?"

Emerson, at rigid attention, said: "Are you Charles Hunter, a citizen of the Massachusetts Bay Colony, and late of His Majesty's Colony in Jamaica?"

Hunter said, "I am." He noticed that despite the cool evening breeze, Emerson was sweating.

"Identify your vessel if you please."

"She is the Spanish galleon known as *El Trinidad.*"

"A Spanish vessel?"

Hunter grew impatient. "She is, plain as your nose."

"Then," Emerson said, taking a breath, "it is my sworn duty, Charles Hunter, to place you under arrest on a charge of piracy—"

"Piracy!"

"—and so, too, all your crew. You will please accompany me in the longboat."

Hunter was astounded. "By whose order?"

"By the order of Mr. Robert Hacklett, Acting Governor of Jamaica."

"But Sir James—"

"Even as we speak, Sir James is dying," Emerson said. "Now please come with me."

Benumbed, moving in a kind of trance, Hunter went over the side, into the longboat. The soldiers rowed ashore. Hunter looked back at the receding silhouette of his ship. He knew that his crew was as stunned as he.

He turned to Emerson. "What the devil is happening?"

Emerson was more relaxed, now that he was in the longboat. "There have been many changes," he said. "A fortnight past, Sir James took ill with the fever—"

"What fever?"

"I tell you what I know," Emerson said. "He has been confined to bed, in the Governor's Mansion, these many days. In his absence, Mr. Hacklett has assumed direction of the colony. He is assisted by Commander Scott."

"Is he?"

Hunter knew he was reacting slowly. He could not believe that the outcome of his many adventures, these past six weeks, was to be clapped in jail—and no doubt hanged—as a common pirate.

"Yes," Emerson said. "Mr. Hacklett has been stern with the town. Many are already in jail, or hanged. Pitts was hanged last week—"

"Pitts!"

"—and Morely only yesterday. And there is a standing warrant for your arrest."

A thousand arguments sprang to Hunter's mind, and a thousand questions. But he said nothing. Emerson was a functionary, a man charged with carrying out the orders of his commander, the foppish dandy Scott. Emerson would do his duty as he was ordered.

"Which jail shall I be sent to?"

"The Marshallsea."

Hunter laughed at the ludicrousness of it. "I know the jailer of the Marshallsea."

"Not anymore, you don't. There is a new man. Hacklett's man."

"I see."

Hunter said nothing further. He listened to the stroke of the oars in the water, and he watched Fort Charles loom closer.

Once inside the fort, he was impressed by the readiness and alertness of the troops. In the past, one could find a dozen drunken lookouts on the battlements of Fort Charles, singing dirty songs. This evening there were none, and the men were neatly dressed in full uniform.

Hunter was marched by a company of armed and alert soldiers into the town, through Lime Street, now unusually quiet, and then north along York Street, past darkened taverns, which normally glowed warmly at this hour. The silence in the town, the desertion of the muddy streets, was striking.

Marshallsea, the men's prison, was located at the end of York Street. It was a large stone building with fifty cells on two floors. The interior stank of urine and feces; rats scuttled through the rushes on the floor; the men in the cells stared at Hunter with hollow eyes as he was marched, by torchlight, to a cell and locked inside.

He looked around his cell. There was nothing inside; no bed, no cot, just straw on the floor, and a high window with bars. Through the window he could see a cloud drifting across the face of a waning moon.

As the door clanged closed behind him, he turned to look at Emerson. "When shall I be tried for piracy?"

"Tomorrow," Emerson said, and then turned away.

THE TRIAL OF Charles Hunter took place on October 21, 1665, a Saturday. Ordinarily, the Justice House did not meet on a Saturday, but nevertheless Hunter was tried on that day. The earthquake-damaged structure was largely empty as Hunter was ushered in, alone, without the rest of his crew, to face a high tribunal of seven men sitting at a wooden table. The tribunal was presided over by Robert Hacklett himself, as Acting Governor of the Jamaica Colony.

He was made to stand before the tribunal while the charge was read to him.

"Raise your right hand."

He did.

"You, Charles Hunter, you and every one of your company, by the authority of our Sovereign Lord, Charles, King of Great Britain, are indicted as follows."

There was a pause. Hunter scanned the faces: Hacklett, glowering down at him, with the faintest trace of a smug smile; Lewisham, Judge of the Admiralty, evidently ill at ease; Commander Scott, picking his teeth with a gold toothpick; the merchants Foster and Poorman, averting their eyes from Hunter's glance; Lieutenant Dodson, a rich officer in the militia, tugging at his uniform; James Phips, a merchant captain. Hunter knew them all, and he recognized how uneasy they were.

"Forasmuch as in open contempt of the laws of your country and the sovereign alliances of your king, you have wickedly united and articled together for the annoyance and disturbance of the subjects and properties of His Most Christian Majesty Philip of Spain upon the land and seas. And have, in conformity to the most evil and mischievous intentions, been to the Spanish settlement upon the island of Matanceros for the purpose of plundering and burning and robbing such ships and vessels as then happened in your way.

"And further ye stand charged with the unlawful opposition upon a Spanish vessel in the straits south of Matanceros, and the sinking of same, with the loss of all lives and properties aboard the ship.

"And lastly, that in the acting and compassing of all this, you were all and every one of you in wicked combination to exert, and actually did, in your several stations, use your utmost endeavors to distress and assault the said Spanish ships and dominions and murder the subjects of Spain. How plead you, Charles Hunter?"

There was a brief pause. "Not guilty," Hunter said.

For Hunter, the trial was already a travesty. The Act of Parliament 1612 specified that the court must be composed of men who had no interest, directly or indirectly, in the particulars of the case being tried. And yet every man on the tribunal stood to gain from Hunter's conviction and the subsequent confiscation of his ship and her treasure.

What confused him was the detailed nature of the indictment. No one could know what had occurred during the Matanceros raid except himself and his men. And yet the indictment had included his successful defense against the Spanish warship. Where had the court gotten its information? He could only assume that one of the crew had talked, probably under torture, the night before.

The court accepted his plea without the slightest reaction. Hacklett leaned forward. "Mr. Hunter," he said, in a calm voice, "this tribunal recognizes the high standing you hold within the Jamaica Colony. We do not wish in this proceeding to stand upon hollow ceremony, which may not see justice served. Will you speak now in defense of your indictment?"

This was a surprise. Hunter paused a moment before answering. Hacklett was breaking the rules of judicial procedure. It must be to his advantage to do so. Nevertheless, the opportunity seemed too good to ignore.

"If it may please the distinguished members of this fair court," Hunter said, with no trace of irony, "I shall endeavor to do so."

The heads of the men on the tribunal nodded thoughtfully, carefully, reasonably.

Hunter looked from one to the next, before he began to speak.

"Gentlemen, no one among you is more thoroughly informed than I, of the sacred treaty lately signed between His Majesty King Charles and the Spanish Court. Never should I break the newly forged ties between our nations without provocation. Yet such provocation occurred, and in abundance. My vessel, the *Cassandra*, was set upon by a Spanish ship of the line, and all my men captured without warrant. Further, two were murdered by the captain of that vessel, one Cazalla. Finally, the same Cazalla intercepted an English merchantman bearing, among other cargoes unknown to me, the Lady Sarah Almont, niece of the Governor of this Colony.

"This Spaniard, Cazalla, an officer of King Philip, destroyed the English merchantman *Entrepid*, killing all those aboard in a bloodthirsty violent act. Among those dispatched was a favorite of His Majesty Charles, one Captain Warner. I am certain His Majesty mourns the loss of this gentleman very much."

Hunter paused. The tribunal did not know this information and it was plain they were not pleased to hear of it.

King Charles took a very personal view of life; his normal good temper might be destroyed if one of his friends was injured or even insulted—let alone killed.

"For these several provocations," Hunter said, "we attacked in reprisal the Spanish fortress at Matanceros, restoring Her Ladyship to safety, and taking as plunder what trifling reparations we deemed reasonable and proper. This is not piracy in the first instance, gentlemen. This is honorable revenge for heinous misdeeds upon the high seas, and such is the substance and nature of my conduct."

He paused and looked at the faces of the tribunal. They stared back at him impassively; they all knew the truth, he realized.

"Lady Sarah Almont can bear witness to this testimony, as can every man aboard my ship, if such be called. There is no truth in the indictment as charged, for there can be no piracy except in the absence of due provocation, and there was indeed most strenuous provocation."

He finished, and looked at the faces. They were bland now, blank and unreadable. He felt chilled.

Hacklett leaned over the table toward him. "Have you any further to speak in your reply to the indictment, Mr. Charles Hunter?"

"Nothing further," Hunter said. "I have spoken all I have to say."

"And most creditably, too, if I may take the liberty to say," Hacklett commented. There were nods and murmurs of assent from the other six men. "But the truth of your speech is another question, which we must all now consider. Be so good as to inform this court under what business your vessel sailed in the first instance."

"The cutting of logwood," Hunter said.

"You had letters of marque?"

"I did, from Sir James Almont himself."

"And where are these documents?"

"They were lost with the *Cassandra*," Hunter said, "but I have no doubt Sir James will confirm that he drew them up."

"Sir James," Hacklett said, "is in great distress of illness, and cannot confirm nor deny any matter at hand before this court. Nonetheless, I feel we can take you at your word that these papers were issued."

Hunter bowed slightly.

"Now then," Hacklett said. "Where were you captured by the Spanish warship? In what waters?"

Hunter instantly sensed the dilemma he faced and hesitated before answering, knowing that the hesitation would damage his credibility. He decided to tell the truth—almost.

"In the Windward Passage north of Puerto Rico."

"North of Puerto Rico?" Hacklett said with an air of elaborate surprise. "Is there logwood in those parts?"

"No," Hunter said, "but we were buffeted by a mighty storm for two days, and sent far off our intended course."

"Indeed, it must have been, for Puerto Rico is to the north and east, while all the logwood is to the south and west of Jamaica."

Hunter said, "I cannot be held accountable for storms."

"What was the date of this storm?"

"The twelfth and thirteenth of September."

"Odd," Hacklett said. "The weather was fair in Jamaica on those days."

"The weather at sea is not always similar to that of the land," Hunter said, "as is well known."

"The court thanks you, Mr. Hunter, for your lesson in seamanship," Hacklett said. "Although I think you have little to teach the gentlemen here assembled, eh?" He chuckled briefly. "Now then, Mr. Hunter—forgive me if I do not address you as Captain Hunter—do you aver that there never was, at any time, an intent of your vessel and its crew to attack any Spanish settlement or dominion?"

"I do so aver."

"You never held counsel to plan such an unlawful attack?"

"I did not." Hunter spoke with as much certainty as he could muster, knowing that his crew dared not contradict him on this point. To admit to the vote that was held in Bull Bay was tantamount to a conviction of piracy.

"On pain of your mortal soul, do you swear that no such intent was ever discussed with any member of your company?"

"I do."

Hacklett paused. "Let me be certain to understand your import. You sailed upon a simple logwood expedition, and by ill fortune were cast far north by a storm which did not touch these shores. Subsequently, you were captured without provocation of any sort by a Spanish warship. Is this correct?"

"It is."

"And further, you learned that this same warship attacked an English merchantman and took as hostage the Lady Sarah Almont, giving you cause for reprisal. Is that so?"

"It is."

Hacklett paused again. "How came you to know the warship captured the Lady Sarah Almont?"

"She was on board the warship at the time of our capture," Hunter said. "This I learned—from a Donnish soldier, who made a slip of the tongue."

"Most convenient."

"Yet that was the truth of the matter. After we made our escape—which is, I hope, no crime before this tribunal—we pursued the warship to Matanceros, and thence saw the Lady Sarah debarked to the fortress."

"So you attacked, for the sole purpose of preserving this Englishwoman's virtue?" Hacklett's voice was heavy with sarcasm.

Hunter glanced from one face to the next on the tribunal.

"Gentlemen," he said, "it is my understanding that the function of this tribunal is not to determine whether I am a saint"—there was amused laughter—"but only whether I am a pirate. I knew, of course, of the galleon within the Matanceros harbor. That was a most estimable prize. And yet I pray the court will perceive that there was provocation for a score of such attacks—and provocation broadly speaking, admitting no legalistic quibbling nor technical point of turning."

He looked toward the court reporter, whose duty it was to make a note of the proceedings. Hunter was astounded to notice that the man was sitting placidly and taking no notes.

"Tell us," Hacklett said, "how you came to escape from the Spanish warship, once captured?"

"It was through the efforts of the Frenchman, Sanson, who performed with most estimable bravery."

"You regard this Sanson highly?"

"Indeed I do, for I owe him my very life."

"So be it," Hacklett said. He turned in his chair. "Call the first witness in evidence, Mr. Andre Sanson!"

"Andre Sanson!"

Hunter turned to the door, astounded again, as Sanson walked into the courtroom. The Frenchman moved quickly, with smooth, liquid strides, and took his place in the witness box. He raised his right hand.

"Do you, Andre Sanson, solemnly promise and swear on the Holy Evangelists to bear true and faithful witness between the king and the prisoner in relation to the fact or facts of piracy and robbery he does now stand accused of, so help you God?"

"I do."

Sanson lowered his right hand, and looked directly at Hunter. The gaze was flat and pitying. He held the glance for several seconds, until Hacklett spoke.

"Mr. Sanson."

"Sir."

"Mr. Sanson, Mr. Hunter has given his own account of the proceedings of this voyage. We wish to hear the story in your own words, as a witness whose valor has already been remarked by the accused. Will you tell us, please, what was the purpose of the voyage of *Cassandra*—as you understood it in the first instance?"

"The cutting of logwood."

"And did you discover differently at any time?"

"I did."

"Please explain to the court."

"After we sailed on September ninth," Sanson said, "Mr. Hunter made for Monkey Bay. There he announced to the several crew that his destination was Matanceros, to capture the Spanish treasures there."

"And what was your reaction?"

"I was shocked," Sanson said. "I reminded Mr. Hunter that such an attack was piracy and punishable by death."

"And his response?"

"Oaths and foul curses," Sanson said, "and the warning that if I did not participate wholeheartedly he would kill me as a dog, and feed me in pieces to the sharks."

"So you participated in all that followed under duress, and not as a volunteer?"

"That is so."

Hunter stared at Sanson. The Frenchman was calm and unruffled as he spoke. There was not the slightest trace of a lie. He looked at Hunter repeatedly, a defiant look, daring him to repudiate the story he so confidently told.

"What then transpired?"

"We set sail for Matanceros, where we hoped to make a surprise attack."

"Excuse me, do you mean an attack without provocation?"

"I do."

"Pray continue."

"While sailing for Matanceros, we came upon the Spanish warship. Seeing that we were outnumbered, we were captured by the Spanish, as pirates."

"And what did you do?"

"I had no wish to die in Havana as a pirate," Sanson said, "especially as I had been forced to do Mr. Hunter's bidding thus far. So I hid, and subsequently enabled my companions to escape, trusting that they would then decide to return to Port Royal."

"And they did not?"

"Indeed they did not. Mr. Hunter, once returned to command of his ship, forced us to set sail for Matanceros to carry out his original intent."

Hunter could stand no more. "I forced you? How could I force sixty men?"

"Silence!" bellowed Hacklett. "The prisoner will remain silent, or he shall be removed from court." Hacklett turned back to Sanson. "How did you fare with the prisoner at this time?"

"Badly," Sanson said. "He clapped me in irons for the duration of the voyage."

"Matanceros and the galleon were subsequently captured?"

"Aye, gentlemen," Sanson said. "And I was placed in the *Cassandra* thusly: Mr. Hunter went aboard the ship and determined that she was unseaworthy, after the attack on Matanceros. He then gave me command of this poor ship, in the manner of marooning, for he did not expect her to survive the open sea. He gave me a small crew of men who felt as I did. We made for Port Royal when a hurricane overtook us, and our ship was shattered with the loss of all hands. I, myself, in the longboat, managed to come to Tortuga and thence here."

"What know you of Lady Sarah Almont?"

"Nothing."

"Nothing at all?"

"Not until this moment," Sanson said. "Is there such a person?"

"Indeed," Hacklett said, with a quick glance at Hunter. "Mr. Hunter claims to have rescued her from Matanceros and brought her safely thus."

"She was not with him when he left Matanceros," Sanson said. "If I were to conjecture, I should say Mr. Hunter attacked an English merchantman and took her passenger as prize, to justify his wrongdoings."

"A most convenient event," Hacklett said. "But why have we not heard of this same merchantman?"

"Probably he killed all hands aboard and sunk her," Sanson said. "On his homeward voyage from Matanceros."

"One final inquiry," Hacklett said. "Do you recall a storm at sea on the twelfth and thirteenth of September?"

"A storm? No, gentlemen. There was no storm."

Hacklett nodded. "Thank you, Mr. Sanson. You may step down."

"If it please the court," Sanson said, and left the room.

There was a long pause after the door slammed with a hollow, echoing sound. The court turned to face Hunter, who was trembling and white with anger, and yet he fought for composure.

"Mr. Hunter," Hacklett said, "can you charge your memory with any particulars to account for the discrepancy between the stories you have related and those of Mr. Sanson whom you have said you respect so highly?"

"He is a liar, sir. A foul and black liar."

"The court is prepared to consider such an accusation if you can acquaint the court with particulars which will serve in evidence, Mr. Hunter."

"I have only my word," Hunter said, "but you may have ample evidence from Lady Sarah Almont herself, who will contradict the French tale in all respects."

"We shall certainly have her witness," Hacklett said. "But before calling her, a perplexing question remains. The attack on Matanceros—justified or no—occurred on September twenty-first. You returned to Port Royal on October twentieth. Among pirates, one expects that such a delay represents a sailing to an obscure island, for the purpose of concealing treasure taken, and thus cheating the king. What is your explanation?"

"We were engaged in a sea battle," Hunter said. "Then we fought a hurricane for three days. We careened in an island outside the Boca del Dragon for four days. Subsequently, we set sail but were besieged by a kraken—"

"I beg your pardon. Do you mean a monster of the depths?"

"I do."

"How amusing." Hacklett laughed, and the others on the tribunal laughed with him. "Your imagination to explain this monthlong delay gains our admiration, if not our credence." Hacklett turned in his chair. "Call the Lady Sarah Almont to give evidence."

"Lady Sarah Almont!"

A moment later, looking pale and drawn, Lady Sarah entered the room, took the oath, and awaited her questions. Hacklett, with a most solicitous manner, peered down at her.

"Lady Sarah, I wish first to welcome you to the Jamaica Colony, and to apologize for the dastardly business which must be your first encounter with society in these regions."

"Thank you, Mr. Hacklett," she said, with a slight bow. She did not look at Hunter, not once. That worried him.

"Lady Sarah," Hacklett said, "it has become a question of importance to this tribunal whether you were captured by Spaniards and then released by Captain Hunter, or whether you were captured by Captain Hunter in the first instance. Can you enlighten us?"

"I can."

"Please do so freely."

"I was aboard the merchantman *Entrepid*," she said, "bound from Bristol for Port Royal when . . ."

Her voice trailed off. There was a long silence. She looked at Hunter. He stared into her eyes, which were frightened in a way he had never seen.

"Go on, if you please."

". . . When we spotted a Spanish vessel on the horizon. It opened fire upon us, and we were captured. I was surprised to discover that the captain of this Spanish ship was an Englishman."

"Do you mean Charles Hunter, the prisoner who stands before us now?"

"I do."

"Please continue."

Hunter hardly heard the rest of her words: how he had taken her onto the galleon, then killed the English crew and set the ship afire. How he had told Lady Sarah that he would pretend he had saved her from the Spaniards, in order to justify his raid on Matanceros. She delivered her story in a high-pitched, taut voice, speaking rapidly, as if to finish the matter as quickly as possible.

"Thank you, Lady Sarah. You may step down."

She left the room.

The tribunal faced Hunter, seven men with blank, expressionless faces, examining Hunter like a creature already dead. A long moment passed.

"We have heard nothing from the witness of your colorful adventures with the Boca del Dragon, or the sea monster. Have you any proofs?" Hacklett asked mildly.

"Only this," Hunter said, and, swiftly, he stripped to the waist. Across his chest were the tears and scars of giant, saucerlike suckers, an unearthly sight. The members of the tribunal gasped. They murmured among themselves.

Hacklett banged his gavel for order.

"An interesting amusement, Mr. Hunter, but not persuasive to the educated gentlemen present. We can all surely imagine the devices you employed, in your desperate predicament, to re-create the effects of such a monster. The court is not persuaded."

Hunter looked at the faces of the seven men, and saw that they were persuaded. But Hacklett's gavel banged again.

"Charles Hunter," Hacklett said, "this court finds you justly convicted of the crime of piracy and robbery upon the high seas, as charged. Do you wish to say any reason why sentence shall not be carried out?"

Hunter paused. He thought of a thousand oaths and expletives, but none would serve any purpose. "No," he said softly.

"I did not hear you, Mr. Hunter."

"I said no."

"Then you, Charles Hunter, and all your crew, are adjudged and sentenced to be carried back to the place from whence you came, and thence on Monday next to the place of execution, the High Street Square in the town of Port Royal, and there to be hanged by the neck till dead, dead, dead. And after this, you and each of you shall be taken down and your bodies hanged from the yardarms of your vessel. May God have mercy upon your souls. Take him away, jailer."

Hunter was led out of the Justice House. As he went out the door, he heard Hacklett laugh: a peculiar, thin, cackling sound. Then the door closed, and he was returned to jail.

CHAPTER 35

HE WAS TAKEN to a different cell; apparently the jailers of Marshallsea did not care one from another. He sat in the straw on the floor and considered his plight with care. He could hardly believe what had happened, and he was angry almost beyond understanding.

Night came, and the jail turned quiet except for the snores and the sighs of the inmates. Hunter himself was falling asleep when he heard a familiar hissing voice: "Hunter!"

He sat up.

"Hunter!"

He knew the voice. "Whisper," he said. "Where are you?"

"In the next cell."

The cells all opened at the front; he could not see the next cell, but he could hear well enough, if he pressed his cheek close to the stone wall.

"Whisper, how long are you here?"

"A week, Hunter. Were you tried?"

"Aye."

"And judged guilty?"

"Aye."

"So also me," Whisper hissed. "On a charge of theft. It was false."

Theft, like piracy, had a fatal outcome.

"Whisper," he said, "what has happened to Sir James?"

"They say he is ill," Whisper hissed, "but he is not. He is healthy, and under guard, in peril of his life, at the Governor's Mansion. Hacklett and Scott have taken control. They tell all in the town he is dying."

Hacklett must have threatened Lady Sarah, Hunter thought, and forced her to testify falsely.

"There is more rumor," Whisper hissed. "Madam Emily Hacklett is heavy with child."

"So?"

"So, it appears that her husband the Acting Governor never performs his uxorial duties upon the wife. He is not so capable. Therefore her condition is irksome to him."

"I see," Hunter said.

"You have cuckolded a tyrant, and all the worse for you."

"And Sanson?"

"He came alone, in a longboat. There was no crew. He told the story that all died in a hurricane, save him alone."

Hunter pressed his cheek against the stone wall, feeling the cool dampness. It provided a kind of solid comfort to him.

"What day is this?"

"Saturday."

Hunter had two days before his execution. He sighed, and sat back, and stared out the barred window at the clouds across a pale and waning moon.

THE GOVERNOR'S MANSION was constructed of solid brick, a veritable fortress at the north end of Port Royal. In the basement, under heavy guard, Sir James Almont lay feverish upon a bed. Lady Sarah Almont placed a cool towel across his hot forehead, and bid him breathe easily.

At that moment, Mr. Hacklett and his wife strode into the room.

"Sir James!"

Almont, his eyes glazed with fever, looked over at his deputy. "What is it now?"

"We have tried Captain Hunter. He will hang on Monday next, as a common pirate."

At this, Lady Sarah looked away. Tears came to her eyes.

"Do you approve, Sir James?"

"Whatever . . . you think . . . is the best course . . ." Sir James said, breathing with difficulty.

"Thank you, Sir James." Hacklett laughed, spun on his heel, and left the room. The door closed heavily behind him.

Instantly, Sir James was alert. He frowned at Sarah. "Take this damnable cloth from my head, woman. There is work to be done."

"But Uncle—"

"Damn it all, do you understand nothing? All the years I have spent in this godforsaken colony, waiting and financing privateering expeditions, and all for this one moment, when one of my buccos would bring back a Donnish galleon, laden with treasure. Now it has happened, and do you not comprehend the outcome?"

"No, Uncle."

"Well, a tenth will go to Charles," Almont said. "And the remaining ninety percent will be divided between Hacklett and Scott. You mark my words."

"But they warned me—"

"Hang their warnings, I know the truth. I have waited four years for this moment, and I will not be cheated of it. Nor will the other good citizens of this, ah, temperate town. I'll not be cheated by a pimple-faced moralistic knave and a dandified military fop. Hunter must be freed."

"But how?" Lady Sarah said. "He is to be executed in two days' time."

"That old dog," Almont said, "will not swing from any arm, I promise you. The town is with him."

"How so?"

"Because if he returns home, he has debts to pay, and handsomely, too. With interest. To me, and to others. All he needs is a setting free . . ."

"But how?" Lady Sarah said.

"Ask Richards," Almont said.

And then a voice from the gloom at the back of the room said, "I will ask Richards."

Lady Sarah whirled. She looked at Emily Hacklett.

"I have a score to settle," Emily Hacklett said, and she left the room.

When they were alone, Lady Sarah asked her uncle, "Will that suffice?"

Sir James Almont chuckled. "In spades, my dear," he said. "In spades." He laughed aloud. "We will see blood in Port Royal before dawn, mark my words."

"I AM EAGER to help, my lady," Richards said. The loyal servant had been smarting for weeks under the injustice that had placed his master under armed guard.

"Who can enter Marshallsea?" Mrs. Hacklett asked.

She had seen the building from the outside, but had not, of course, ever entered it. Indeed, it was impossible that she ever do so. In the face of criminality, a high-born woman sniffed and looked away. "Can you enter the prison?"

"Nay, madam," Richards said. "Your husband has posted his special guard; they'd sight me at once, and bar my way."

"Then who can?"

"A woman," Richards said. Food and necessary personal articles were brought to prisoners by friends and relatives; it was ordinary custom.

"What woman? She must be clever, and avoid search."

"There's only one I can think," Richards said. "Mistress Sharpe."

Mrs. Hacklett nodded. She remembered Mistress Sharpe, one of the thirty-seven convict women who had made the crossing on the *Godspeed*. Since then, Mistress Sharpe had become the most popular courtesan in the port.

"See to it," Mrs. Hacklett said, "with no delay."

"And what shall I promise her?"

"Say that Captain Hunter will reward her generously and justly, as I am sure he shall."

Richards nodded, then hesitated. "Madam," he said, "I trust you are aware of the consequence of freeing Captain Hunter?"

With a coldness that gave Richards a shudder down his spine, the woman answered, "I am not only aware, I devoutly seek it."

"Very good, madam," Richards said, and slipped off into the night.

IN THE DARKNESS, the turtles penned in Chocolata Hole surfaced and snapped their sharp beaks. Standing nearby, Mistress Sharpe, flouncing and laughing, giggled and twisted away from one of the guards, who fondled her breast. She blew him a kiss, and continued on to the shadow of the high wall of Marshallsea. She carried a crock of turtle stew in her arms.

Another guard accompanied her to Hunter's cell. This one was surly and half-drunk. He paused with the key in the lock.

"Why do you hesitate?" she asked.

"What lock was ever opened without a lusty turning?" he asked, leering.

"The lock is better for a proper oiling," she leered back.

"Aye, lady, and for a proper key as well."

"I judge you to have the key," she said. "But for the lock, well, that must wait the proper time. Leave me a few minutes with this hungry dog, and then we shall have ourselves a turning such as you will not forget."

The guard chuckled and unlocked the door. She went in; the door was locked behind her, and the guard remained.

"A few minutes with this man," she said, "as decency permits."

"'Tis not allowed."

"Who cares for that?" she said, and licked her lips hungrily at the guard.

He smiled back at her, and walked away.

As soon as he was gone, she set down the pot of stew on the floor and faced Hunter. Hunter did not recognize her but he was hungry, and the smell of the turtle stew was strong and agreeable.

"You are most kind," he said.

"You hardly know," she replied, and, in a quick gesture, lifted her skirts from the hem, pulling them up to her waist. It was an astonishingly lewd movement, but more astonishing for what was revealed.

Strapped to her calves and thighs was a veritable armory—two knives, two pistols.

"My secret parts are said to be dangerous," she said, "and now you know the truth."

Quickly, Hunter took the weapons and stashed them in his belt.

"Do not, sir, discharge prematurely."

"You may count upon my staying power."

"How long may I count?"

"To a hundred," Hunter said, "and there's a promise."

She looked back in the direction of the guard.

"I shall hold you to your word, at another time," she said. "In the meanwhile, shall I be raped?"

"I think it is best," Hunter said and flung her to the ground.

She squealed and screamed, and the guard came running. He saw the import of the scene in a moment, and hastily unlocked the door, running into the room.

"You damnable pirate," he growled, and then the knife in Hunter's fist was buried in his neck, and he staggered back, clutching at the blade beneath his chin. He pulled it free and blood gushed out, a hissing fountain, and then he collapsed and died.

"Quickly, lady," Hunter said, helping Anne Sharpe to her feet. All around them, the men jailed in Marshallsea were silent; they had heard, and they were utterly quiet. Hunter went around, opening cell doors, then he gave the keys to the men and let them finish the task.

"How many guards at the gates?" he asked Anne Sharpe.

"I saw four," she said, "and another dozen on the ramparts."

This presented a problem for Hunter. The guards were English, and he had no stomach for killing them.

"We must have a ruse," he said. "Call the captain to you."

She nodded, and stepped out into the courtyard. Hunter remained behind, in the shadows.

Hunter did not marvel at the composure of this woman, who had just watched a man brutally slain. He was not accustomed to the faintheartedness of women, so fashionable in the French and Spanish courts. English women were tough-minded, in some ways tougher than any male, and it was equally true of low- and high-born women.

The captain of the Marshallsea Guard came over to Anne Sharpe, and at the last moment saw the barrel of Hunter's pistol protruding from the shadows. Hunter beckoned him over.

"Now hear me," Hunter said. "You may call your men down, and have them throw their muskets to the ground, and no lives shall be lost. Or you can stand and fight, and all surely die."

The captain of the guard said, "I've been awaiting your escape, sir, and I hope you will remember me in the days to come."

"We shall see," Hunter said, promising nothing.

In a formal voice, the captain said, "Commander Scott shall have his own action upon the morrow."

"Commander Scott," Hunter said, "shall not live to see the morrow. Now take your stand."

"I hope you will remember me—"

"I may," Hunter said, "remember not to slit your throat."

The captain of the guard called his men down, and Hunter supervised their locking up in the Marshallsea jail.

MRS. HACKLETT, HAVING given her instructions to Richards, returned to her husband's side. He was in the library, drinking after dinner with Commander Scott. Both men had in recent days become enamored of the governor's wine cellar, and were engaged in consuming it before the governor recovered.

They were, at this moment, deep in their cups.

"My dear," her husband said, as she entered the room, "you come at a most opportune moment."

"Indeed?"

"Indeed," Robert Hacklett said. "Why, just this very moment I was explaining to Commander Scott the manner of your getting with child by the pirate Hunter. You understand, of course, that he will soon swing in the breeze until the flesh rots off his bones. In this beastly climate, I am told that happens quickly. But I am sure you know of haste, eh? Why, speaking of your seduction, Commander Scott was not previously acquainted with the details of the event. I have been informing him."

Mrs. Hacklett flushed deeply.

"So demure," Hacklett said, his voice taking a nasty edge. "One would never think her a common bawd. And yet that is what she is. What would her favors fetch, do you think?"

Commander Scott sniffed at a perfumed handkerchief. "Shall I be frank?"

"By all means, be frank. Be frank."

"She is too lean for the usual taste."

"His Majesty liked her well enough—"

"Perhaps, perhaps, but that is not the usual taste, eh? Our king has a preference for hot-blooded foreign women—"

"So be it," Hacklett said irritably. "What would she fetch?"

"I should think, she would fetch not above—well, considering she has tasted the royal lancet, perhaps more—but in no case above a hundred reales."

Mrs. Hacklett, very red, turned to leave. "I shall attend no more of this."

"On the contrary," her husband said, leaping from his chair and barring her way. "You shall attend a good deal more. Commander Scott, you are a gentleman of worldly experience. Would you pay a hundred reales?"

Scott gulped his drink and coughed. "Not I, sir," he said.

Hacklett gripped his wife's arm. "What price would you make?"

"Fifty reales."

"Done!" Hacklett said.

"Robert!" his wife protested. "Good gracious God, Robert—"

Robert Hacklett struck his wife in the face, a blow sending her across the room. She collapsed into a chair.

"Now then, Commander," Hacklett said. "You are a man of your word. I shall accept your credit in this matter."

Scott looked over the brim of his cup. "Eh?"

"I said, I shall accept your credit in this matter. Have your money's worth."

"Eh? You mean, ah . . ." he gestured in the direction of Mrs. Hacklett, whose eyes were now wide with horror.

"Indeed I do, and quickly, too."

"Here? Now?"

"Precisely, Commander." Hacklett, very drunk, staggered across the room and clapped his hand on the soldier's shoulder. "And I shall observe, for my own amusement."

"No!" shrieked Mrs. Hacklett.

Her voice was piercingly loud, but neither man appeared to have heard her. They stared drunkenly at each other.

"Faith," Scott said, "I'm not sure 'tis wise."

"Nonsense," Hacklett said. "You are a gentleman of reputation and you must uphold that reputation. After all, this is a consort worthy of a king—well, at least once worthy of a king. Go to it, man."

"Damn me," Commander Scott said, getting unsteadily to his feet. "Damn me, I shall do, sir. What's good enough for a king is good enough for me. I shall do." And he began to unbuckle his breeches.

Commander Scott was exceedingly drunk, and his buckles proved difficult. Mrs. Hacklett began to scream and her husband crossed the library and struck her in the face, cutting her lip. A trickle of blood ran down her chin.

"A pirate's whore—or a king's—can have no airs. Commander Scott, take your pleasure."

And Scott advanced upon the woman.

"MOVE ME," WHISPERED Governor Almont to his niece.

"But Uncle, how?"

"Kill the guard," he said, and handed her a pistol.

Lady Sarah Almont took the pistol in her hands, feeling the unfamiliar shape of the weapon.

"You cock it thus," said Almont, showing her. "Now careful! Go to the door, ask to go out, and fire—"

"Fire how?"

"Directly into his face. Make no mistake here, my dear."

"But Uncle . . ."

He glared at her. "I am a sick man," he said. "Now help me."

She stepped a few paces toward the door.

"Right down his throat," Almont said, with a certain satisfaction. "He's earned it, the traitorous dog."

She knocked on the door.

"What is it, miss?" said the guard.

"Open up," she said. "I wish to leave."

There was a scraping, and a metallic click, as the lock was turned. The door opened. She had a glimpse of the guard, a young man of nineteen, fresh-faced and innocent, his expression bemused. "Whatever Your Ladyship desires . . ."

She fired at his lips. The explosion rocked her arm, and blew him backward. He twisted and slid to the ground, then rolled onto his back. She saw, with horror, that he had no face left, just a bloody pulp mounted on his shoulders. The body writhed on the ground for a few moments. Urine leaked down the leg of his trousers, and she smelled defecation. Then the body was still.

"Help me move," croaked her uncle, the Governor of Jamaica, sitting up painfully in his bed.

∞

HUNTER ASSEMBLED HIS men at the north end of
Port Royal, near the mainland. His immediate problem
was wholly political, to reverse a judgment against him.
As a practical matter, once he escaped, the townspeople
would rally around him, and he would not again be jailed.

But equally practical was the question of his response
to unjust treatment, for Hunter's reputation within the
town was at stake.

He reviewed the eight names in his mind:

> Hacklett
> Scott
> Lewisham, the judge of the Admiralty
> Foster and Poorman, the merchants
> Lieutenant Dodson
> James Phips, merchant captain
> And last, but not least, Sanson

Each of these men had acted with full knowledge of the
injustice. Each stood to profit from the confiscation of his
prize.

The laws of the privateers were solid enough; such
chicanery inevitably meant death and confiscation of the
share. But at the same time, he would be obliged to kill
several highly placed members of the town. That would be

easy enough, but he might have a bad time of it later, if Sir James did not survive unscathed.

If Sir James were worth his salt, he would have long since escaped to safety. Hunter would have to trust to that, he decided. And in the meantime, he would have to kill those who had crossed him.

Shortly before dawn, he ordered all his men into the Blue Hills north of Jamaica, telling them to remain there for two days.

Then, alone, he returned to the town.

CHAPTER 36

FOSTER, A PROSPEROUS silk merchant, owned a large house on Pembroke Street, northeast of the dockyards. Hunter slipped in through the back, passing the separate kitchen block. He made his way upstairs to the master bedroom on the second floor.

He found Foster asleep in bed with his wife. Hunter awoke him by pressing a pistol lightly against his nostrils.

Foster, a fattish man of fifty, snorted and sniffed and rolled away. Hunter jammed the pistol barrel up one nostril.

Foster blinked and opened his eyes. He sat up in bed, not saying a word.

"Be still," his wife muttered sleepily. "You toss so." Yet she did not wake up. Hunter and Foster stared at each other. Foster looked from the pistol to Hunter, and back again.

Finally, Foster raised a finger in the air, and gently eased out of bed. His wife still slept. In his nightgown, Foster padded across the room to a chest.

"I shall pay you well," he whispered. "See here, look." He opened a false compartment and withdrew a sack of gold, very heavy. "There is more, Hunter. I shall pay you whatever you want."

Hunter said nothing. Foster, in his nightshirt, extended his arm with the sack of gold. His arm trembled.

"Please," he whispered. "Please, please . . ."

He got down on his knees.

"Please, Hunter, I pray you, please . . ."

Hunter shot him in the face. The body was knocked back, the legs thrown up in the air, the bare feet kicking space. In the bed nearby, the wife never awoke, but turned sleepily and groaned.

Hunter picked up the sack of gold and left as silently as he had come.

POORMAN, BELYING HIS name, was a rich trader in silver and pewter. His house was on High Street. Hunter found him asleep at a table in the kitchen, a half-empty bottle of wine before him.

Hunter took a kitchen knife and slashed both Poorman's wrists. Poorman awoke groggily, saw Hunter, and then saw the blood pouring over the table. He raised his bleeding hands, but could not move them; the tendons had all been cut, and the hands flopped lifelessly, rag-doll fingers, already turning grayish-white.

He let his arms drop again to the table. He watched the blood pool on the wood and drip through the cracks to the floor. He looked back at Hunter. His face was curious, his expression confused.

"I would have paid," he said hoarsely. "I would have done what you . . . what you . . ."

He stood up from the table, weaving dizzily, holding his injured arms bent at the elbows. In the silence of the room, the blood spattered with an odd loudness on the ground.

"I would have . . ." Poorman began, and then rocked back and fell flat on the floor.

"Ye, ye, ye, ye," he said, fainter and fainter. Hunter turned away, not waiting for the man to die. He went back into the night air and slipped silently through the dark streets of Port Royal.

HE ENCOUNTERED LIEUTENANT Dodson by accident. The soldier was singing a song, stumbling drunk through the streets with two whores at his side. Hunter saw him at the end of the High Street and turned back, slipping down Queen Street, turning east on Howell Alley, just in time to meet Dodson at the corner.

"Who goes there?" Dodson demanded, speaking loudly. "Know you that there is a curfew? Be gone else I shall clap you in the Marshallsea."

In shadow, Hunter said, "I have just come from there."

"Eh?" Dodson said, tilting his head toward the voice. "What means your churlish speech? I shall have you know——"

"Hunter!" shrieked the whores, and they both fled. Deprived of their support, Dodson fell drunkenly down into the mud.

"Damn you for uncertain quim," he grunted, and struggled to get up. "Look at my uniform now, damn you all." He was covered in mud and manure.

He had already gotten to his knees when the words of the women suddenly reached his alcohol-fogged brain. "Hunter?" he asked softly. "You are Hunter?"

Hunter nodded in the shadows.

"Then I shall arrest you for the scoundrel and pirate that you are," Dodson said. But before he could get back to his feet, Hunter kicked him in the stomach and sent him sprawling.

"Ow!" Dodson said. "You hurt me, damn you."

They were the last words he spoke. Hunter gripped the soldier by the neck and pressed his face into the mud and dung of the street, holding the squirming body, which struggled with increasing force and, finally, toward the end, with violent wrenchings and twistings until at last it did not move.

Hunter stepped back, gasping for breath with the exertion.

He looked around the dark, deserted town. A marching patrol of ten militiamen went by; he stepped back into the shadows until they had passed.

Two whores came by. "Are you Hunter?" one asked, with no sign of fear.

He nodded.

"Bless you," she said. "You come see me, and you'll have your way without a farthing spent." She laughed.

Giggling, the two women disappeared into the night.

HE STOOD INSIDE the Black Boar tavern. There were fifty people there, but he saw only James Phips, dapper and handsome, drinking with several other merchantmen. Phips's companions immediately slipped away, showing aspects of terror on their faces. But Phips himself, after an initial shock, took on a hearty manner.

"Hunter!" he said, grinning broadly. "Damn my eyes, but you have done what we all knew you would. A round for everyone, I say, to celebrate your new freedom."

There was utter silence in the Black Boar. No one spoke. No one moved.

"Come now," Phips said loudly. "I call for a round in honor of Captain Hunter! A round!"

Hunter moved forward, toward Phips's table. His soft footsteps on the dirt floor of the tavern were the only sound in the room.

Phips eyed Hunter uneasily. "Charles," he said. "Charles, this stern countenance does not become you. It is time to be merry."

"Is it?"

"Charles, my friend," Phips said, "you surely understand I bear you no ill will. I was forced to appear on the tribunal. It was all the work of Hacklett and Scott; I swear it. I had no choice. I've a ship to sail in a week's time, Charles, and they would not give me embarkation papers, so they said. And I knew you would make good your escape. Only an hour ago, I was telling Timothy Flint that very expectation. Timothy: answer true, was I not telling you that Hunter would be free? Timothy?"

Hunter took out his pistol and aimed it at Phips.

"Now Charles," Phips said. "I beg you to be reasonable. A man must be practical. Do you think I would have condemned you if ever I believed sentence would be carried out? Do you think so? Do you?"

Hunter said nothing. He cocked the pistol, a single metallic click in the silence of the room.

"Charles," Phips said, "it does my heart good to see you again. Come, have a drink with me, and let us forget—"

Hunter shot him, full in the chest. Everyone ducked away as fragments of bone and a geyser of blood blew outward from his heart in a hissing rush. Phips dropped a cup that had been raised in one hand; the cup struck the table and rolled to the floor.

Phips's eyes followed it. He reached for it with his hand and said hoarsely, "A drink, Charles . . ." And then he collapsed on the table. Blood seeped over the rude wood.

Hunter turned and left.

As he came out on the street again, he heard the tolling of the church bells of St. Anne's. They rang incessantly, the signal for an attack on Port Royal, or some other emergency.

Hunter knew it could have only one meaning—his escape from the jail of Marshallsea had been discovered.

He did not mind at all.

LEWISHAM, JUDGE OF the Admiralty, had his quarters behind the courthouse. He awoke to the church bells in alarm, and sent a servant out to see what was the matter. The man returned a few minutes after.

"What is it?" Lewisham said. "Speak, man."

The man looked up. It was Hunter.

"How is it possible?" Lewisham asked.

Hunter cocked the gun. "Easily," he said.

"Tell me what you wish."

"I shall," Hunter said. And he told him.

COMMANDER SCOTT, DROWSY with drink, lay sprawled on a couch in the library of the Governor's Mansion. Mr. Hacklett and his mistress had long since retired. He awoke to the church bells and instantly knew what had happened; he felt a terror unlike any he had ever known. Moments later, one of his guard burst into the room with the news: Hunter had escaped, all the pirates were vanished, and Poorman, Foster, Phips, and Dodson were all dead.

"Get my horse," Scott commanded, and hastily arranged his disarrayed clothing. He emerged at the front of the Governor's Mansion, looked around cautiously, and jumped on his stallion.

He was unhorsed a few moments later, and flung rudely to the cobblestones no more than a hundred yards from the Governor's Mansion. A contingent of vagabonds led by Richards, the governor's manservant—and directed by Hunter, that scoundrel—clapped him in irons and took him away to Marshallsea.

To await trial: the nerve of the ruffians!

∽

HACKLETT AWOKE TO the tolling of the church bells, and also guessed their meaning. He leapt out of bed, ignoring his wife, who had lain the whole night, wide awake, staring at the ceiling, listening to his drunken snores. She was in pain and she had been badly humiliated.

Hacklett went to the chamber door and called to Richards.

"What has transpired?"

"Hunter escaped," Richards said flatly. "Dodson and Poorman and Phips are all dead, perhaps more."

"And the man is still loose?"

"I do not know," Richards said, pointedly failing to add *Your Excellency.*

"Dear God," Hacklett said. "Bolt the doors. Call the guard. Alert Commander Scott."

"Commander Scott left some few minutes past."

"Left? Dear God," Hacklett said, and slammed the chamber door, locking it. He turned back to the bed. "Dear God," he said. "Dear God, we shall all be murdered by that pirate."

"Not all," his wife said, pointing a pistol at him. Her husband kept a brace of loaded pistols by the bed, and she now held them aimed at him, one in each hand.

"Emily," Hacklett said, "don't be a fool. This is no time for your silliness, the man is a vicious killer."

"Come no closer," she said.

He hesitated. "You jest."

"I do not."

Hacklett looked at his wife, and the pistols she held. He was not himself skilled with weapons, but he knew from limited experience that a pistol was extremely difficult to fire with accuracy. He did not feel fear so much as irritation.

"Emily, you are being a damnable fool."

"Stay," she commanded.

"Emily, you are a bitch and a whore but you are not, I'll wager, a murderer and I will have—"

She fired one gun. The room filled with smoke. Hacklett cried aloud in terror, and several moments passed before both husband and wife realized that he had not been hit.

Hacklett laughed, mostly in relief.

"As you see," he said, "it is no simple matter. Now give me the pistol, Emily."

He came quite close before she fired again, hitting him in the groin. The impact was not powerful. Hacklett remained standing. He took another step, coming so near her that he could almost touch her.

"I have always hated you," he said, in a conversational tone. "From the first day that I met you. Do you remember? I said to you, 'Good day, madam,' and you said to me—"

He broke off into a coughing fit, and collapsed on the ground, doubled over in pain.

Blood was now seeping from his waist.

"You said to me," he said. "You said . . . Oh damn your black eyes, woman . . . it *hurts* . . . you said to me . . ."

He rocked on the ground, his hands pressed to his groin, his face twisted in pain, eyes shut tightly. He moaned in time to his rocking: "Aaah . . . aaah . . . aaah . . ."

She sat up in the bed and dropped the pistol. It touched the sheet, so hot that it burned the imprint of the barrel into the fabric. She quickly picked it up and flung it on the floor, then looked back at her husband. He continued to rock as before, still moaning, and then he stopped, and looked over at her, and spoke through clenched teeth.

"Finish it," he whispered.

She shook her head. The chambers were empty; she did not know how to load them again, even if there were spare shot and powder.

"Finish it," he said again.

A dozen conflicting emotions pressed in her mind. Realizing that he was not soon to die, she went to the side table, and poured a glass of claret, and brought it to him. She lifted his head, and helped him to drink. He drank a little, and then a fury overcame him, and with one bloody hand he pushed her away. His strength was surprising. She fell back, with a red imprint of a flat hand on her nightdress.

"Damn you for a king's bitch," he whispered, and took up his rocking again. He was now absorbed in his pain, and seemed to have lost any sense that she was there. She got to her feet, poured a glass of wine for herself, sipped it, and watched.

She was still standing there when Hunter entered the room half an hour later. Hacklett was alive, but wholly ashen, his actions feeble except for an occasional spastic twitch. He lay in an enormous pool of blood.

Hunter took out his pistol and moved toward Hacklett.

"*No,*" she said.

He hesitated, then stepped away.

"Thank you for your kindness," Mrs. Hacklett said.

CHAPTER 37

ON OCTOBER 23, 1665, the conviction of Charles Hunter and his crew on a charge of piracy and robbery was summarily overturned by Lewisham, Judge of the Admiralty, meeting in closed session with Sir James Almont, newly restored Governor of the Jamaica Colony.

In the same session, Commander Edwin Scott, Chief Officer of the Garrison of Fort Charles, was convicted of high treason and sentenced to be hanged the following day. A confession in his own handwriting was obtained on the promise of commutation of sentence. Once the letter was written, an unknown officer shot Scott to death in his cell in Fort Charles. The officer was never apprehended.

For Captain Hunter, now the toast of the town, one final problem remained: Andre Sanson. The Frenchman was nowhere to be found, and it was reported that he had fled into the inland hills. Hunter put out the word that he would pay well for any news of Sanson, and by mid-afternoon he had a surprising report.

Hunter had stationed himself publicly in the Black Boar, and soon enough an old bawdy woman came to see him. Hunter knew her; she ran a whoring house, her name was Simmons. She approached him nervously.

"Speak up, woman," he said, and he called for a glass of kill-devil to ease her fears.

"Well, sir," she said, drinking the liquor, "a week past, a man of the name of Carter comes to Port Royal, desperate ill."

"Is this John Carter, a seaman?"

"The same."

"Speak on," Hunter said.

"He says he has been picked up by an English packet boat from St. Kitts. They had spotted a fire on a small uninhabited cay, and, pausing to investigate, had found this Carter marooned, and brought him thence."

"Where is he now?"

"Oh, he has fled, he has. He's terrified of meeting with Sanson, the Frenchy villain. He's in the hills now, but he told me his story, right enough."

Hunter said, "And that is?"

The bawdy woman told the story quickly. Carter was aboard the sloop *Cassandra*, carrying part of the galleon treasure, under Sanson's command. There had been a fierce hurricane, in which the ship was wrecked on the inner reef

of an island, and most of the crew killed. Sanson had gathered the others together, and had salvaged the treasure,
which he directed them to bury on the island. Then they
had all built a longboat with the flotsam of the wrecked
sloop.

And then, Carter had reported, Sanson had killed them
all—twelve men—and set sail alone. Carter had been
badly wounded, but somehow survived and lived to return
home and tell his story. And he said further that he did not
know the name of the island, nor the exact location of the
treasure, but that Sanson had scratched a map on a coin,
which he then hung around his neck.

Hunter listened to the story in silence, thanked the
woman, and gave her a coin for her trouble. More than
ever, now, he wanted to find Sanson. He sat in the Black
Boar and patiently listened to every person with a rumor of
the Frenchman's whereabouts. There were at least a dozen
stories. Sanson had gone to Port Morant. Sanson had fled to
Inagua. Sanson had gone into hiding in the hills.

When finally the truth came, it was stunning. Enders
burst into the tavern:

"Captain, he's on board the galleon!"

"What?"

"Aye, sir. There were six of us set as guard; he killed
two, and sent the rest in the boat to tell you."

"Tell me what?"

"Either you arrange his pardon, and discard openly your feud with him, or he'll sink the ship, Captain. Sink her at anchor. He must have your word by nightfall, Captain."

Hunter swore. He went to the window of the tavern and looked out at the harbor. *El Trinidad* rode lightly at anchor, but she was moored well offshore, in deep water— too deep to salvage any treasure if she were sunk.

"He's damnably clever," Enders said.

"Indeed," Hunter said.

"Will you make your reply?"

"Not now," Hunter said. He turned away from the window. "Is he alone on the ship?"

"Aye, if that matters."

Sanson alone was worth a dozen men or more in an open battle.

The treasure galleon was not moored close to any other ships in the harbor; nearly a quarter mile of open water surrounded it on all sides. It stood in splendid, impregnable isolation.

"I must think," Hunter said, and went to sit again.

A SHIP MOORED in open, placid water was as safe as a fortress surrounded by a moat. And what Sanson did next made him even safer: he dumped slops and garbage all around the vessel to attract sharks. There were plenty of sharks in the harbor anyway, so that swimming to *El Trinidad* was a form of suicide.

Nor could any boat approach the ship without being easily spotted.

Therefore, the approach must be open and apparently harmless. But an open longboat gave no opportunity for hiding. Hunter scratched his head. He paced the floor of the Black Boar and then, still restless, he went out into the street.

There he saw a water-spouter, a common conjurer of the day, spouting streams of multicolored water from his lips. Conjuring was forbidden in the Massachusetts Colony as tending to promote the work of the devil; for Hunter, it had an odd fascination.

He watched the water-spouter for several moments, as he drank and spewed different kinds of water one after another. Finally, he went up to the man.

"I want to know your secrets."

"Many a fine woman in the Court of King Charles has said as much, and offered more than you have offered."

"I offer you," Hunter said, "your life." And he pressed a loaded pistol in his face.

"You'll not bully me," the conjurer said.

"I fancy, I will."

And a few moments later, he was back in the conjurer's tent, hearing the details of his exploits.

"Things are not as they seem," said the conjurer.

"Show me," Hunter said.

The conjurer explained that before a performance, he swallowed a pill confected of the gall of a heifer and baked wheat flour. "This cleanses my stomach, you see."

"I do. Go on."

"Next, I take a mixture of brazil nuts and water, boiled until it is dark red in color. I swallow this before I work."

"Go on."

"Then I wash the glasses with white vinegar."

"Go on."

"And some glasses not so washed."

"Go on."

Then, the water-spouter explained, he drank water from clean glasses, and regurgitated the contents of his stomach, producing glasses of bright red "claret." In other glasses, which had a coating of vinegar, the same liquid became "beer," of a dark brown color.

Drinking and regurgitating more water produced a lighter red color, which was called "sherry."

"There's no more trick to it than that," said the conjurer. "Things are not as they seem, and that's an end to it." He sighed. "It's all in directing attention to the wrong place."

Hunter thanked the man, and went off to search for Enders.

"DO YOU KNOW the woman who enabled our release from Marshallsea?"

"Anne Sharpe is her name."

"Find her," Hunter said. "And get for the longboat crew six of the best men you can muster."

"Why, Captain?"

"We are going to pay a visit to Sanson."

CHAPTER 38

ANDRE SANSON, THE lethal, powerful Frenchman, was not accustomed to the sensation of fear, and he did not feel afraid as he saw the longboat put out from shore. He observed the boat carefully; from a distance, he could see six oarsmen and two people sitting in the bow, but he could not discern who they were.

He expected some ruse. The Englishman Hunter was crafty, and he would use his craft if he could. Sanson knew that he was not clever, as Hunter was. His own talents were more animal, more directly physical. And yet he was confident that there was no trick Hunter could play upon him. It was, very simply, impossible. He was alone on this ship and he would remain alone, safely, until night fell. But he would have his freedom by dusk or he would destroy the ship.

And he knew Hunter would never let the ship be destroyed. He had fought too hard and suffered too much for that treasure. He would do anything to keep it—even to the point of releasing Sanson. The Frenchman was confident.

He peered at the approaching longboat. As it came nearer, he saw that Hunter himself stood in the prow, along with some woman. What could be the meaning of this? His head ached to wonder what Hunter had planned.

Yet, in the end, he contented himself with the reassurance that no trick was possible. Hunter was clever but there was a limit to cleverness. And Hunter must know that even from a distance, he could be picked off as quickly and simply as a man brushes a fly from his sleeve. Sanson could kill him now if he wished. But there was no reason. All he wanted was his freedom, and a pardon. For that, he needed Hunter alive.

The longboat came closer, and Hunter waved cheerfully. "Sanson, you French pig!" he called.

Sanson waved back, grinning. "Hunter, you English pox of a sheep!" he shouted with a joviality that he did not feel at all. His tension was considerable, and increased as he realized how casually Hunter was behaving.

The longboat pulled alongside *El Trinidad*. Sanson leaned over slightly, showing them the crossbow. But he did not want to lean too far, though he was eager for a look inside the boat.

"Why are you here, Hunter?"

"I have brought you a present. May we come aboard?"

"You two only," Sanson said, and stepped back from
the railing. He quickly ran to the opposite side of the ship,
to see if another longboat was approaching from another
direction. He saw nothing but calm water, and the rip-
pling fins of cruising sharks.

Turning back, he heard the sound of two people clam-
bering up the side of the ship. He aimed his crossbow as
a woman appeared. She was young and damnably pretty.
She smiled at him, almost shyly, and stepped to one side as
Hunter came on deck. Hunter paused, and looked at Sanson, who was twenty paces away, with the crossbow in his
hands.

"Not a very hospitable greeting," Hunter said.

"You must forgive me," Sanson said. He looked at the
girl, then back to Hunter. "Have you arranged to meet my
demands?"

"I am doing so, even as we talk. Sir James is drawing
up the papers, and they shall be delivered in a few hours."

"And the meaning of this visit?"

Hunter gave a short laugh. "Sanson," he said, "you
know me for a practical man. You know that you have all
the cards. I must agree to anything you say. This time, you
have been too clever, even for me."

"I know," Sanson said.

"Someday," Hunter said, his eyes narrowing, "I shall find you and kill you. I promise you that. But for now, you have won."

"This is a trick," Sanson said, with the sudden realization that something was very wrong.

"No trick," Hunter said. "Torture."

"Torture?"

"Indeed," Hunter said. "Things are not always as they seem. So that you may spend the afternoon in pleasurable pursuits, I have brought you this woman. Surely we can agree that she is most charming—for an Englishwoman. I will leave her here for you." Hunter laughed. "If you dare."

Now Sanson laughed. "Hunter, you are the devil's own servant. I cannot take this woman without ceasing to keep watch, yes?"

"May her English beauty torment you," Hunter said, and then, with a short bow, he climbed over the side. Sanson listened to the thud of his feet on the hull of the ship, and then a final thump as Hunter landed in the longboat. He heard Hunter order the boat to put off, and he heard the stroke of the oars.

It was a trick, he thought. Somehow, a trick. He looked at the woman: she must be armed in some fashion.

"Lie down," he growled harshly.

She seemed confused.

"Lie down!" he said, and stamped the deck.

She lay on the deck, and he moved cautiously over to her, then frisked her through her garments. She had no weapons. Yet he was sure it was a trick.

He went to the railing and looked out at the longboat, now pulling strongly for shore. Hunter sat in the bow, facing land, not looking back. There were six oarsmen. Everyone was accounted for.

"May I get up?" the girl asked, giggling.

He turned back to face her. "Yes, get up," he said.

She stood and straightened her clothes. "Do I please you?"

"For an English pig," he said harshly.

Without another word, she began to undress.

"What are you doing?" he demanded.

"Captain Hunter said I should remove my clothes."

"Well, I am telling you to leave them as they are," Sanson growled. "From now on, you will do as I tell you." He scanned the horizon in all directions. There was nothing except the departing longboat.

It must be a trick, he thought. It *must* be.

He turned and looked again at the girl. She licked her lips, a fetching creature. Where could he take her? Where would he be safe? He realized then that if they went up to the aft castle, he would be able to look in all directions, and still enjoy this English whore.

"I shall have the better of Captain Hunter," he said, "and of you as well."

And he marched her up to the aft castle. A few minutes later, he had another surprise—this demure little creature was a screaming, passionate hellion, who yelled and gasped and clawed, much to Sanson's happy satisfaction.

"You are so big!" she gasped. "I did not know Frenchmen were so big!"

Her fingers raked his back, painfully. He was happy.

He would have been less happy to know that her screams of ecstasy—for which she was amply paid—were a signal to Hunter, who was hanging just above the waterline, holding on to the rope ladder, and watching the pale shapes of the sharks slip through the water all around him.

Hunter had hung there since the longboat cast off. In the bow of the longboat was a scarecrow dummy, previously concealed under a tarp and erected while Hunter had been aboard the ship.

It had all worked exactly as Hunter planned. Sanson dared not look down too carefully into the longboat, and as soon as it pushed off, he had been obliged to spend some moments searching the girl. By the time he got around to looking at the departing boat, it was far enough away that the dummy was convincing. At that time, had he looked directly down, he would have seen Hunter dangling there. But there was no reason to look directly down—and, in any case, the girl had been instructed to distract him as soon as possible.

Hunter had waited, hanging on the ropes, for many minutes before he heard her shouts of passion. They were coming from the aft castle, as he had expected. Gently, he climbed to the gunports, and slipped onto *El Trinidad* belowdecks.

Hunter was not armed, and his first task was to find weapons. He moved forward to the armory, and found a short dagger and a brace of pistols, which he loaded and carefully wadded. Then he picked up a crossbow, bending his back to the metal, and cocking it. Only then did he move up the gangway to the main deck. There he paused.

Looking aft, he saw Sanson standing with the girl. She was arranging her clothing; Sanson was scanning the horizon. He had spent only a few minutes in lusty action, but it had been a fatal few minutes. He watched Sanson climb down to the waist of the galleon, and pace the decks. He looked over one side, then the other side.

And then he stopped.

He looked again.

Hunter knew what he was seeing. He was seeing the

wet marks on the hull that Hunter's clothing had left in an erratic pattern moving up the side of the ship to the gunports.

Sanson spun. "You bitch!" he shouted, and fired his cross-bow at the girl still on the castle. In the heat of the moment, he missed her; she shrieked and ran below. Sanson started after her, then seemed to think better of it. He paused, and reloaded the crossbow. Then he waited, listening.

There was the sound of the girl's running feet, and then a bulkhead door slammed. Hunter guessed she had locked herself into one of the aft cabins. She would be safe enough for the moment.

Sanson moved to the center of the deck, and stood by the mainmast.

"Hunter," he called. "Hunter, I know you are here." And then he laughed.

For now, the advantage was his. He stood by the mast, knowing that he was out of range of any pistol, from any direction, and he waited. He circled the mast cautiously, his head turning in slow, even motions. He was perfectly alert, perfectly aware. He was prepared for any tactic.

Hunter was illogical: he fired both his pistols. One shot splintered the mainmast, and the other struck Sanson in the shoulder. The Frenchman grunted, but he hardly seemed to notice the injury. He spun and fired the crossbow, and the arrow streaked past Hunter, burying itself in the wood of the companionway.

Hunter scrambled down the steps, hearing Sanson running after him. He had a glimpse of Sanson, both pistols out, charging forward.

Hunter stepped behind the companionway ladder, and held his breath. He saw Sanson running down, directly over his head, hastening down the ladder.

Sanson reached the gun deck, his back to Hunter, and then Hunter said in a cold voice, "Stand there."

Sanson did not stand. He spun, and discharged both pistols.

The balls whistled over Hunter's head as he crouched near the ground. Now he stood, holding the crossbow ready.

"Things are not always as they seem," he said.

Sanson grinned, raising his arms. "Hunter, my friend. I am without defense."

"Go up," Hunter said, his voice flat.

Sanson began to climb the steps, still holding his hands out. Hunter saw that he had a dagger at his belt. His left hand began to drop toward it.

"Don't."

The left hand froze.

"Up."

Sanson went up, with Hunter following him.

"I will still have you, my friend," Sanson said.

"You will have only a shaft up your bum hole," Hunter promised.

Both men came onto the main deck. Sanson backed toward the mast.

"We must talk. We must be reasonable."

"Why?" Hunter said.

"Because I have hidden half the treasure. Look here," Sanson said, fingering a gold coin about his neck. "Here I have marked where the treasure is located. The treasure from the *Cassandra*. Does that not interest you?"

"It does."

"Well then. We have reason to negotiate."

"You tried to kill me," Hunter said, holding the crossbow steady.

"Would you not try the same, in my place?"

"No."

"Of course you would," Sanson said. "It is sheer impudence to deny it."

"Perhaps I would," Hunter said.

"There is no love lost between us."

"I would not have crossed you."

"You would, if you could."

"No," Hunter said, "I have something like honor—"

At that moment, from behind him, a female voice squealed, "Oh, Charles, you got him—"

Hunter turned fractionally, to look at Anne Sharpe, and in that moment, Sanson lunged.

Hunter fired automatically. With a *whish!* the crossbow arrow was released. It shot across the deck, catching Sanson in the chest, lifting him off his feet and pinning him to the mainmast, where he swung his arms and twitched.

"You have done me wrong," Sanson said, with blood dripping from his lips.

Hunter said, "I was fair."

Then Sanson died, his head slumping on his chest. Hunter plucked out the crossbow arrow, and the body fell to the ground. Then he pulled the gold coin with the treasure map etched in its surface from around Sanson's neck. While Anne Sharpe watched, with her hand covering her mouth, Hunter dragged the body to the side of the ship, and pushed it overboard.

It floated on the water.

The sharks circled it warily. Then one came forward, tugged at the flesh, tore away a piece. Then another, and another; the water churned and foamed blood. It lasted only a few minutes, and then the color dissipated, and the surface was still, and Hunter looked away.

Epilogue

ACCORDING TO HIS own memoirs, *Life Among the Privateers of the Caribbean Sea*, Charles Hunter searched for Sanson's treasure during all of the year 1666, but never found it. The gold coin did not have a map scratched on its surface; instead, there was a funny series of triangles and numbers, which Hunter was never able to decipher.

Sir James Almont returned to England with his niece, Lady Sarah Almont. Both perished in London's Great Fire of 1666.

Mrs. Robert Hacklett remained in Port Royal until 1686, when she died of syphilis. Her son, Edgar, became a merchant of substance in the Carolina Colony. In turn, his son, James Charles Hacklett Hunter, was governor of the Carolina Colony in 1777, when he urged that the colony side with the northern insurgents against the English army under the command of General Howe in Boston.

Mistress Anne Sharpe returned to England in 1671 as an actress; by that time, women's parts were no longer played by boys, as they had been earlier in the century. Mistress Sharpe became the second most famous woman from the Indies in all Europe (the most famous, of course, being Madame de Maintenon, mistress of Louis XIV, who had been born on Guadeloupe). Anne Sharpe died in 1704, after a life of what she herself described as "delicious notoriety."

Enders, the sea artist and barber-surgeon, joined Mandeville's expedition on Campeche in 1668 and perished in a storm.

The Moor, Bassa, died in 1669 in Henry Morgan's attack on Panama. He was run down by a bull, one of the many animals Spaniards released in an attempt to protect the city.

Don Diego, the Jew, lived on in Port Royal until 1692, when, at an advanced age, he died in the earthquake that destroyed the "wicked city" forever.

Lazue was captured and hanged as a pirate in Charleston, South Carolina, in 1704. She was said to have been a lover of Blackbeard's.

Charles Hunter, weakened by malaria during his searches for Sanson's treasure, returned to England in 1669. By that time, the raid on Matanceros had become a political embarrassment, and he was never received by

Charles II, nor accorded any honor. He died of pneumonia in 1670 in a cottage in Tunbridge Wells, leaving a modest estate and a notebook, which was stored at Trinity College, Cambridge. His notebook still exists, as does his grave, in the cemetery of the Church of St. Anthony in Tunbridge Wells. The stone is nearly worn smooth, yet it can still be read:

HERE LYES

CHAS. HUNTER, CAPT.

1627–1670

HONEST ADVENTURER AND SEAMAN

BELOVED OF HIS COUNTRYMEN

IN THE NEW WORLD

VINCIT